A Wicked Way to Burn

a Mischief in the Snow

Margaret Miles

Bantam Books

New York   Toronto   London
Sydney   Auckland

A MISCHIEF IN THE SNOW

PUBLISHING HISTORY
A Bantam Book / March 2001

ISBN 0-553-58288-7

Published simultaneously in the United States and Canada

Bantam Books are published by Bantam Books, a division of Random
House, Inc. Its trademark, consisting of the words "Bantam Books"
and the portrayal of a rooster, is Registered in U.S. Patent and
Trademark Office and in other countries. Marca Registrada. Bantam
Books, 1540 Broadway, New York, New York 10036.

PRINTED IN THE UNITED STATES OF AMERICA

OPM   10   9   8   7   6   5   4   3   2   1

For Paula and Tom

To mourn a mischief that is past and gone
Is the next way to draw new mischief on.

— WILLIAM SHAKESPEARE, *Othello*

Prologue

IN THE COLONY of Massachusetts, a few miles north of the village of Bracebridge, a large thrusting of rock rises up from the sighing marshes of the Musketaquid. While familiar to the village from afar, its interior remains, to most, a mystery.

Little in this rugged spot shows Nature's gentler side. But between steep walls graced only by slanting hemlock, and the peeling, aerial vine of native grape, a few bowers do lie scattered here and there, secret chambers whose floors may glint with wildflowers.

Though it is a subject frequently debated, the origin of Boar Island (for so the place is called) remains unresolved. Such discussions may be heard especially during long winter evenings at the Blue Boar tavern. Some suppose the curious formation to be of weathered lava, concluding from its shape that it must once have oozed from infernal regions, as Etna continues to do. Some claim it is no more than the start of a mountain range little different from others in New England. One elder blessed with a classical bent has stated that the great mass could well be an expired head, evidence of Demeter's savage attempt to bring forth a new Giant. A few more speculate fairies may have had something to do with it. But most agree the rock was set down by the hand of God, as was the rest of the world.

Certain things, however, are beyond all dispute. The isle boasts an impressive dwelling resembling a Rhenish fortress, set near the top of a crag, guarded by nodding firs. One Johan Fischart, of Hanover, built this structure to crown his water-bound estate . . . which, strangely, no one had claimed before him. His new home yet unfinished, Fischart invited many guests from across the sea, and imported fierce Harz boars to give them sport. Unhappily, such rough entertainment often turns to tragedy, and in fact blood was spilled here, on both sides of the lance. *"May the next to visit you be the very Devil himself!"* was the curse one dying gentleman aimed at his cruel host.

Still, John Fisher, as the Teutonic lord soon came to be known, allowed his favorite creatures to tread paths between the precipices, breeding freely, feeding in the secret glens on whatever they most desired.

Gone, now, are Fisher and his huntsmen, yet the descendants of the first boars continue to roam. From the land, one can sometimes hear them screaming. Fisher, too, left a part of himself behind; his only child, a daughter, inherited his private isle. For years she remained there with an unfortunate relation, shunning the rough company of men. While their situation was considered wrong, none in Bracebridge attempted to alter it. Perhaps, it is whispered even now, this was because of the widespread belief that Boar Island is haunted.

Surely, across the faint breath of the marshes, one

does occasionally seem to hear spectral shouts and laughter, the clatter of swordplay, a harpsichord's metallic chime. Then, a few may recall stories of lusty men and women, whose amusements in the great house at one time sent forth true sounds of revelry. There are regular reports, as well, of phantom figures that come out to cavort in the mist, and lights that flare up magically, to bob along the shore. A few who trust in Science smile and say the basis for these occurrences is no more than marsh gas, or the cries of night birds, or the reverberating croaks of frogs. Most still have doubts sufficient to cause them to give the area a wide berth, adding to its natural isolation. Some things, it is said, no one can know for sure.

But other, recent occurrences have helped to illuminate, to some extent, the island and its inhabitants. These events took place early in the year of 1766, during days of cold and storm. These days, too, will long be remembered in Bracebridge, for they gave rise to murder.

Chapter 1

FINISHED WITH A hearty dinner of beef stew and brown bread, Charlotte Willett sat by the fire in the low-beamed kitchen of her farmhouse. Carefully, she inserted her stockinged feet into slippers double-cut from discarded silk, stuffed with a layer of feathers. These she covered with another pair of woolen stockings. With both feet well protected, she pulled on her stoutest leather boots, and laced them tight.

At the opposite side of the hearth, Lem Wainwright had barely lifted his face from a worn volume of *Gulliver's Travels*. While he attempted to hide his concern, he could hardly imagine any other woman of the village following Mrs. Willett's lonely example that afternoon—if conditions did seem perfect for her plan.

"You'll take care?" he finally asked, as the dappled dog at his feet raised his head to watch.

"I will," she replied with good cheer. She clomped across the sanded pine floorboards, to find mittens in a woven basket full of winter apparel.

"How far do you mean to go?"

"Well—I don't know."

"You'll be back before dark?"

Now it was Charlotte's turn to worry, for she'd again heard a note that had lately begun to grate. Lem's new inquiries into her actions seemed to have started in August when he'd returned from Boston, where he'd been tutored for a first term at Harvard College. For a number of reasons he'd abandoned his plans to attend. Instead, he'd come home.

She knew she could hardly expect him to speak to her as he had at the age of twelve—it was then that his parents, whose house on the road to Concord was still full of children, had sent him to help in her dairy. Today her small herd and barn were largely Lem's responsibility, an arrangement that freed Charlotte to follow other pursuits. But if that gave him a new privilege to question her plans, why was it that her growing curiosity about *his* affairs so often went unsatisfied? Still, young men deserved an additional degree of privacy, she'd decided, and this, she was determined to give.

"Sunset must be three hours away," she said now, after taking a peek through to the large room with south-facing windows. "I suppose," she continued, moving toward the back door, "that by then I'll have had enough. If I haven't *quite* managed to freeze my toes and fingers." She bent briefly to pat Orpheus, giving him soft instructions to return to the hearth, for he could not come with her.

Lem seemed about to give a further warning, but seeing one of her strange new looks, he reconsidered and retreated into his storybook.

Charlotte tied a linen cap over her head and ears. She drew on a hooded cloak, and picked up a long muff of spotted lynx, something her mother had been given years before by her new husband, and had cherished. It was still as useful as it was beautiful. Yet how sad, Charlotte reflected, that none saw such beauty alive today, roaming the remaining acres of transparent winter wood near the village. It was often remarked that old ways disappeared with the trees. Yet others insisted new ideas so improved their lives that the future was bound to be a great deal better than the past. She doubted either statement was entirely true. But the world did revolve swiftly, and with that thought in mind, she set the muff over one mittened hand. With the other she took up two joined objects made of wood, leather, and steel.

Minutes later, Charlotte accepted a ride on a neighbor's passing sleigh. It then continued on along hard-packed snow, down the hill that led to the village. They first passed between Richard Longfellow's impressive house and the Bracebridge Inn across the way. After a few hundred yards of open fields, the sleigh reached tree-lined lanes, and came to the closely huddled dwellings of the village proper.

At the stone bridge over the Musketaquid River, Charlotte gave the driver her thanks, and hopped down. For a moment she stood gazing at the milky surface below. What current still flowed was covered, she supposed, by several inches of ice, and two would be sufficient. For weeks she'd missed her usual walks, and was not about to spend the entire winter inside. Ice, bare and beautiful, gave her a rare chance to glide like a swallow into a part of the countryside that was usually inaccessible, to see what she could see.

By the river's edge she sat and attached two wooden plates filleted with leather straps to her boot soles—plates set with curl-fronted, sharp-backed blades. Rising, she tested her work, maneuvering away from the shore. Soon leaving the houses behind, she flew through the bright winter sunlight, under an azure sky. Nothing in the bleached stalks on either side of the ice distracted her; no reflection but her own came from a sparkling surface. Though numerous avenues branched off into barely glimpsed pockets, she avoided them, keeping to the good sense of the broadest path. Lulled by the singing of her skates, she let her mind, instead, wander.

She had come out hoping to relieve a sadness that had settled within her. Recalling the painful news once more, Charlotte felt a wave of sympathy. She willed it away. Diana would not be comforted by her sighs.

Grief! How much of it she'd felt in her own short life. First, her parents had gone; then illness had taken her sister Eleanor, soon to have become the wife of their new neighbor. And in the same dreadful week, six years ago, her own husband, Aaron. . . .

Then, she and Richard Longfellow had mourned together. He, too, must now be remembering that terrible time, having learned only the week before that Diana's child had died. Two days after the letter reached them, his sister was brought to Bracebridge by a coachman, accompanied by a small coffin, without her husband, Edmund Montagu. She requested they bury the boy among Charlotte's family, atop a knoll on the Howard farm bordering her brother's own. Diana knew that Richard and Charlotte often visited the graves there. She told them Captain Montagu spoke increasingly of taking her to London. Should they go, she feared a Boston burial might mean their child would lie forgotten. And that was a thing she could not bear to imagine.

The morning after Diana's arrival, Richard, with Lem's help, had carried the coffin up the snowy slope of the knoll, as Charlotte and Diana followed. At the top they covered the small box with a layer of balsam, and then a cairn of stones. As soon as the earth could be broken in the spring, the coffin would be lowered into a permanent grave.

The child's death was tragic—yet they'd known from the first that Charles Douglas had come into the world too early, and was not strong. Dr. Warren warned them the boy might fall prey to a winter fever, a malady that gave cherubic faces a heavenly touch of blue, even while their mothers rocked them before high fires. Such women were frequently reminded new life can never be certain, and that they bore no blame. But the six weeks of life allotted to the boy had made his parents grow ever fonder, so they felt his passing most keenly. At least, Diana assured them with marked coldness, this was true for one.

She told them, too, that Edmund refused to allow himself to share her grief, no doubt for the sake of his duties. The captain was a King's officer, of course. But could this have hardened him to the death of his firstborn son and heir? Considering his respect for his own noble family, and his love for Diana, Charlotte could not bring herself to believe it. Though she had no way of knowing the real reason for his absence, she did know that heartlessness was not a part of Edmund Montagu's character.

At the moment, there *was* a great deal in Boston to distract him. Bales of Parliament's new revenue stamps had arrived; still, they sat unopened in Castle William, out in the bay. These blank paper sheets of several denominations, their corners variously stamped with figures of red ink, were ready for sale and use, and were now required for the printing of newspapers, as well as for documents including deeds, degrees and licenses, court writs, manifests, and port clearances. The main objection to the stamps (beyond their added cost to business) was that for generations the colonial assemblies had raised royal revenues themselves. This new order given by a distant body—one that lately seemed to ignore the pleas of America's own popular houses—was not only an insult, but a threat to liberties long enjoyed in all the provinces. The people of Boston had made it clear enough that any official attempting to support or sell the stamps would be sorry for it—which was why Governor Bernard had gone to sit in his castle as well, comforted by two British men-of-war anchored nearby. Meanwhile, trade and legal business had come to a halt.

Lieutenant Governor Thomas Hutchinson had closed civil and admiralty courts, and promised he would keep them closed, as long as the stubborn colonists prevented the implimentation of the new law. While more distant counties might choose to ignore his wishes, Suffolk County could not. In Boston, without properly stamped and filed papers, it became increasingly difficult to borrow, and shipping languished; without the civil courts, merchants could no longer legally enforce the collection of debts. And with trade disrupted, the price of flour, which was usually imported from the colonies to the south, shot up like a rocket. There was good reason to fear that more riots, resembling the one that had destroyed Hutchinson's home the previous August, were in store for the new year. This much Charlotte knew from her glances at Longfellow's weekly copies of the *Boston Gazette*.

But who in Boston, she wondered, could predict what might happen next? Surely not Governor Bernard, nor Mr. Hutchinson; each had incorrectly gauged the feelings of the town before. Yet did Sam Adams, John Hancock, or Joseph Warren know better? She imagined that this time there was likely to be a long, stubborn stand-to, before all arms were grudgingly lowered.

On the other hand, each year brought times of trouble, set between more encouraging days. In every season, she reminded herself, some would suffer under clouds of sorrow, while others celebrated the rebirth of hope and happiness. Diana and Edmund had experienced their loss as a storm that had driven them apart. But one day soon, they might begin to drift back together again—especially if they had help.

Bringing herself to a halt, Charlotte looked about the blank ice. She took a deep breath of the chill air, feeling it sear its way into her chest. Perhaps she and Richard could find some way to restore Diana's tranquillity. Then, they might recover their own.

For it seemed they, too, had grown apart. Frequently she expected to hear footsteps at her kitchen door, as before. Lately, they rarely came. Out on a solitary walk, she sometimes glimpsed her neighbor approaching; more than once, he had then turned away. Now, she hesitated to set her feet on the path between their houses.

No more did they picnic on the grass, or walk together through the fields, nor did they often spend quiet evenings before a fire. Instead, after the summer visit of his friend Signor Lahte, they seemed uneasy with one another. Lately, she even imagined a hint of suspicion in her neighbor's inquisitive gaze.

Had her admitted interest in the *musico* offended him? It had certainly done *her* little good. But it might be that the winter's tedium, its lack of immediate employment, was to blame for Richard's inattention. She knew he tended to black moods; perhaps this was an unusually long and gray one. At least he had extended an invitation to visit this evening, so that they might cheer Diana.

Charlotte stamped her feet onto the ice, attempting

to loosen her stiffening limbs. This caused her hood to fall. In a burst of exasperation, she pulled at her cap, freeing a pinned knot of hair to glint like clear cider.

Why bother to think about trouble? *Freedom* was what she'd come out to find today! And was it not all around her? Nature was an anodyne, always ready to offer comfort if one would only look around. Full of beauty and surprises, it wove life into patterns, maintained its own balances, followed observable laws. Richard often impressed the last idea upon her. Charlotte knew she had an ample sense of life's harmony, while his interests tended to be a bit more precise.

For instance, he would have noted that there, surrounded by marsh, stood a group of elms resembling frozen fountains. They had lost not only their leaves, but most of their outer bark. Each had dropped several branches, too, now embedded in ice. All were dead, surely. What in the Great Design had doomed them? She skated closer to find out.

Looking up, she was surprised to see a red hawk seated on a high branch. She squinted to see it more clearly. It appeared to watch her as well. The heavy bird lowered its head and raised its tail, cocking its thick, powerful body. She wondered if they might be acquainted. She'd frequently seen one like him in the white oak of her barnyard, watching her chickens. Cap in hand, she glided on, warmed by the feeling that she was somehow welcome in the silent grove.

Unfortunately, her curiosity caused her to forget her footing, and disaster then found its chance. In the next instant, Charlotte felt herself sink abruptly, even as she heard a brittle crack. At once she knew she'd skated over ice too thin to support her. Instinctively, she threw her lynx muff far away, so that this, at least, would stay dry. While the air beneath her skirts buoyed her momentarily, she realized she would have little time to escape.

She'd encountered a deep pool, created by a wandering spring—something from which the elms might have saved her, had she heeded their warning. The subterranean water's heat had made the ice about her rotten. She drew off her mittens, then tried to kick and claw her way onto a sustaining shelf—bit by bit, the ice continued to break away under her weight.

There was no use calling for help; she knew no creature but the hawk could see her. Then the bird gave a piercing cry, flapped its wings, and lifted up. With long, regular strokes it flew away in silence, leaving Charlotte utterly alone. She began to gasp, her heart sinking further as she felt her chest tighten with the cold.

Sodden wool skirts now began to work against her, pulling her down. Her feet found no bottom. Already, her aching legs seemed unwilling to help, though she knew they must. A cry welled within her, as she imagined an inevitable end to her folly. And yet—?

Gathering her remaining strength, she forced her feet to kick vigorously, while she leaned back to clasp one knee. She tried to wrench a skate from her booted foot, bobbing under the water through three attempts, coming up to gasp for air as loose hair floated about her face. Then, by twisting, she had what she wanted. She readjusted the long leather strap and hurtled the wooden plate before her, in an arc above the ice. It landed a yard away; the pointed blade seemed to bite. She pulled, and found she'd won a small amount of purchase.

By repeating her earlier motions she made the second skate ready. This she sent out to the side of the first. It, too, bit. Pulling gently as she kicked, she gained a foot, then another, and yet another. The shelf of ice sagged and sighed, but held. It was nearly enough. She tried to re-plant the blades, but found that now, while the slab ahead promised to bear more of her weight, it was also better able to repel the metal points. Suddenly the ice groaned, and she found herself sinking back into the freezing marsh.

Just out of reach was a thick branch, partly submerged. With a last inspiration, Charlotte knotted both of her skates together, and threw one of them. As she'd hoped, it entangled itself in the dead wood. Slowly she pulled herself forward, until at last she knelt on soft plates of fungus, and could crawl to further safety.

She was again able to stand upright, but she knew she must find some way to warm herself, and quickly. Her muscles were cramped, her legs nearly crippled. She'd skated for half an hour from the village bridge to come to her present position. It would take even longer, in her new situation, to return. Would she be able to complete the journey? Exercise promised some relief, but with wet boots, her toes might yet freeze. The thought frightened her—but at least, she told herself, she was alive! Taking another precious moment she threw back her head, and sent silent thanks toward the sky.

Someone nearby began to laugh; a moment later, she knew she had heard the sound of her own voice. Had the shock of the water affected her mind, too? Spinning about, she looked desperately for help.

Through the elms, she recognized Boar Island. She knew its house, closer than her own, sheltered two women. They would have a fire, and could surely offer her cups of hot tea, while she had the chance to dry. Neither had a friend in the village, but Charlotte recalled meeting old Catherine Knowles some years before. Even a recluse who guarded her privacy would not refuse another in such desperate need.

There was, however, a further danger worth considering. *What of the boars?* It would be a long climb to the house, with no one to protect her from the savage creatures. But then she recalled that for a year at least, a youth had made lone visits to the island. And she'd not heard that Alexander Godwin had ever been injured.

Beggars could not be choosers, she decided at last. With slow fingers, she'd managed to re-attach both skates to her soggy boots. Regaining her feet, she imagined her friends in Bracebridge would be less likely to learn of her accident if she *did* visit Mrs. Knowles and her companion, for then she might return home in a more presentable state. What would the future hold if Lem, Richard, or even Christian Rowe, the village minister who seemed overly fond of watching her, found further cause to worry?

She might tell Hannah of her adventure, though, after swearing her to secrecy. For years her helper had repeated strange tales of things said to have occurred on Boar Island, told by those living nearby. Lately, these stories had become more frequent, so that Charlotte wondered if they might not have some basis in fact after all. But ghosts, she thought, would be the least of her problems this afternoon.

Shuddering, she skated back and circled carefully, until she'd retrieved the lynx muff. Thrusting her hands into its glossy fur, she took a final look at the spot where she'd nearly drawn a last breath of black water.

Then she forced her quaking legs to take her off in long, smooth glides, toward the dark rock that loomed ahead.

Chapter 2

FEELING A GOOD deal warmer, Charlotte reached what was left of an old landing at the edge of the rocky shore. Little more than a few boards that jutted out over the ice, the silver planks still offered a place to sit comfortably while she removed her skates. These she slipped into the shadows beneath her.

She began to climb along the broad path, glad that a portion, at least, had been packed down by someone pulling a sled. She supposed the occasional footprints to one side were those of Alexander Godwin. How strange that he, and no one else, came here. Most of the village saw little of Alex, and liked what they saw even less. An over-plump, unsmiling young man of seventeen or so, he had an unfortunate face that erupted regularly; seeing him, one couldn't help but think of an unbaked bun studded with red currants. Yet his lack of friends was due not to his appearance, but to a pose of superiority—something remarked upon whenever the youth's name was mentioned.

Why was it, Charlotte wondered again, that he'd returned to Bracebridge, after all?

Once, Alex's father had supplied John Fisher, who then owned the island, with the special ales, wines, and spirits he'd required, ordered from agents across the sea. When Fisher died the trade stopped and the Godwins went off to Worcester. Alex could barely have been born. But little more than a year ago, when he was just old enough to find his own way in life, the young man had come back. Since then he'd paid rent for an extra room in Bracebridge, yet Charlotte had heard he spent many days away from it. She guessed his absences had something to do with the job he'd taken soon after the death of Alaric Jones, an ancient who'd lived along the north road. It was now up to Alex to fetch supplies, do heavy chores, and carry whatever messages Catherine Knowles might have. It was understood in the village that she would tolerate no other man on her island. Was it possible Alex enjoyed this work? Mrs. Knowles, it was widely held, had been born with a fiery temper. But she might also pay well, like her father before her, for what she wanted.

After pausing at a final terrace, Charlotte wound her way to the top of the long trail. She was then able to peer into a strip of snowy yard. Two ravens, strutting as though they might be gatekeepers, hopped off, and her eyes rose further to gaze at the startling edifice before her.

Regaining her breath, she studied its many peculiarities. Longer than the houses she knew, this one had a dozen dark windows in each of two stories; then, perhaps forty feet from the ground, a steep roof began with eaves that were studded with horrible heads, their mouths agape, each carved from stone. Above stretched decorative turrets, which she guessed concealed several chimneys. Leading up to these foreign features, gray facing stones, many

carved to suggest thick, twining vines, were well joined
but ignobly stained with patches of frozen damp and
lichen.

Just ahead, flanked by holly trees with tiny red eyes, a
pair of doors met in a high point. On their oaken faces,
appropriate brass ornaments seemed to warn as much as
welcome.

Charlotte approached hesitantly, and took the tusk of
a boar's head in her hand. She lifted it, and let go. A muffled boom sounded inside, followed by an echo, and silence.

She heard footsteps approaching. Hinges creaked, then
one of the doors swung open to reveal a tall woman, her
gown plain white linen, with a heavy gray shawl. Though
her eyes were wide, her face showed no other sign of animation. Charlotte thought this more than strange, for she
imagined herself to be something of a spectacle.

"I've met with an accident on the ice," she finally
managed. The woman watched her for another moment.
"Come to the fire," she then whispered. Reaching out a
quivering hand, she touched Charlotte's trembling fingers
with her own. Once her unexpected guest had come inside, she turned to push the groaning door shut behind
them.

Charlotte looked first to the top of a vaulted central
hall—it seemed to separate two halves of the house—
then down one of a pair of broad staircases made entirely
of stone. Behind these steps, thin windows of colored
glass directed north light into the murk below, where it
reflected on what appeared to be ancient weapons of war.
Lining a series of alcoves were lances, swords, shields,
even a wicked crossbow, all hung above empty candle
sconces, each one under a thin canopy kept by attentive
spiders. Charlotte quickly realized these things must have

been used in the days of John Fisher, by the visiting huntsmen she'd heard of.

Even more astounding were the immense tapestries
she now saw, high on the stone walls. Fisher must have
brought these, too, from Europe; they could hardly have
been made in the colonies. Their colors were muted by
the poor light, and possibly by time—but how alive their
subjects seemed! Robust men and women, perhaps gods
and goddesses—all were nearly naked, leering and blush-
ing at one another while they stood or reclined in forest
and field. Did their knowing smiles speak of past revels, or
did they anticipate new ones? For now, thankfully, they
only consumed glowing fruits, or fingered other delicacies.

The woman in white seemed to float to the right, into
a short passage. Charlotte followed, giving a last glance
above as she walked under several hanging wheels of
iron, all devoid of candles.

They passed into a dark room decorated with var-
nished portraits, and what Charlotte guessed were scenes
of Teutonic woods and peaks. In the shadows stood seats
constructed largely from the intertwined horns of animals. The room had no fire, but through a low arch that
led into the next, Charlotte saw a hearth blazing. A few
rays of sunlight lay ahead, venturing through curtains not
completely shut against the cold. Into this pocket of rela-
tive warmth she followed her silent guide.

In what might once have been a ballroom, massive
old settles and sofas stood against the long walls. Before a
distant ceremonial hearth, an old woman appeared to
doze in one of a half-dozen walnut chairs, beautifully upholstered, their delicately curved arms and legs carved
with shells. These seemed to make up most of the furniture in use; one supported a stack of books topped with

unfinished needlework, another held a plate with the remains of a candied orange. On a third, Charlotte saw to her joy, a tray bore cups and saucers, and a painted teapot.

But the obvious pride of the room hung all the way across its impressive expanse. This was a tall painting of a figure larger than life. The subject was a young woman, her face and tresses fair, who stood before a mountainous terrain, adorned in nearly regal fashion. In a dark gown and furs she seemed elegantly serene. Charlotte also supposed her smile was a little haughty. Perhaps she had reason to feel far above her audience. Youthful and confident, she must have assumed she held the future in her gloved palm.

Today, however, Catherine Knowles sat below her own image in a dirty woolen blanket of an uncertain color, draped about her like a cocoon. All that remained to suggest wealth and fashion was a cap of moss velvet edged with lace, drawn over hair now resembling foam on a stormy sea. Her back was bent, and Charlotte quickly supposed Mrs. Knowles suffered acutely from swollen joints, possibly due to long years spent in damp surroundings.

"What?" the old woman cried. She tilted her head, listening to the approaching footsteps. "It's not the boy? A woman, then! Come closer, whoever you are. With the web over both my eyes, I see very little. It's a rather simple woman, I think, by the sound of her—at least, she's not seen fit to affront me with her voice. What's this, Magdalene? Found a little friend at last, to come and drink my tea?" The old woman leaned forward with a cackle, but a fit of coughing forced her to sink back into her chair.

"Mrs. Knowles, I'm so sorry to intrude—" Charlotte began. She was stopped by a gesture of displeasure. Her hostess tapped at the knobbed arm of her chair and then extended a wreathed limb, its exposed finger not unlike a parrot's claw.

"Sorry? So you should be, young woman, so you should! You have the advantage of me, *as you were not invited*. But what's this? Do I hear you drip, madam? Do I smell the bog?"

"If you'll allow me to approach your hearth, I'll do my best to dry."

"Approach, then. It's been years since anyone melted before me." Another cackle forced itself from the stooped chest, only to be allayed by a new thought. The old woman strained forward, nearly upsetting herself from her rococo perch. "But I know you after all, do I not? Charlotte Howard—or Willett, now. What other female would have the courage to come here alone? Or even in company, for that matter! You see, your sullied reputation precedes you—and I think I can guess what you've been up to . . ."

While the old woman's eyes, nearly white, continued to gleam in the firelight, Charlotte was surprised to observe the beginnings of a smile. Catherine Knowles went on without waiting for an explanation.

"I recall a little girl—nearly twenty years ago. It was on one of my visits to Bracebridge, and beyond, when I still made such excruciating journeys. You were walking down the road with your mother. A decent woman, I supposed, and brave enough to say a kind word when others feared me—probably for good reason! Is she dead? I thought so. Those I knew are all gone, or very nearly. You were an unusual child . . . obedient, with fair braids, and eyes bluer than the North Sea. And now?"

Charlotte reached up to push her loose hair away from her face, wishing she'd not lost her cap in the marsh below. The woman before her did not seem to notice.

"But I hear you've managed to lose a husband," Mrs. Knowles continued. "As have I . . . as have I. Quite recently, too. You're puzzled by that, I suppose. Good! Come and sit by the fire, in Magdalene's chair. She will bring another pot of tea. And a cake from the storeroom," the old lady ordered.

Charlotte watched as Magdalene finished adding a pair of logs to the fire and moved off without a word. Then, for several minutes, while her outer garments began to drip in earnest, Charlotte found herself answering more questions concerning her family. At Magdalene's return she was directed by her hostess to take up a cup of tea and a lap robe, and go into an adjoining room to await a change of clothing. She went at once, while old Mrs. Knowles whispered a new set of instructions, sending Magdalene off in a different direction.

Chapter 3

THE SMALL ROOM appeared to serve as a poor sort of kitchen. No doubt it was more convenient than the one Charlotte guessed lay beneath the rest of the house. Over a fire simmered soup in an iron kettle. This she swung out of the way to add sticks from a nearby bin, feeling a twinge of conscience for the liberty she took. She removed her cloak and boots, stripped off her skirts and all the rest, and wrapped herself in the lap robe she'd been given. Everything else she put onto a rack standing to one side, which already supported a woman's cloak.

Later, while noting that her hair had nearly dried, she saw Magdalene come in with an armful of surprisingly fine garments. Careful hands helped her to put them on. At last, both reentered the larger room. Moving slowly in a trained gown of heavy green silk, Charlotte imagined she might have gained the approval of a duchess. The long silk gloves she'd been given were welcome for their warmth, but she hardly knew what to make of their many buttons, every one a pearl. Walking toward the fire with a rustling sound, she wobbled in shoes that held her heels three inches from the floor.

Over the mantel hung a gold-framed mirror, its silver backing speckled with dark spots that proved its age, the rest tinted to reflect a rosy world. In it, Charlotte saw enough to ensure her embarrassment. Mrs. Knowles, however, seemed satisfied, and bid her guest come close so she might touch the smooth fabric of the gown.

"What a pleasure it is to enjoy something bright!" she said decidedly. "For color, at least, I *can* see. Magdalene wears dull things, as she is determined to save her best robes—though of course no one ever gave her many. But I think you're less than sure of your feet, madam. Have you perhaps found a forgotten bottle of wine? In my time, that robe did not drag so in the front. Today it would be a different story—it is why I have abandoned my own finery, of which this is a small part. The longer the life God grants you, Mrs. Willett, the shorter you, too, will become. Despite the high source, I do not find the joke amusing. But my mind has not withered, I assure you! A good thing, too. Growing old graciously demands strength of will, a quality I suspect you yourself enjoy. Without such a thing, you might well have perished this very afternoon."

Charlotte felt a new discomfort, as she realized the old woman had guessed at her swim. She explained the reason she'd arrived in such a disheveled state.

"Well done!" cried Catherine Knowles, wringing her hands once she'd heard the exciting story to its end. "We've heard from young Godwin that you are a woman who makes a habit of falling into trouble. You do know Alexander?"

"Not well, I'm afraid."

"Though the boy came well recommended, he is no

better than most poor things others praise. At least he gives me someone to tease when I tire of trying to improve Magdalene. That is one of the few things youths are good for. How odd that so few grow to be true men—and those who do may be the worst of the lot. How they admire their own sex, and value their male spawn. This one, I think, will one day receive something of a shock . . ." Catherine paused to give another unpleasant chuckle before moving on.

"But you have found a way to lead a useful life yourself, have you not? Or has Alexander exaggerated, in the same way he magnifies his own accomplishments? I see you have sense enough to admit nothing—you have no wish to tell me you make a habit of exposing the criminal acts of others. Such a rescue as you do admit to is remarkable enough! I, myself, can no longer boast of such abilities. Perhaps Magdalene, though, would have survived, as you did. Vigorous health is some compensation, I suppose, for a weak mind . . . and a foolish heart."

A small sound came from Magdalene, but she continued to stare toward an east facing window, its curtains parted. In the light beyond, Charlotte saw the small plateau where the blue shadow of a track had been trampled into the snow. This led to a rocky point. Beyond, she was sure, was a long drop to the marshes.

Charlotte shuddered and looked back, startled anew by a feeling that they had been joined by someone else. She had glimpsed an odd movement; though perhaps it had been no more than a reflection of her borrowed splendor as she'd turned.

"We'll have no more," said Mrs. Knowles, "on *that* subject. Instead, let me tell you something of my younger days. You may be interested to learn I was once little more than a prisoner here, kept by my father. *There* was a strong, ruthless man! It was he who caused me to be straddled by a strutting fool of a husband. For twenty-two years, I endured those miserable men! Finally, my father died, and Peter's family agreed to a new arrangement. What a glorious day it was, when they came to cart home the heir! Magdalene stayed, for there was no reason for her to live in a fine city—and she had become useful to me here. You may not know she is my husband's sister, born much later than he, sent here twenty years ago by relations who thought her mad. Her elder brother was little better, I assure you! Such things follow the blood. Godwin tells us it's even said that the present monarch—"

"For whose recent recovery we're all thankful?" Charlotte suggested. She had no wish to trade speculations on the King's illness. Her hostess dismissed this with a snort, and moved on.

"My marriage was arranged solely for financial gain, Mrs. Willett, and proved to me that in the eyes of men, a woman's soul is worth nothing. At least marriage is one insult Magdalene has been spared. After all, she could hardly be left anything of value. You, too, I suppose, though for different reasons, had no worries in that respect." Despite her proud words, the old woman's tone became almost wistful. "Were you allowed to marry a man of your own choosing, my dear? For love?"

Charlotte had been momentarily distracted. Again, the mirror showed movement; this time, she could not account for it at all. She began to wonder if the shock of the icy water had affected her eyes—perhaps it even portended the beginning of a fever? At any rate, the rosy glass now contained numerous flecks of light, as if the room held many candles, and over these, colors that seemed to swirl.

"Mrs. Willett!" Catherine chided her. "Pay attention, please! I asked if you were wed for love."

A sudden flood of memories from the brief days of her marriage gave Charlotte new resolve. Pushing away her new concern, and her misgivings at being so oddly entertained, she confirmed the old woman's suspicion. She then helped herself to another slice of cake, and continued with her answer.

"My husband came from a large family of Friends who live in Philadelphia. We met in Boston, and Aaron visited my own family in Bracebridge. He stayed, and with our parents' approval—"

Catherine Knowles interrupted her with a sharp look. "Philadelphia, you say. My husband recently died there, among his own family. We may have more in common than I had assumed. But are these Willetts wealthy?"

"They have more than enough."

"More than enough? A strange answer, madam. Can they not *count*? You say your husband chose to stay in your village out of love for you. Well, without a fortune of your own, I suppose you would not have been welcome in his home . . ."

Though this was far from the truth, Charlotte felt it better to make no answer.

"My own husband," Mrs. Knowles continued, "loved nothing beyond stalking about in his hunting boots and leather doublet, crop in hand. Yet both of us honored the wishes of our parents. In Hanover, I received my training for life, and Hanover sees little point in giving young people choices—especially when they are female. So, it was entirely my father's decision to move his wife and child here to the Bay Colony, after our Elector was crowned Britain's *first* George. He hoped for some advancement. None ever came. The move killed my mother, I'm sure—though little he cared for that! But I was introduced to gentlemen with fine titles, invited, they believed, for the hunting. They were never rich enough, or generous enough, in my father's eyes. Until I was nearly thirty, he made me wait—and then, what did I get? Fortunately I did enjoy an English tutor, a pretty fellow . . ."

The old woman's voice trailed away, though a smile lingered on her lips. Charlotte wondered at the freedoms such a life might have allowed, or even encouraged, despite its restrictions.

"Do what you like, Mrs. Willett! But know this. We live with what we have done. Sometimes, we find we regret our actions—though occasionally, amends may be made for our errors."

Catherine Knowles contemplated something unspoken, while Charlotte gave further consideration to what had been hinted. It surely had some value; it came from long experience. Yet she could not help hoping that her own clothing would now be dry enough to wear.

"But you would do well, my girl, to be less sure of yourself than Magdalene—for years, *she* has not allowed her desires to alter a whit! Every day it is the same thing—she walks to the cliff's edge, and stands staring. Even now, you see, she watches from her seat. She hopes for a lover. But do you think such a woman should be allowed to marry, and to breed? Beyond that, would anyone have her now? It is a futile hope, and it only proves her madness."

Again the old woman received no answer. Charlotte

thought these hurtful words unnecessarily cruel. She began to wonder, too, if such harsh judgments were often made in this lonely place.

Magdalene lifted a hand to support her head, yet she attempted no more in her own defense.

"I found marriage to be a disaster, unmitigated by pleasure," Catherine said firmly. "Magdalene, too, would have found it so. But I'll say no more. If you do not start for your village soon, Mrs. Willett, you'll be forced to stay the night. Is that something you would like? We have many sleeping chambers above, you know. However, we would have to send you to work with a broom first, to clean a few nests from a mattress. No? I thought not."

This time the familiar cackle seemed less than pleased, perhaps because Mrs. Knowles recalled how far the standards of her house had fallen.

As Charlotte stood, she saw a new flash in the old mirror. Her heart pounding, she remained stock-still; further perplexed, she listened to faint notes of music. Meanwhile, colors continued to swirl relentlessly in the glass, almost as if revolving skirts surrounded them.

She tore her gaze away, and found the somber room the same, except that its fire had waned. Her hands trembling, she set down her china cup and retreated.

A few minutes later she returned, glad to be dressed in her own simple garments.

"I must thank you for your help . . . for the fire, the cake and tea," she told her hostess, while she carefully kept her eyes from the hearth.

"Magdalene," Mrs. Knowles said, "her voice tells me she still shivers. Give her one of your cloaks to wear over her own."

Magdalene went quietly.

"Is there something I might send back with the

cloak?" Charlotte asked politely. "Something from my dairy, or the village shop?"

"The goods Emily Bowers has to offer," Catherine retorted, "are homespun or pinchbeck, as she is! You are a woman of more character. But I find your dead husband's name a fitting one. Even in my finery, I am afraid, you were a plain little willet, rather than a nobler swan."

With a grateful smile, Charlotte took the cloak Magdalene offered. "It will soon be returned," she murmured, ignoring the foregoing comment.

"But perhaps you know that swans are not the most reliable of birds," Mrs. Knowles insisted. "As a child I watched one attack and drown a small dog, of which I was foolishly fond. But we mustn't keep you from your journey. May it be uneventful, for I would enjoy seeing you another time."

"Thank you, again," said Charlotte. "And good day."

"You do possess a sense of what is amusing, Mrs. Willett! Good day to you, madam. Come back whenever you're passing. We will be here. Though what *goodness* will be found in our remaining days it is difficult to imagine. Now be off!"

Dropping a curtsy for them both, Charlotte took up the lynx muff from a walnut chair, and went to the door through which she'd first entered the strange room. She turned to look back at the long portrait; it seemed to watch from across the room. She could still admire its strong-willed subject—beautifully dressed, carefully protected, with little say in the life that lay ahead.

Charlotte traversed the entry hall alone, and let herself out. Enjoying the crisp air, she started down the path, watching the ruby remains of the winter sun. At the bank, she retrieved one of the skates slipped earlier under the landing; she pulled a clammy leather strap through its buckle, and reached for the other. Unfortunately, the action caused a splinter to enter her bare finger. She dropped the skate abruptly. It skittered, and came to rest beneath the boards. When she bent to retrieve it, she saw something else glimmer faintly, beside the blade. She retrieved this as well. And then she stopped to stare at the object she held.

What was a spoon doing here? And it was no ordinary pewter spoon, but one of silver, perfectly cast. It also had a flower, quite possibly a tulip, chased into its bowl. Stranger still, it was untarnished. Someone must have dropped it recently, she decided. Yet why here, in the dead of winter? Surely no one had come this way looking for a place to picnic! Although perhaps poor Magdalene? . . .

Charlotte smiled uncomfortably, recalling her earlier embarrassment for both women, and her pain at the treatment of the younger. She'd pitied Mrs. Knowles, hearing of her youthful difficulties. But then she'd seen her lead a merry dance at the expense of a silent partner.

The thought of dancing caused her skin to prickle, for it reminded her of the uncanny mirror, with its strange lights and colors.

Just then, she heard a rustling behind several fallen rocks only a few yards away. It sounded as if something large moved there. A deer? Or one of the boars, like the painted sign that hung over the door of the village tavern? That colorful representation included a pair of gruesome tusks, curling about a face whose intentions seemed plainly evil.

Even if she hurried, she would barely be home before twilight turned to darkness. Nothing would be wrong with bringing the spoon back some other time, with the borrowed cloak. Perhaps with Lem, too, and a pair of good, long sticks. Had she not been encouraged to return?

Charlotte placed the spoon in the bottom of her muff, then quickly attached her second skate. With this accomplished, she sank her bare hands into the circle of spotted fur, and set off on the long journey home.

Chapter 4

ONE OF THE most worthless things I've ever read,"
Richard Longfellow declared, holding the floor in his
candlelit study. "Claptrap, written to gain the applause of
idiots," he went on, clarifying his position. With a wry
smile he raised high the volume in his hand, then gave it
to Mrs. Willett for her own evaluation.

Moments earlier Charlotte had taken off her cloak.
Now she sat in an armchair and began to examine *The
Castle of Otranto*, a lovely book whose title was pressed in
gold onto an ochre calf-skin cover.

"If that is true, then I wonder why you bought it," she
answered.

"Bought it? Hah! The thing was sent to me from
London, by an acquaintance whose character I've begun
to reconsider. I suppose he may have hoped to gain some
satisfaction by passing it on as an annoyance."

In a few healthy strides, Longfellow crossed over a
Turkey carpet to examine the portrait John Copley had

painted not long before; this showed his sister Diana during happier days.

"What can be so wrong with it, I wonder?" Charlotte asked herself softly.

"What is right, you may as well ask," he replied as he gazed, his features set. "Mr. Walpole, it seems, has lost what little sense he once enjoyed. Unless he seeks to influence others of doubtful mental abilities. Possibly, to extend his own political influence? . . ." he mused.

"I'm afraid that I don't see—"

"Hmm?"

"Which Walpole is it?"

"Certainly not the former prime minister, who's been dead for twenty years, Carlotta." Her neighbor turned back, his handsome features softening in a tolerant smile. "But since you sensibly refuse to follow the latest fashions, allow me to explain. The novel you hold was written by Horace, the son—a Parliamentary representative of the Whig party. Their claim to him proves how little that collection of traders and adventurers has left to recommend it—though lately they've managed to outwit the old Tories, that stubborn horde of country squires, who it seems have become impotent as a working body."

"Oh."

"Well. At any rate, Society knows Walpole as a scribbler, and something of a fop. An elder brother has inherited the old earl's title. But here's a detail you'll find interesting. Horace is a friend of a favorite of yours, the poet Thomas Gray. It was Walpole who first arranged to have his works published."

"That, at least, shows some wisdom," Charlotte answered, looking across the room to see if Diana might agree. Young Mrs. Montagu, wrapped in a cashmere shawl, reclined on an upholstered couch. For many minutes, she'd been staring into the starry night through a cleft in a pair of curtains—not unlike another woman she'd encountered that day, Charlotte thought uneasily.

"They were at Eton together," Richard continued, "where, incidentally, Walpole was a friend to a pair of Montagus. Edmund told me their early alliance then deteriorated into a feud."

"A feud, between Edmund and Mr. Walpole?" Charlotte immediately suspected the trouble had something to do with the captain's quiet work for the Crown, for whom he gathered information, one way or another. That, she knew, would be unlikely to please anyone with Whiggish sentiments in London or in Boston—or even in Bracebridge. Such men resented the King's increasing power over Parliament at their party's expense—especially while he gave his particular friends opportunities to enrich themselves. Little of this, she thought, had much to do with common people on either side of the ocean. But men would take a stand, though it appeared to do little good.

"No, no—" Longfellow corrected her shortly, "two other Montagus. The captain was well removed from the fireworks, since he belongs to a different branch of the family. But it was for his sake that I read this idiot tale of Walpole's to its conclusion, thinking that one day, as new brothers, Edmund and I might discuss it."

"The feud," she returned, marginally interested as she read a few lines. "What was it about?"

"Well—it appears that Lady Mary Wortley Montagu offended quite a few gentlemen in her time, including Walpole, with her literary prowess. And, I would imagine, the frequent tartness of her observations. Walpole once visited her abroad, then claimed she had become a slattern, or worse. Malicious gossip, no doubt, something she herself was known to enjoy. But it does seem the lady was rather reckless in allowing herself to be hoodwinked and swindled by certain Italian gentlemen she befriended, during long years of solitary travel."

Charlotte looked up suddenly to find Longfellow's hazel eyes appraising her.

"I'm sorry to hear it," she replied, setting the book onto a nearby table.

"What else could be expected of a woman who chooses to ignore convention, and lives alone in a foreign country? Though she may have had one good reason to leave England."

"Oh?"

"She was outshone at last by her own daughter, the woman who married Bute, before he became prime minister."

"Lord Bute," asked Charlotte, "who was seen with the Devil in Boston last summer?" She followed his gaze to the windows. "Hanging in a tree?"

"Our Liberty Boys do such admirable work in papier mâché," he returned, "that all of Boston may soon demand to be copied in the stuff, and painted up for posterity. The ladies, at least. What do you think, Mrs. Willett?"

Despite the bantering tone of Richard's remark, Charlotte saw that Diana was unmoved. Perhaps she still admired the moonlit snow beyond the frosted panes. But it was more likely that her thoughts had drifted back to her lost child. At least there was a marked contrast to her usual impatience with her brother's teasing pronouncements. Until very recently, Diana had been a rising force among the unyielding ladies of Boston, known for her clever tongue and courageous spirit, if her words were sometimes said to have a little too much bite. But now, she seemed a statue of quiet grief.

Charlotte rose and went forward, looking down on loosely curled auburn locks. When these moved, she met a pair of brimming emerald eyes. She pulled a lavender-scented handkerchief from her sleeve. It was taken gladly, and did help to stem a flow of tears that glistened, for a few moments, in the candlelight. Yet Diana's smile of thanks was more pitiful than what had come before.

Charlotte sighed and returned to the fire, where she was surprised to find a bold admiration in her neighbor's steady expression. In a manner she hoped was careless, she settled herself onto the arm of one of his stuffed chairs. Had he finally begun to soften toward her? She felt emboldened by the idea. Then again, she remembered her recent glimpse of Eternity. In recalling the black water that had nearly claimed her, she felt her knees begin to quiver. Should she tell them both what had nearly happened? She decided not.

"Has Edmund described to you, Diana, the visit he made to Walpole's *castellino*?" Longfellow asked a short time later. His sister nodded, and went to pour herself a small glass of sherry from a tea table near the hearth.

"Then I will tell the story to Mrs. Willett. It seems Horace Walpole has been nurturing a monstrosity at Twickenham, near London. Pope is buried there, but may regret it; people regularly come out, not to pay their respects to him, but to see the progress of the 'little castle.' The captain was asked to join one such party arranged by his friend Mr. Goldsmith. Edmund says Walpole adds a tower here, a cloister there—he's caused stained glass windows to be put up, depicting the lives of tormented saints. He's inserted numerous niches into the walls to display ancient weapons, and suits of mail and armor, removed from someone's attic or cellar. If he craves something fanciful that can't be supported by the under-lying structure of his old farmhouse—a battlement, for instance—he simply orders it to be created out of card-board! Wallpaper, too, is used to imitate groined vaults, and stone stairways . . ."

As the description went on, Charlotte grew astonished at the remarkable coincidence. Hadn't she seen some-thing similar that very afternoon, not ten miles away?

"All of this falls, of course, under a term that is well known," Longfellow said at last.

"Gothic?" she suggested, recalling the title page of the book she'd recently put down. She received a smile of approval.

"An architectural style," he went on to explain, "in-volving pointed arches, spires, buttresses, gargoyles—things found in the cathedrals of Europe. Lately, people of ele-vated taste have begun to use the term for a sensibility they link to the romantic temperament; their aim, it seems, is to be thrilled by the fantastic and the grotesque. In fact, a growing number of ladies and gentlemen use 'gothic' as a word of praise, shivering at the supernatural worlds they imagine. Yet these fantasies prove they are no better than untutored children, easily frightened, unable to accept or enjoy the world around them."

Diana sent a query from across the room.

"And what of your own view of the world, Richard? We know you are the opposite, for you would root out all emotion from life, if you could. I wonder what in this novel you most object to. Do the characters speak hon-estly of their fears and sorrows? Do they explore hopes and desires, rather than morality, and your precious Science? Do they even dare, I wonder, to speak passion-ately of love?"

Gladdened by this flash of Diana's old irascibility, Longfellow smiled once more, and fell into an easy chair. Taking up the book from the table, he turned to an early page.

"Since you ask, Mrs. Montagu, one thing to which I object is a hotchpotch of foolish characters, weaker and even more absurd than some of the gentlemen I've seen you bring home to tea. And the so-called *miraculous* happenings of Walpole's plot are unlikely to inspire or improve the reader—which is the whole point of literature. In the beginning, for instance, we're told of a giant statue of black marble, sporting a helmet topped with black plumes—like those one sees on heroes at the opera, I suppose. We hear of this head only because it has fallen into the castle's courtyard and crushed the life out of the young heir, whose existence was first mentioned only a moment earlier. An explanation of how this dreadful thing was accomplished is never attempted. What, I wonder, are we to make of that?"

"It could be a dream," Charlotte said softly, recalling her own waking illusions that day. She also asked herself if the mention of a lost heir might send Diana's mind back to her own pain. Could Richard be completely unaware of his sister's feelings? Or did he only try to provoke Diana's mettle?

"A dream resulting, possibly, from too much goose and cherry sauce," Longfellow returned, remembering an unpleasant evening of his own. "Unfortunately, Mr. Walpole neglects to mention how he came to have his visions, or hallucinations, or whatever they were. The book's first printing even pretended the manuscript had been composed by someone who lived centuries ago! Now that the thing has gained a certain amount of success, he admits he is the author—even puffs that he's unleashed a new Gothic School for our novelists. 'A new species of romance' he says in the preface. He imagines he has only to wish for something to have it so—though we all should know that nothing can exist beyond the laws of Nature."

Charlotte leaned forward to stir the fire. "How does he describe Otranto's castle?" she asked cautiously.

"Where to start, Mrs. Willett! Perhaps at the bottom. It seems Walpole's castle has deep vaults and subterranean passages—one leads conveniently to a convent. Above ground there are massive halls and a long picture gallery. There, from time to time, a man in a portrait climbs down to stroll about. Another ghostly appearance is made by a disembodied leg, clad in armor. When this inexplicably grows huge, it is said to fill one of the private chambers—yet that is less terrifying, apparently, than a giant armored hand which grimly clutches the rail of a staircase."

"Who lives in this castle?" asked Diana, intrigued despite her brother's scoffing.

"An evil usurper, with a wife cruelly ignored; a pair of pathetic princesses, one or two young men. There is also a poor priest nearby with an unspeakable secret. I recall a hermit in a cave, and a few distant Algerian pirates. And there is a prophecy. All that goes on, Mr. Walpole assures us, demands what he calls 'a dreadful obedience' from his characters. His world, I believe, has little room for rational choice. Instead, he presumes some fearful influence guides Fate's hand, as it moves steadfastly against us. Walpole seems to consider this story heroic. I do not. But I think many *will* find guilty pleasure in riding their passions through his pointless hell . . . those who do not rise to their feet after a quarter of an hour, and wisely throw the thing into the fire."

Longfellow got up and crossed to his own hearth to

pour out three more glasses of his best sherry. "Now what," he then asked, "do you say to that, Carlotta?"

"It may be easier to take a novel apart than to put one together," she decided.

"A laudable answer. However—?"

"However—perhaps I should read it for myself."

"Could any of us rest, imagining you *dreadfully obedient* to Mr. Walpole? But I imagine you are far too sensible to be impressed by such fare. No—I would like to test this new work on a mind of lesser capacity. For that, I plan to give *Otranto* to our friend Jack Pennywort."

Charlotte's eyes widened. "Jack Pennywort!"

"As a fellow prone to superstition, he should be a proper audience for Walpole's litany of horrors. I will offer a reward, of course—after all, he will be plowing rather stony ground. Jack's wife could no doubt use something extra for her pocket, with the price of food and fuel steadily increasing."

"I'm sure she could," said Charlotte, appreciating his kinder motive. For many, life *had* lately become more difficult. "Still, do you think it's sensible to plant such seeds, in such a place?"

"It was you who showed us that while Jack may be gullible, he is no simpleton. Let us see if he trusts his reason this time, or falls prey to the fantastic. In any event, he'll earn a good supply of punch at the Blue Boar as he reveals the astounding contents of each new chapter. At least it will be entertainment for a winter's eve."

"Well—"

"I shouldn't be surprised if the village clamors for more—showing itself no different from London's best society. But there is a chance our neighbors will show more discretion, which would be amusing. I only wish Edmund were here to wager on the outcome."

Charlotte was struck anew by Longfellow's apparent callousness to his sister's discomfort. Yet winter's short days and long nights did cause many to seek diversions. She'd seen enough of superstition in the village where she'd been born (and Longfellow had not) to doubt the wisdom of fostering more. But what he'd described seemed something even the least reasonable among them would hardly swallow whole. And there could be little harm in chewing over literature, great or not, she supposed.

"Would you enjoy more energetic entertainment, Mrs. Willett?" Longfellow asked, as if he read her thoughts. "I've come up with still another good idea today. You might even guess what it is before I tell you. No? I have heard that you were off skating, after dinner. Even the memory of your exercise gives your cheeks a healthy glow! It should also have given you some idea of the state of the ice."

"I believe most of the river to be well frozen," she answered evasively.

"Which is why I sent word flying while you were at play, to organize a day of ice-cutting. I've found my pond solid to a depth of fourteen inches. Tomorrow, anyone who cares to take ice home, or who is willing to move the stuff for others for a few shillings, is invited to come up to Pigeon Creek. Diana shall see that working together is a far better thing than setting neighbor against neighbor, which seems the new style in Boston."

"Richard . . ." Diana replied with a sigh, as if she believed such a social event still beyond her. Again, her face seemed drawn.

"But it will mean early work, so we should prepare for bed," he finished easily.

On this, they all agreed. Charlotte bid them both goodnight, kissing Diana's forehead before she retired.

When she had entered Richard's house earlier, she'd seen its eldest inhabitant reading in the kitchen, next to a pair of curled and sleeping cats. Now, as she left, Cicero still sat quietly at his own fire, his head covered by a tasseled red toque.

"How is Mrs. Montagu this evening?" he asked. His dark face held the strain of long concentration, for he'd been amusing himself by poring over Milton's conversations with Satan.

"Tearful, I'm afraid. Did she seem to you any better today?"

Cicero thought this over, then cleared his throat. "She still neglects to order me to straighten a room, improve her tea, or feed the fire. That, you will agree, is unusual. No complaints, either, about the news her brother brings us from the village. And, no word from Boston." Laying his book aside, the old man shook his head with a frown.

Charlotte shared Cicero's sense of helplessness. Both of them knew that mourning for a young child should not be encouraged; such deaths happened far too often. For the sake of the living, one was expected to return to normal patterns of life as soon as possible. But the former major-domo and guardian of what was once the Longfellow establishment in Boston—who knew well that its junior member would often surprise them—had found something else to worry him.

"What are we to do," he asked, "if she decides to stay?"

"Stay? Here? You don't really think—?"

"Today," he returned, "if she were asked, I believe she would refuse to go to London. Yet it seems the governor may be off before long, and so I wonder about the captain . . ."

"Oh!" The new thought saddened Charlotte further—and she could imagine why Cicero found it alarming. Diana was willful and did tend to be inconsiderate, though the happiness she'd found with Edmund seemed to improve the common faults of a child raised by doting women. The captain had been able to moderate his wife's quick opinions by exposing her to his own, which were generally more charitable. But if he were to go—?

"In that event," she asked, "do you really think Diana would choose to live here with Richard, rather than return to her mother's house in Boston? Since she dislikes the country, such a course would hardly seem prudent."

"No," Cicero agreed with a sharp look, until she saw his point. Prudence was not always Diana's guide, especially when her feelings offered to lead the way.

But were any of them different, when something threatened the flame at the core of one's heart? Then, did wisdom or reason offer the best protection? When she'd lost Aaron, she'd wished it wasn't so—wished so hard it seemed he'd returned to comfort her. If his imagined presence was not exactly real, it was certainly *something*. To this day, she might find herself surprised by an unexpected touch, a familiar scent, the sound of steps, or rustling . . . things that had been born of great need, she suddenly saw, as much as by desire.

Knowing she would think more on each of these matters as the night wore on, Charlotte bid Cicero a fond good evening, and set off for her own fireside.

Chapter 5

IT WAS REFRESHING to walk out into the dark, past the bare, pruned stubs of Longfellow's mulched roses, and on to her own kitchen garden. Again, Charlotte found the cold air useful for clearing her thoughts. She stopped a moment to appreciate the hour, pleased with the warmth her wool cloak gave her, and the smoothness of the silk scarf she'd wrapped about her throat.

Something new attracted her attention—something not right. The sky had flickered, as if it were lit by lightning high above the clouds. But there *were* no clouds this evening, except for a single mare's tail that glowed faintly in the starlight. But there it was again—an illumination that might have come from a giant lamp, held high above the northern pole. With this thought, she knew that what she saw was a pale form of the aurora. Fascinated by this rare display, she watched vague patches of light scurry back and forth across the heavens.

Though the *aurora borealis* did seem magical, it was a natural occurrence. She'd heard it said these northern lights, particularly when beautifully colored, were an omen of evil. She did not believe it. Why they came and went, none knew exactly, but she thought them lovely. Yet they did nothing to combat the cold, and so at last she lifted her door's latch and went inside.

In the kitchen, her nose twitched at the scent of hanging herbs and a pine fire, while her eyes enjoyed a scene she'd expected. Lem was engrossed in a book. Orpheus, who'd been asleep, got slowly to his feet. Shaking his speckled fur, he approached and put his soft muzzle against her hand, while his feathery tail and hind quarters wagged a further welcome.

At the sound of her voice, Lem got up, took her cloak, and hung it on a peg behind the door.

Charlotte removed her shoes and sat with her skirts drawn in, until Lem had tossed another log into the fire.

"How was the ice this afternoon?" he asked, taking a seat beside her.

When she'd arrived earlier he'd been in the barn, busy with the evening milking. He'd not seen her run swiftly up the stairs to change her clothing, and re-pin her hair.

"Exhilarating," she said at last, glad to have found a truthful answer. She *had* been cheered to find the outcome no worse.

There seemed to be a further query in his eyes. If, she thought once more, she planned to return to the island, Lem would be a logical companion. Or, she might ask him to give the spoon and cloak to Alexander Godwin. She decided she would tell him something more of her day after all.

"I paid a visit to Boar Island."

"What! I'd no idea you were acquainted with those women. Were you invited?" he asked, suddenly suspicious.

"Well . . . I'd met Mrs. Knowles before. And I've been asked to return."

"Huh!"

"They're lonely, Lem, as you might suppose. An occasional visit could make their lives easier. Would you like to go back with me?" The new look on his face caused her to suspect he kept something interesting from her. "What?" she asked.

"You already know, I guess, that it's dangerous to go up there."

"Is it?"

"There are the boars, for one thing. And then . . ."

"Then you believe the other stories, too?"

"About supernatural beings? I'm open to the possibility," he replied.

"You might bring that up in conversation with Mr. Longfellow one day. I'm sure we'd all find such a discussion extremely stimulating," she said, in a way that made Lem wonder if she was serious.

"It's got a reputation, and it's had one for years," he maintained stubbornly. "My grandfather told me men in his time were aware of lights floating around, and fires that would come and go, the sound of the huntsmen, strange music . . ."

"Have you seen or heard such things?"

"Well, no. But I do think it's a dangerous place, one way or another." Her face told him she still required convincing, or at least something for her curiosity. "I can tell you a little about the rest of it," he offered.

"You've been there, too?" Charlotte asked in surprise.

"My brothers and I were warned to stay away. I did go once, though, when I was twelve."

"You never told me."

"I took an oath to keep mum."

"But how did you get there?"

"That summer, Ethan made a kind of bark canoe. Not a very good one, but it could float for an hour or two. Then we had to stop the new leaks with more pitch. My mother was forever asking why she found it on our breeches, and each time, she'd tell my father." Recalling the outcome, Lem shifted in his seat.

"What were you planning to do?" Charlotte asked, feeling a forgotten thrill herself. Once she, too, had hoped to reach the island and explore it, no matter what others told her. She'd even supposed she might find plants and animals related to those in Spanish America, or India, or other places she'd read of.

"We had no real plan," Lem continued, "but we crossed the water and a few patches of reeds, and landed at a place we were sure couldn't be seen from the house. Walking along the shore, we found a crack in a face of rock, covered by a lot of vines. That took us into something like a little meadow, with cliffs all around. There was a sort of hut there, no more of it left than stone walls and a chimney. It made us imagine we might meet a castaway, like Robinson Crusoe—but all we did was eat our bread and cheese, climb the cliffs a while, and then paddle home."

"I would like to see it for myself—though perhaps in summer, as you did."

"I've heard the island's boars killed a man once, who went walking alone. I wouldn't advise it, Mrs. Willett. Nor, I think, would Mr. Longfellow. After all, he's warned me his own pigs can be dangerous."

"That's true . . ."

"But just visiting the house might be safe enough. If they really are lonely. How did it look? How were the ladies? 'Old Cat and Mad Maud,' my father used to call them, though I'd never call them that to anyone else."

"I'd say Mrs. Knowles is not without thorns. But she was kind to me. Maud's given name is Magdalene. It seems she was born with an affliction which causes her to lack judgment; Catherine also hinted she's not always been in her right mind. I suppose that's one reason they've kept to themselves for so long. But today, when we took tea together, everything went well enough."

"Is the house full of relics, from the Crusades?"

"I don't think they're quite that old," she said with a gentle smile.

"Alex Godwin swears they are. But he often says things he knows aren't true, and then mocks anyone who believes him."

"An annoying habit," said Charlotte, in sympathy with one she assumed had been such a victim. "I would say the furnishings are something like those of an English gentleman's country manor. Or one from Hanover, which is where John Fisher came from."

Here she stopped, unwilling to put into words further ideas she'd had about Mrs. Knowles's father, remembering the tapestries she'd seen, and the tales she'd heard.

"Perhaps one day," Lem said, "when the old woman dies, the village can see what it's like before it's sold."

"I hope that won't be any time soon."

"Few will regret it when it does happen," Lem told her. "Except, possibly, the 'Little Lord.'"

"Who?"

"It's what some of us call Godwin. I've heard it said the fool believes the island will be left to him, one day."

Charlotte recalled something else Mrs. Knowles had told her, concerning a surprise in the boy's future. Could what Alex believed be true?

"That's why he always has airs," Lem said, with an

expression that made Charlotte laugh as she rose from her seat.

"Since we'll be busy again tomorrow, I think I'll go up to bed."

"Pleasant dreams."

"And you," she replied.

"Though I hope you're not troubled by thoughts of the river."

"The river? How do you mean?" She watched as Lem bent to retrieve one of the boots she'd removed that afternoon, and left behind a broom at the edge of the hearth.

"Still not dry," he informed her.

So he'd known all along! But would he say more? At the moment, it appeared not.

For his observation, her friend received a pained look from another who did not enjoy being deceived. Charlotte made her way out of the kitchen, into the front room. She walked past the tall clock, patting it out of habit. Finally she climbed the stairs to her chilly bed chamber, clucking her tongue while Orpheus padded softly behind.

Chapter 6

P ULL!" CALLED A chorus of voices.

The two horses on the bank strained at first, snorting bursts of breath that hung in the morning air. The slide did its job, and the long sledge, laden with blocks of ice, began to inch from the pond. Soon it reached the back of a waiting wagon. More men sent the slippery blocks— each a double hundredweight, two feet square and the depth of yet another—up an incline of planks. Pulled with iron prods and pincers, the blocks tumbled at last into a straw-lined bed to form a single layer, enough for the wagon's axles.

The horses were now hitched to the front, ready for another trip to Richard Longfellow's nearby ice house. Several years before, he'd supervised the diverting of a part of the creek that ran through his meadow, to create the shallow pond. For that reason, his claim came first. But once the blockhouse behind his stone barn was full, more ice would flow into Jonathan Pratt's storehouse, next to the stables that stood behind the inn. Then, smaller cellars about the village would open their doors.

As things proceeded, Longfellow felt the cold, and again donned his long coat and fur-lined hat. He spoke with a few of the loaders and packers preparing to walk by the wagon's side. Out on the ice, others stripped of outer clothing continued in pairs to wield their long, pointed saws with double handles.

Longfellow had earlier lent a hand in cutting the first two parallel lines two feet apart. These had run out into the pond for sixty feet. Crosscuts turned the ice between into blocks, which were pushed beneath the opposite lip, to create a trough of open water. Then a further line and crosscuts freed more blocks that were floated to shore and hauled out, until the first course was finished. The men moved back, sawed a new parallel line, and began to cut more ice from where they'd stood before. As soon as a wagon on the shore was filled, another moved forward to take its place in a changing row.

Longfellow turned to see a number of young women in full cloaks, most often scarlet, lining the shore, cheering as a competition began to see which of the current crews could cut the most blocks before they came together. Older women and small girls arranged food on trestle tables, keeping baskets full of the rolls donated by the Bracebridge Inn's landlord, Jonathan Pratt, serving soup from pots in double-tiered tin boxes lined with coals. Not far off, by a snapping bonfire, jugs offered a more pungent form of refreshment.

Shifting his attention away from the main bustle, Longfellow watched the adjacent ice, dotted with low islands of blueberry scrub. Here, skaters raced or circled one another on blades of steel, antler, or bone. Boys bundled until they resembled sheep romped nearby, awaiting turns. Waging serious battle, the eldest threw hard missiles of old snow and fell according to the rules of the game; younger brothers simply rolled about on their own.

One of these, Longfellow saw, was Mrs. Willett's occasional assistant Henry Sloan, happily at war with associates from the village dame school. Henry's sister Martha skated by with Lem Wainwright. The pretty pair passed Rachel Dudley, newly arrived, who stood watching with her children Winthrop and Anne. As yet, all three seemed uncertain about what to do with their rare holiday. Considering what he knew of their daily lives, Longfellow was sure they richly deserved a reprieve.

It occurred to him that this winter scene resembled a Flemish village he'd enjoyed while on a visit to the Continent—one painted by the Elder Brueghel, who'd lived two centuries before. Not a great deal seemed to have changed, though Richard believed his own countrymen to be more sober and attractive than old Peter's peasants. Yet to be fair, he had to take into account some of the least fastidious members of the village—for instance, Jack Pennywort and his friends.

Where was Jack? Hadn't word reached him of an exciting tale awaiting his perusal, offering him employment? Longfellow patted his pocket to make sure he still had the wretched book, then looked back along the road. He could see several figures climbing the long slope—and there was the pair he sought, one weaving, one with a foot dragging a little behind. Longfellow presumed Dick Craft had tested the cold that morning, and had then taken several nips before venturing out. At least he would make some honest effort on the ice, if pocket silver performed its usual magic. After that, Longfellow supposed, Dick and his club-footed companion would enjoy the evening hours the more, on returning as usual to Phineas Wise's snug tavern across the river.

Deciding their approach would take some time, Richard ambled over to a trio of older men who sat beside the blazing fire, deep in conversation with a lad.

"What is the news today, gentlemen?" Longfellow asked, bowing generously to age.

"Nothing of great interest, sir," Thaddeus Flint assured him. A regular patron of the Blue Boar, he'd come up early with a friend named Tyndall, long known as Tinder. Between this quail-like pair sat another elder of somewhat smaller stomach, though he had a chest shaped like a barrel. Jonah Bigelow gave a gap-toothed grin. He attempted to stand so that he might return the courtesy of one of their selectmen, newly reelected. The effort caused him to wheeze, and he sat down again. The ancient complaint in his lungs was one well known to the village; none grew alarmed, nor did they think to ask particularly after his health. Still, it seemed to Longfellow that Jonah Bigelow's grandson, who stood listening, gave a worried look at his grandsire.

"Are we to have music, Ned?" Longfellow asked, eying a battered wooden box at the young man's feet. This sat next to an open canvas seed bag from which peeped a wooden handle, and a brown scarf with white snowflakes. He realized the latter was Mrs. Willett's work, for he'd watched her knit it the year before.

"Music it shall be, sir, if my fingers cooperate." With a slow smile sometimes called charming, sometimes roguish, and often enough both, Ned bent to open the box's brass latch. Inside, on well-rubbed velvet, lay a softly glowing violin, and a horsehair bow. He lifted both, and set the instrument against his chin and shoulder. His knowing fingers drew the bow slowly across the strings. The resulting tone caught the attention of many; after a curious pause, pleased voices and laughter arose.

"Music," Longfellow commented, "is useful in lifting both heart and load—as I believe Hesiod once remarked, did he not, Ned?" He smiled as he received a rivulet of joyous notes in reply.

Ned now began to bend and saw in earnest, producing a popular tune. For the amusement of those near the fire and to return feeling to his toes, Mr. Tinder got on his feet and jigged about. He was joined for a moment in a jesting gavotte by Mr. Flint; Jonah Bigelow slapped his knees and cried out his approval until a fit of coughing stopped him. Then all three, quite winded, resumed their neat row, like so many kegs on a tavern shelf.

Turning to leave, Longfellow caught sight of something in the snow. He stooped to retrieve it. Moments earlier, it seemed, a shilling had been dropped.

"I assume this belongs to one of you?" he asked. Their response was curious. Each stared at the thing, and then back to his inquiring face. They next glanced furtively toward one another.

"Come, now—it must belong to one of you?" he tried again.

"I came out with none today, sir," said Tinder, "thinking I'd not need money." Mr. Flint nodded absently as he dug around in his coat for his long clay pipe, which he finally pulled out. Jonah Bigelow seemed to take refuge in a cough, while Ned tuned his fiddle.

"Well, then," said Longfellow, "I'll give it to Mr. Rowe, for the poor box." He put the shilling into his coat pocket.

"A good idea, sir," said Tinder.

"Thankee, sir," said Jonah Bigelow, for no apparent reason.

Another friend now sought Longfellow's attention, this one using an insistent nose. This greeting from Orpheus led Richard to suspect Charlotte would not be far away. He patted the dog's head, and went to where Charlotte stood at a trestle table, holding a plate containing crusted wedges of cheese from her dairy. Richard waited patiently while she exchanged greetings with old Sarah Proctor, a tall, officious matron he knew to have a tough crust of her own. Standing by Sarah was her frequent companion and devoted follower, twittering Jemima Hurd, today covered by a vivid cape of Scots plaid.

When he supposed his neighbor had heard enough, Longfellow went closer, and pulled her away. The others quietly withdrew to their own business, though they remained, perhaps, close enough to listen.

"How goes the morning?" he asked.

"Hannah and I are baking. You may try our maple rolls in a few more hours."

"Good. The high clouds increase, and I suspect the wind has something new in it. This morning, too, my barometer began to drop. I don't believe our work could have waited another day," he decided, gazing to the sky.

"Then since we *are* here, everything is as it should be."

"As much as it ever is," he returned.

"Have you brought Diana?"

Longfellow looked back toward the knoll that rose between their houses. "My sister has gone to visit Charles

Douglas, on the hill. I doubt it will help her, though walking may do some good. My advice was to join us later. We'll see if she humors me."

"Mr. Longfellow!" A cry announced the arrival of Jonathan Pratt. The rotund landlord walked before a sled pulled by Tim the message boy. Peeping out from a swathe of blankets was a familiar metal urn, sure to be filled with sweet tea. A few steps behind, Rebecca, the cook's daughter, carried a frosted raisin cake.

Tim and Jonathan lifted the urn to the planks of a table; Rebecca increased the opening in the wrappings, to expose a spigot.

A commotion arose as the men on the ice put down their tools and came for a warming mug. Most were soon taught to select what was best—usually that made by the hands of each fair instructor. In the midst of all this, Ned Bigelow played on, a trio of dogs revolving around his feet.

"Where do the wagons go now?" Jonathan Pratt asked Longfellow, after the two had stepped back to make room for others.

"This next load will go to you. A good many, it seems, are already wagering away the silver we'll be giving them for the day's work."

"Well, John Dudley would have taken most of it anyway," said the landlord, not without reason. Longfellow, who had no love for the new constable responsible for collecting taxes, let out a groan. Jonathan grinned his agreement, and went on.

"Come June, I suppose I'll be repaid one way or another. Then our local friends, like my stopping guests, always begin to drool for ices and frozen creams, which they'll find some way to pay for."

June was also the time when fresh meat in storage

rooms became foul from the heat, Longfellow knew. He'd certainly noticed a stink coming from Jonathan's when he first moved into his house, across the road from the inn. Since the smell seemed to bring on the summer flux, he'd then decided to encourage the use of ice, hoping to protect the entire village.

While the two men continued to converse, Charlotte moved off to speak with Lem, who stood next to Alexander Godwin. Seeing them close in some private discussion, she stopped and waited. Today, Alex wore a round hat with a fringe of striped grouse feathers. His coat, though now unfashionable, was elegantly tailored. Its long doubled sleeves and huge buttons marked it as an old one, and she wondered if it had once been the property of John Fisher. This took her thoughts back to Boar Island. Shivering, she looked to the sun, noticing that it had lost some of its earlier strength.

She finally walked closer to the two youths, and began to make out hot words, delivered in snarls and harsh whispers.

"Not if you know what's good for you, you won't, Godwin!" Lem said to the fat boy.

"And if I do?" came a quick answer. "You'll *beat* me, I suppose?" It was said with a sneer. Alex rightly imagined he had little reason, at the moment, to fear a blatant attack.

"See if I don't!" Lem growled, his voice betraying rising fury.

"Then you are *both* going to be sorry." Alex took a step forward, his hands clenched into threatening fists. "Give me any more trouble, and I'll gladly tell the whole world that you—"

He had no chance to finish, for Lem gave him a shove that knocked the wind from his body.

In a few moments more they circled one another. Then they came together in what might have seemed, from a distance, to be a clasp of friendship. Yet Charlotte could see sharp blows were being delivered, as first one and then the other took a turn. Both tried to hide what they were up to, but it was no good—Sarah Proctor and Jemima Hurd turned shocked faces.

Martha Sloan hurried forward, her cardinal cloak flying, her displeasure apparent. Fearing what might come next, Charlotte interrupted the young men herself.

"Good day, Mr. Godwin!" she called out loudly. They stopped, exchanged a few more words in threatening undertones, and took several steps apart. Lem stooped to retrieve his hair ribbon, while Alex turned to pant and glower.

"I've been hoping we'd find a chance to speak," Charlotte said more gently.

"Then I'm sorry, madam! For I am off to write something down, as I should have done *before*."

Why, she asked herself, did she suddenly think the same? Wasn't there something she, too, had meant to write down, and remember?

"Could we talk later?" she asked. "When you have a moment to spare? You'll return this afternoon?"

"I most certainly will," Godwin assured her with a fresh sneer. "And then, I will have something for Mr. Longfellow! Good day to you, madam," he said, touching his hat to her, giving no sign to Lem or to Martha Sloan as he stalked away.

Mattie stood at Lem's shoulder, her pale blue eyes snapping, though she somehow managed to hold her tongue.

"I see," said Charlotte, breaking the charged silence,

"that you've given Henry his chance on the ice—and this year, he's learned to stop himself before charging into others. An accomplishment to be proud of."

"Agreed," Lem answered, addressing her thoughts rather than her exact words. "Yet sometimes, a *man* has no choice."

"Lem Wainwright," Martha exploded, "what could be lost in one turn with him, out on the ice?" He looked at her in some confusion.

"Nothing, I suppose," he finally answered. "Was it what you wanted, Mattie?"

"No—but just how should I have refused? You'd already gone off to prove you skate better than I do. Didn't you? *Didn't you?*"

"What if I did?"

The girl turned her face to the sky, her lips pressed tightly together.

"Well," said Lem at last, "there's nothing to be done about any of it now, I suppose. And all that skating has made me hungry."

"Go on, then, and try my suet cakes. My sisters may say I made them for you, but we all know how fond of them *my father is*."

Imagining they must have further words meant only for one another, Charlotte turned away to examine ideas of her own. The exchange she'd heard earlier had been a curious one; she wondered just what Alex Godwin had suggested. She also asked herself if Lem would one day come to real blows with his apparent rival, or with any other. She hoped not, though lately she'd seen his capacity for anger grow with the rest of him. So, too, did his pride.

They would *both* be sorry, Alex had said. Did he also

threaten to make Mattie suffer? For what? And what good would it do to write his thoughts down for Richard Longfellow, instead of telling her father, or even Hannah? Was Alex about to make a bid to court Mattie himself? Or did he feel, perhaps, that she had led him on, only to make Lem burn with jealousy? If that had been the case, she'd apparently succeeded! Hardly an official matter, but such were the games, Charlotte recalled uneasily, that often occupied young men and women whose lives were still unsettled.

She wished she'd been able to ask Alex about the spoon she'd found beneath the dock, below the house he often visited. Later, she would also ask what the two women needed most, before she chose something to repay their kindness. He might tell her more about their strange companionship, and how he'd become a part of their lives. Yet to ask would intrude on things that were no concern of hers—even if he wanted to give her answers, which she doubted.

Deciding the island would remain a mystery on many fronts, Charlotte heaved a sigh and went to join Richard Longfellow. She found him still with Jonathan, discussing the state of the roads from Worcester and Concord, and the highway that led to Boston. But she soon discovered an even better reason to go back up the hill. Along the well-trampled track came a man she preferred to avoid.

In dark woolen leggings and a black great coat, Christian Rowe sidled toward the ice pond in his usual disjointed manner, watching for anything amiss. Charlotte feared he might resume his peculiar attempts to please her with unctuous praise, unnecessary advice, and comfort, the last aimed at her lengthening term of widowhood. These things she found even more unpleasant than his previous disapproval, which had been bad enough.

She made a sign to Longfellow. In a moment, he and Jonathan saw what she did. Then the little party dissolved, as each hurried off in a different direction, seeking some distant occupation.

Chapter 7

WITH A LONG wooden paddle, Hannah Sloan finished pulling a row of brown loaves from the deep oven next to the hearth. Her face was damp and red, her linen sleeves pulled up to reveal the strength of her broad arms. She turned with the loaves, and slid them off onto a cooling board. This accomplished, she set the paddle down and went to re-latch the oven door.

"How warm it is!" said Charlotte happily, closing the door to the outside.

"It is, indeed!" said Hannah, with quite a different perspective on the matter. She wiped her brow and considered the state of her younger friend. Charlotte suspected Hannah had come to think of her as almost a part of her own family—it was not surprising, since they'd worked together for many seasons, taking care of the Howard farm. "You must be nearly frozen," Hannah scolded. "And those boots will only hold the cold."

Knowing it was true, Charlotte sat and removed them, and put on softer house shoes.

"Is anything worth hearing about going on down there?" Hannah asked.

"The usual." Charlotte had already decided to keep to herself Lem's heated words with Alex Godwin, and Mattie's part in the fracas. No doubt the girl's mother would learn of it soon enough.

"The first loaves were good; these, I think, are better. Now the oven feels nearly right for rolls."

Charlotte looked to the pan she'd filled earlier—bread dough smoothed thin, covered with a generous layer of butter, maple sugar, nuts, and cinnamon. She'd rolled it up, cut the soft log into small pieces, and placed these into a pan. They'd doubled in size.

"They'll be gobbled up in no time," Hannah predicted.

"But what *is* it I've forgotten?" Charlotte murmured to herself. "I can't help feeling there's something."

"Didn't you mean to start a stew?"

"Oh, yes. But still—" She went toward the cellar door. Another question from Hannah stopped her.

"That reminds me—the spoon there, on the table. That isn't one you've bought for yourself recently?"

"No. I'll tell you an interesting story—"

"I've been asking myself if it might be one of those gone missing."

"Missing? . . ."

"Stolen, it's said, from Rachel Dudley. Though it's hard to believe, when you consider her husband's constable this year. Why *he* was ever elected—"

"Stolen! When, Hannah?"

"Rachel couldn't say. They've always been kept in a cupboard, locked up tight—her one small security, too valuable to use. You know the Dudleys are often in straits. But it would take some persuading to get Rachel to sell them. That set of spoons was the one fine thing given to her by her mother on her wedding day."

"What does her husband say?"

"John Dudley claims to know nothing, and says there's little he can do about it! Given the fact that he's often in his cups—my Samuel sees him drinking often enough at the Blue Boar—it's hard to say *what* could have happened."

"But you do think this is one of Rachel's spoons?" Charlotte picked it up.

"Emily Bowers told me yesterday each had a flower etched onto its bowl. There was also said to be a guild mark, and that of a London maker, like what you see there."

"Locked in a cupboard, but loved . . . which might explain why it was recently polished. That surprised me, when I found it."

"Where?"

"Beneath a landing. On Boar Island."

"What on earth were you doing *there*?"

"I went skating yesterday afternoon," Charlotte returned mildly. Her heart, however, began to beat quickly.

"Ah, my joints ache just to think of it . . . did you decide you'd climb up and have a chat with the two old women?" Hannah asked with growing disbelief.

"Magdalene is several years younger than you."

"Thank you for that bit of information. If you found the spoon on the ice there, why did you not take it up to them?"

"I found it when I was about to leave, at sunset."

Hannah considered the travels of the young woman before her, as well as those of the missing spoon, now found. "I've long told you," she said at last, "eerie things happen near that accursed place—probably in the great house, as well. Though no worse than the high times once had there, I'm sure. Another Merry Mount, they used to say it was. Lately, Samuel says, men have seen the strange lights again."

"Lights and colors," Charlotte murmured, recalling the rose mirror she'd seen over the hearth.

"Colors? I don't know about that—but I wonder what Samuel would say to hear of this?" Hannah contemplated the spoon Charlotte had just set down.

"I hope he doesn't hear of it. I'll take it to Rachel when I go back to the pond, to see if it's hers after all."

Still pondering, Charlotte went down the cellar steps, candle in hand. Below, she bent over a barrel of sand and removed a layer of carrots, then chose two papery spheres from a nearby nest of onions, each held from touching the next by wood shavings. She took up a pan of dried cod set to soak the night before, and a small bowl of salt pork she'd cut from a hanging leg. Balancing carefully, she took these things upstairs.

On a further trip to one of the cold bedrooms above, she picked out the most shriveled potatoes in store. Soon after, the kitchen began to fill with the smell of crisping pork and fresh-cut onions. Then, she heard a knock on the back door.

Wiping her hands and face, Charlotte went to see, expecting to find women from the ice coming to visit and warm themselves. Instead, to her embarrassment, she found the answer to her earlier question. There *had* been something important, and she'd forgotten all about it— an appointment with the man who had acted as Aaron's attorney. Moses Reed had written earlier in the month from Boston, saying he wished to bring her papers to transfer a small legacy from her late husband's family.

"Mr. Reed!" she exclaimed.

The pleasant-looking man stepped inside, allowing

the door to be swiftly shut behind him. He was a few years past forty, but still quite fit; his upper face showed he'd taken the smallpox. His jaw was of greater interest, for it was covered with an amusing beard—soft curls of dark brown hairs a few inches long. Both women stared at this sight, for it was something rarely seen on the face of a gentleman, at least in New England. If beards were the fashion in other lands, here they marked men who had no fear of taunting children, or of more subtle disapproval from their peers.

Charlotte took her visitor's hat and heavy coat, noticing a glint of appreciation for her own appearance in his darting eyes. At the same time she heard Hannah hurry through one of the doors that flanked the hearth.

"Am I too early, Mrs. Willett? I fear I've startled you. Perhaps I've been somewhat forward in coming to your back door," Moses Reed apologized. "But I see your kitchen is warm and snug, as well as busy." He continued to assess the industry around him with his eyes and nose.

"I'm glad to see you, sir, of course! But I'm afraid, well, the truth is—"

"You had forgotten me! Never mind. There was a good chance the weather would delay my arrival, but I'm glad to say I reached Bracebridge last evening, as planned. I've since been presuming on the kindness of your minister."

"You chose to stay with Reverend Rowe?"

"Less of an expense than the Bracebridge Inn, and more comfortable than the Blue Boar. With a large house at his disposal, I felt sure Mr. Rowe would not object . . . after I told him I intend to leave a donation."

Charlotte still had to wonder at his choice, and only hoped her expression didn't reveal this fact. Moses Reed smiled, and explained further.

"I thought I might also look over the village records

kept there. Lawyers, you know, take pleasure in poking into the past. And since this was my early home, I have decided to follow the example of our lieutenant governor, and write a small history—as he has so admirably done for the whole of Massachusetts. I'm sure my work will never be as fine, but it could be useful one day. And, I have time on my hands, since that same gentleman balks at re-opening Boston's courts."

"How well I remember the day you left us, sir!" said Hannah, returning from the front room. "We were nearly young together," she added with a silly smile.

"Yet most would swear, Mrs. Sloan, that you are no older than my daughter," the lawyer countered, "if, indeed, I had one."

Charlotte now smiled as well, noticing that Hannah's apron was straighter than it had been, and her hair tidier.

"Someone with bats' eyes might be fooled," Hannah returned. "I am a *few* years older than you, sir, I'll admit." Following Charlotte's example, she lowered her substantial body onto a chair. "We were sorry when you left us to read the law; my husband and I have followed your successes lately in the *Gazette*. But do you recall one winter day twenty years ago, when you and Samuel went out into the west hills together, and came back with a bear? Didn't we grow heartily sick of it, long before the fat ran out!"

"We did. We've faced lean years together, it's true. But I've also heard your good husband has since prospered— and, that more than the family purse has grown!"

"I have seven children now, including unmarried daughters. I take it, sir, that you have not yet married?"

"That is so. Might I come and meet the family a little later, Mrs. Sloan?"

"You would be most welcome! But you once called me Hannah."

"Then Hannah it shall be again."

"And I must see to the baking," Hannah reminded herself, rising. "Or would you like me to leave you here?" she asked Charlotte.

"I'd better take Mr. Reed to my study, where there's sunlight."

With the matter settled, Charlotte and Moses Reed spent the next hour warming the blue room with a fire, while examining his papers. These concerned a profit lately realized from the sale of land, a portion of which, Aaron's family had decided, must go to his widow. Since they continued a warm correspondence, Charlotte had been pleased but hardly surprised by their generosity.

"Now," she said, after he'd explained everything to her satisfaction, and she had signed the necessary papers, "have you seen what goes on in the village today?"

"Yes, on my way here . . ."

"Would you consider walking back with me, by way of Mr. Longfellow's ice pond?"

"I should like that!"

"If you'll enjoy our fire here a little longer, I'll see if the baking is done."

Moses Reed got up to examine shelves full of volumes while Charlotte left the study. She passed through the front room, then re-entered the kitchen.

"I could hardly restrain myself," Hannah confessed moments later, "after I'd mentioned that bear! I'm sure I thought of it after taking a good look at the stuff all over his face. Why ever did he grow such a thing, do you suppose?"

"I asked him that question myself."

"You didn't!"

"Oh, I did." Charlotte's eyes were bright with amusement. "After all, he sat there stroking it as if he wanted to explain."

"He answered you, then?"

"He told me it's considered impressive by the juries he addresses, and he's found it a help when he attempts to worry witnesses. He also told me that while few have yet emulated him in Boston, he hopes to set a new style, to save importing razors."

"Politics," Hannah intoned darkly.

"I wonder if I should ask Richard if he'd consider joining Mr. Reed in a more natural state . . . to disappoint London's merchants?"

"Far too natural, if you ask me! Would it be any different, I wonder, from kissing a puppy?" Hannah covered a basket by now filled with rolls, each well drizzled with sugar frosting. "Here, take these off while they're hot. And tell my children, if you see any of them still out, they should be home doing their chores!"

"Of course," Charlotte said, planning to do no such thing. "Oh—I nearly forgot the spoon!" She took up the shining object, and nestled it gently in a corner of the basket. Then, she went back to fetch Moses Reed.

Chapter 8

Q
UITE A GATHERING!" the lawyer exclaimed as they left the main road and walked onto a white expanse of field, along a track increasingly muddied and marked by horses.

"The ice harvest has become a favorite day for us," Charlotte agreed.

"Please tell me something of the village. I rarely have time to visit, and it's been too long since I saw many of my acquaintance. Hannah mentioned unmarried daughters at home. What of her sons? Are they married?"

"One of three lives in Concord now—he's expected to wed soon. The eldest brother is in Lexington, learning a trade with a cousin. Martha seems to have made her choice, but the others are still waiting."

"Mr. Rowe tells me you've taken one of Cyrus Wainwright's children into your own home."

"Lem is a great help—especially in the work of the dairy."

"A promising boy, is he?"

"Interested in scientific studies, as well as husbandry."

"Your brother's farm seems well cared for, while he's abroad."

"I hope so."

"Where is Jeremy now?"

"In Geneva. He's become secretary to a banker. He managed to visit us this spring, and said he approved of what we've done—but with only two mouths to feed, it's not difficult."

"No?" Moses Reed replied with a squint. "A good many I come upon these days seem to find it hard to survive. But let me see . . . what has become of my old neighbors, the Bigelows?"

"Jonah suffers from a permanent congestion of the lungs, as you'll probably remember. But it hasn't yet proven to be consumptive."

"He lost a fine wife some years ago. Nabby Bigelow would often give a good boy a ginger snap," he smiled. "But then, Jonah was left alone with a young child in his care."

"Ned is eighteen now, and takes care of his grandfather."

"The way of the world. Born to a young sister of Mrs. Bigelow who lived to the west, I recall, and died in childbirth."

"You know more of the family's history than I."

"Possibly. We realize we're growing old when we discover we're founts of information, much of it unimportant, most unasked for," he replied with a chuckle. "Tell me, what kind of employment supports them? Even before I left Bracebridge, Jonah could do little more than sit in the sun."

"It's said Ned follows in Jonah's footsteps. I've even heard some remark that he resembles the grasshopper in the fable, while he should emulate the ant. But he pleases us with his violin," she added, now that they had begun to hear the fiddle's strains. "And he's read a great deal. They say, too, the stories he often tells at the Blue Boar are well received."

"It sounds as if he might come to Boston, and take up the law."

"By staying here with his grandfather, I think he may well have added years to Jonah's life. I sometimes suppose we give too little praise to those who make joyful noises."

"*Go to the ant, thou sluggard; consider her ways, and be wise,*" the lawyer quoted in ringing tones. "Yet for pleasure, I doubt I would choose to watch an ant for any length of time, myself. A fiddle brings us all far better amusement."

They began to encounter a number of villagers, and as they neared the ice, Charlotte was glad to see Diana among the crowd. Greetings were exchanged between the lawyer and Richard Longfellow, who'd earlier become acquainted in Boston; Mr. Reed bowed to Mrs. Montagu, who had heard of him. As soon as her brief smile faded, Longfellow led Reed into a discussion of town matters, which somewhat excluded the ladies.

Charlotte held out the basket she'd brought and encouraged Diana to take a maple roll, noting that she appeared wan when compared to those around them. Diana nibbled, giving only a small indication of her approval.

Moses Reed went to speak with his old friend Jonah Bigelow who sat by the fire, warming himself inside and out. Then Longfellow turned to give his attention back to his sister, but saw that she'd moved off to stand alone. In spite of his determined efforts to enjoy the day, he found himself glowering.

A year ago, Diana would have found words to describe any situation in which she found herself. Now, it seemed, she cared little for what others around her said or did. Was that the fault of her marriage? More and more, it was a thing he considered to have been ill-advised. Yet how could anyone have stopped her from accepting the captain, the year before? A brother, surely, could hope to do no more than guide a determined young heiress of nearly twenty, especially when her own mother, his stepmother, was pleased with Diana's choice. And what further trouble might Diana have found for herself, had she *not* married? Edmund Montagu did have much to recommend him, Longfellow had to admit. And they had been quite happy together, all in all, until this tragic business with the child. But he would like to know where the devil the man was now, when his wife had need of him!

"Richard?" Charlotte asked quietly.

"Hmm? Oh, thank you, Carlotta. I could use something sweet."

"Your thoughts have soured you?"

"Once again," he sighed.

"I'd hoped to speak with Rachel Dudley. Is she about, do you know?"

"I suppose she is. John is sitting there by the fire, next to his jug."

Charlotte's plan was further delayed, for she'd been seen by someone else.

"Mrs. Willett! I'm pleased to find you at last," crowed Christian Rowe, slipping beside her. "I myself have been here for hours, to make sure the day's festivities do not become *too* merry. We all know men tend to exceed propriety when they gather together, especially when they are without ecclesiastic guidance. In fact, I've heard your young charge became involved in some form of violence earlier in the day . . . but what have you there?"

"Maple rolls."

"Oh, quite wholesome! There is reason to suspect the motives of those who prepare more elegant fare—trifles, French jelly tarts, or rum balls. Those should never, I think, be served in public. I much prefer the plain delights born of our own countryside to the contrivances of more fashionable society."

While speaking, the minister had removed a pair of dog-skin gloves. He then gave a thin smile, and blew on his exposed fingers. Taking a chance, he patted Charlotte's cheek. She stood stoically while he took his time choosing from her offered basket.

"I believe," Rowe went on, once he held his selection between crooked digits, "that Lemuel would behave with more decorum, if he saw daily the example of an older and wiser man. Someone close by, who could instruct him in the responsibilities of manhood."

"Closer than I, sir?" Longfellow asked sharply. It was known in the village that he'd taken Lem under his protection, if not his roof. And his situation as Mrs. Willett's nearest neighbor did give him a natural interest in the boy's welfare, as well as her own. His irritation caused him to shove his hands into his pockets; in one, he felt the shilling he'd picked up earlier. Peevishly, he decided against handing it over to the cleric.

"Yes, even closer than you, Mr. Longfellow," Rowe returned solemnly, while he continued to watch the selectman. His stained teeth bit into the roll he held, and came up sporting small pieces of walnut.

"Have you *another* suggestion, sir?" asked Longfellow.

"I believe a husband would be more efficacious than a

neighbor, for a number of reasons. If only this lady would put her mind to accepting one, I am quite sure—"

"That is something she must decide for herself, when she is ready."

"There's another thing I wish to accomplish at the moment, gentlemen," Charlotte interrupted. "I will go and speak with Mrs. Dudley, as I was about to do when you first joined us, sir. Though I am honored at having my future discussed by such notable persons, at tea time. Please feel free to continue, once I've gone."

Laughing silently, Longfellow admired her determined eyes. He also knew they had trouble with distances, so he assisted her by pointing.

"Rachel is over there with young Anne."

"Then you'll excuse me," she said as she walked away.

"Will I see you later?" Longfellow called, causing her to turn around.

"Whenever you wish," she answered firmly.

"Good," he said, giving the minister a triumphant smile.

CHARLOTTE MADE HER way through the crowd. At the edge of the pond, she touched a bending woman on the shoulder. Rachel Dudley looked up in surprise. Then she, too, beamed to see a friendly face.

"Mrs. Willett! I'm freeing my daughter from what she likes to call her new set of pattens. She assures me she longs to be a lady now, though you see she's made a large hole in the knee of one of her stockings this afternoon."

Rachel took a frozen strap from its buckle. Showing new front teeth, Anne smiled with relief as the heavy blade dropped off. The two women watched as the blonde-headed girl chased after her older brother. Charlotte could not help remembering that there were once three children in the family. She was careful, however, to give no sign to remind Rachel.

"Is there something I can do for you?" Mrs. Dudley asked, while she stood and slipped her mittens back onto her hands. Each year, she seemed a little more absent, a little more tired. It was an effect less of age than of care, and perhaps too frequent quilting, Charlotte supposed; that was how the family made ends meet, beyond consuming or trading what her husband scratched from poor farmland.

"I hope you can tell me something of this." Charlotte reached into her basket, and pulled out the spoon.

"Well, however did you—! Where *was* it?" Rachel asked, nearly overcome with amazement.

"I happened to find it . . . while skating on the marsh."

"On the marsh! But—"

"Hannah told me you lost several spoons, and I thought this could be one of them. I'm sorry I can't tell you anything about the rest." Again Charlotte hesitated, hoping she would not be asked to explain further. Rachel's pleading look forced her to add something more. "It wasn't far from your home. It was—on Boar Island."

At this news, Rachel was speechless, and it was several moments before she nodded. She took the spoon and slipped it into her pocket.

"Thank you—very much, indeed! I feared they would all be in the hands of someone in Boston by now," she added, her tone lowered. "At least I have one back, to help me remember. As if I could forget! You've so often been a help to us, Mrs. Willett."

Charlotte now noticed several knots of people preparing to leave, in conveyances that had arrived to take them home. "Will you visit me, Rachel, one morning or afternoon? When you can steal an hour or two from your house and children?"

"My husband may soon be doing the housework—at least until my temper cools," Rachel Dudley replied, gazing toward the bonfire.

"The sun is setting . . ."

"Yes. In January, it often comes as a surprise. Many things do, it seems. We will have to walk a few miles if I don't urge John to find us a ride. Good-bye, and oh— thank you!" Rachel stepped forward and gave her friend an impulsive embrace. She then hurried off, calling for her children.

Charlotte was glad she did not depend on any one man for her survival—especially a man like John Dudley. For bread and shelter, many women made similar bargains. For them, pity was hardly enough.

She noticed half a dozen lanterns had been lit to combat the coming darkness. The remaining haulers would need some illumination while they finished loading. Though the cutters had already gone off to enjoy their suppers, much ice lay on a long bed of straw, awaiting a final wagon. It would be a while before the last man would leave.

She saw Longfellow take a lantern to his sister, who sat on a makeshift seat at the edge of the pond, gently rocking. Was Diana weeping? Richard helped her to her feet, giving her his arm as she walked forward, awkward as a goose. In an amazing transformation, she seemed to become a weightless sprite, drifting about the gloom.

"I thought she might like to try a pair of skates,"

Longfellow commented at Charlotte's approach. "Nothing else I do seems to improve her spirits." They walked slowly along the bank while they waited, gaining a little warmth.

"It takes time, as you know. But a kind of peace should come before long."

"A kind, yes."

They moved on in silence. Despite a feeling of renewed companionship that she'd missed in recent weeks, Charlotte also felt something nearly its opposite— something unexplained, and distinctly chilly. Though she hardly supposed this to be Richard's fault, it stopped her from speaking further.

What, she wondered, could have begun to bother her now? Looking around, she saw the last of the revelers depart, while the men by the pool of light continued their work. One walked from the others, toward a copse of dark firs. She soon saw him return to the rest and resume his efforts. Orpheus was disturbed as well, his attention directed to the same trees, which grew blacker by the minute. Charlotte lowered her head and suggested he take a look. He whined, his eyes going from hers to the copse, and back again. Though he continued to watch intently, the old dog refused to leave her.

With the fading of the last light in the west, Diana reappeared. By the lantern's glow they saw that her features were quite different from what they'd been before.

"How magical it was!" she gasped. "And just as I remembered! Thank you, Richard," she added breathlessly.

"You're quite welcome, Diana. Now, perhaps, you'll be pleased to try what Cicero has for us at home. Your lack of interest in his culinary efforts has caused him some concern lately."

"Then I'll eat enough to bend my stays! How good it

is to be among friends. I almost feel as if everything will be all right . . ."

"Of course," said her brother, kneeling to remove her skates.

Charlotte made no answer of her own. At that moment, for no apparent reason, she felt far from sure.

Chapter 9

THE WINTER SKY was still dark when Charlotte opened her eyes to a new morning. Refreshed, she looked forward to rising.

The first thing her nose told her, as she moved the linen sheet curled about her face, was that the air was less dry, and a little warmer. It also blew steadily, and had begun to whistle around a corner of the house as it made its way inland from the sea. Before long, it would bring snow. She was glad she'd moved to the middle bedroom, next to the kitchen's chimney. Richard had been right, she thought, when he'd predicted the weather would worsen.

She stretched out her feet, and smiled as they encountered a large ball. Orpheus had crept softly onto the sagging bed, burrowing under its covers like a sapper. Surrounded by feathers, he no doubt dreamed of chasing after ducks or geese, along the Musketaquid's noisy marshes. That might explain the frantic quivering of his paws.

The thought of the marshes reminded her of the ice pond, and the curious feeling she'd had the night before.

Today it was gone; she supposed it had been no more than fatigue from a long day. And the new suggestion of snow on the way gave her a pleasant sense of exhilaration.

After a warning word to Orpheus, she took a breath. She lunged from beneath the covers, and leaped to the chair to grab hold of her morning gown. When she'd slipped into its soft warmth, she sat on the side of the mattress and pulled on her slippers. By now, her companion had emerged to watch intently.

"Run!" she called a moment later, bolting for the door. There was a scrabble of claws behind her on the newly sanded pine floor. While she regretted its marring, she laughed as she led the way down the narrow, twisted stairs.

FROM THE NEARBY dairy, Lem Wainwright watched the light increase while he went about the morning milking. At last he blew out the flame in his lantern, and lifted a final bucket from the straw. As the cows, hayed and watered, continued to chew, he carried the warm milk down several steps to the spring room. He would deal with it later. Now, he intended to make a quick trip back to the scene of yesterday's excitement.

After he'd walked the small herd across the yard to the barn, he went out into the wind once more. Pushed by the increasing gale, he made his way to the Boston-Worcester road, and then took the track that ended by the ice. This morning, it was deserted.

Minutes later, he looked carefully around the fire, no more than dead ashes and the ends of logs. Somewhere he'd left his canvas seed bag, and the woolen scarf Mrs. Willett had knitted for him. The bag also held the ice hatchet he'd borrowed from the barn's supply of tools. Neither, of course, could be lost. Anyone finding them would know where they belonged—the scarf, since they'd all seen it around his neck, and the hatchet because it had "Howard" carved into its handle.

Several minutes later he was about to give up, having found nothing more than some paper and broken china, and one small mitten. Then he saw company, and help, approaching. Orpheus had been let out of the house to begin his own morning duties. He loped down the track, a single bark announcing his pleasure at finding a friend.

With the dog at his side, Lem re-walked the entire area of stamped snow. He investigated a few clumps of blueberries, thinking the wind might have taken the scarf, at least, on its own. Still, nothing useful came to light. They found only scraps of discarded food, another bright mitten (not a match), and a child's stocking.

Then Orpheus's head shot up, for the shifting wind had brought something new to his nostrils. With Lem following, he led the way to a spot behind a small copse of firs, where the snow had been altered in curious ways. Here and there, bright yellow seemed to have blossomed over the white. Other visitors had written bits of messages in the unblemished snow. And one large frozen puddle, Lem thought with a smile, had been made by the more community-minded. It might have been seen as an interesting study of dispositions, he supposed, if one cared to think about such things.

After adding his mark to the others, Orpheus was still not content. His ears pointed with new alertness. He began to whine softly. He moved to the edge of the copse, and uttered a low growl. In another moment he stepped hesitantly into the trees, and disappeared between their singing limbs. A mournful howl then rose above the wind.

With misgiving, Lem strode to the trees and plunged inside. When his eyes had adjusted to the dimness, he saw that someone lay sleeping—a young man stretched out on his chest, on top of a soft bed of needles. A second later he realized he'd been wrong. With a worse shock, he knew by the frost covering its exposed flesh that the body was no longer alive—and, that it was Alex Godwin. He touched a hand, and found it icy cold, hard as marble.

The poor fool must have returned after all, and gotten drunk by the end of the afternoon, Lem imagined with a shudder. Very drunk indeed to fall asleep here, and stay long enough to freeze! It was a terrible thing—and yet, perhaps, a fate that was not entirely unjust.

As this seemed a shameful conclusion, Lem began to look about for something to make him feel more charitable toward his former rival. There was his ridiculous hat, with its fringe of grouse feathers. Odd that it appeared to have been tossed down onto the back of his head, hardly as if he'd put it there himself. With the beginning of a new suspicion, Lem bent to move the hat, and then felt true horror at the sight of a dark hole in the soft base of Alex Godwin's skull. It looked to be deep. There was little blood about—so he'd died quickly, or perhaps somewhere else. But how? Lem soon found the answer. Beneath a fir branch lay an ice hatchet—one all too familiar.

He reached out, but drew back. He could see the damage hadn't been caused by the bite of the flat blade. But the back of the hatchet had a wicked point, now stained with something. Someone must have found it, and brought it here. Who? And why would anyone have wanted to use it for *this*?

Yet as he straightened, he had to ask himself if some in the village might not rejoice to have Godwin out of the way. And then it came to him where he'd left the canvas bag the day before. He'd set it down near the bonfire—not long before his fight with Alex, in front of several women! Mrs. Willett, as well as a couple of the old village hens, had heard them arguing. And Mattie! What would Mattie think when she heard of what had happened *now*?

Feverishly, he began to ask himself if there could be a simple way out. What if Mattie never heard? Maybe none of them had to—at least not any time soon. After all, they might think Alex went off in one of his high and mighty moods, as he often did. He only boarded in the village—he might not even be missed, if someone went in quietly, one day soon, and took away his things. Only yesterday there had been plenty of open water in the pond. It probably hadn't frozen much. With the hatchet, he could open up a hole and slide the body in. It might not be found for months.

But it would be found eventually. And then, Richard Longfellow wouldn't be happy to learn what someone had done to his ice pond. Lem wondered, too, if he could keep such a thing hidden from Mrs. Willett. She already suspected there was something he wouldn't tell her. Keeping this, too, a secret would be next to impossible.

Orpheus began to whine again, then allowed himself to be led out through the branches, back into the streaming wind.

Lem knew he would have to go to them both, and explain what he could. Mr. Longfellow, as one of the village selectmen responsible for seeing to the peace, would have an idea of what to do next. With Mrs. Willett helping him, he might even discover who had done this thing—and why.

Hoping for the best, the young man began to jog back toward the track, glad he'd decided to do what was right. Still, he imagined that a small, nagging devil, as well as a large dog, kept him company.

"WHAT?" ASKED LONGFELLOW, setting down a pen. "*What* did you say?"

"Dead, sir," Lem repeated. Suddenly remembering his manners, he grabbed his cocked hat by one of its corners, and stuffed it under an arm.

"Alexander Godwin? And you say you found him *in my ice pond*?" A ghastly thought had become even worse.

"In some nearby fir trees, sir. You would have seen them when—well, it was where men went to piss yesterday."

"Yes, a small stand, relatively young."

"Littered with needles inside, so a darkly clad body didn't show through."

"An interesting observation. Just how did he die, do you suppose?" The selectman leaned back, hoping for a flow of more useful information.

"His neck was punctured."

"Punctured? Punctured *how*?"

"In the back. It was done with—with an ice hatchet."

"An ice hatchet! Whose?"

"Mine."

Again, Longfellow waited.

"Or rather, Mrs. Willett's," said Lem. He gave a sigh that ended in a moan.

"Does she know about this?"

"I didn't ask to borrow it, but I often use tools left in the barn by her father," said Lem. "I'm sure she won't mind."

"That part, no."

"I didn't do it myself! Yesterday morning, I left the hatchet in the canvas bag we use for scattering seeds—along with my scarf—before I went off to skate with Mattie."

"Where, exactly, did you last see this bag?"

"I set it down when I went to talk to Ned Bigelow, seeing he arrived just after I did. I knew the hatchet would be safe there from children since they wouldn't be allowed to play too near the large fire. Several men were already sitting around it."

"Mr. Flint and Mr. Tinder I saw myself, only a little later."

"And Jonah Bigelow between them?"

"John Dudley came over some time later . . ." Longfellow mused.

"The constable?" Lem hardly knew whether to feel better or worse. "Do you think he saw the hatchet?"

"I doubt he noticed much of anything."

"But the others—someone must know what happened to the bag."

"Now I think of it, I do remember the scarf, and seeing some sort of handle. Lem—how long do you think Alex Godwin has been dead?"

"All night, I'm sure. He's stiff with cold. Frozen, in fact."

"You tried to move him?"

"No, sir. I thought . . . but I decided to leave him. All I moved was his hat."

Longfellow sat up with new purpose. "Do you know of anyone who might have felt he had reason to do such a thing? Even someone who might have wished only to frighten him, but went too far?"

Lem considered carefully. "Many of us might have

wanted to do a little something to him, sir, from time to time."

"I see. But could he have had any real enemies here?"

"He must have. He's dead, after all." This nice bit of logic forced Longfellow to take another tack.

"I'll go and see for myself. No reason to call John Dudley just yet. He'll have a sore head this morning, I'm sure. Go across to the inn. Tell Tim to take his time, but to let the constable know he needs to pay a visit to Reverend Rowe in the next few hours. Then, I want you to tell Mrs. Willett about this. When you've done that, follow her back here. You've told no one else?"

"No, sir!" Lem assured him. At a further sign from Longfellow, he turned and hurried out.

"Young fools," he heard from behind. Striding through the hall, he asked himself who, besides Alex, the select-man could have in mind.

Chapter 10

"A t first, they'll think the worst," said Charlotte, once she'd made her way to Longfellow's warm kitchen.

"I wouldn't be surprised," her neighbor agreed.

"Lem will be suspected, unless—"

Lem sat and watched; he had nothing more to say, now that he'd told Mrs. Willett, too, about the body he'd discovered in the trees, but it seemed to him that things had taken a decidedly unpleasant turn.

"—unless we find a witness who saw someone else pick up the seed bag," Longfellow finished for her. "Or the hatchet alone, though I would guess both were taken together. If not, the bag and scarf would have been found by now."

"Someone could have found them abandoned at the end of the day, and might have taken them home for safe keeping."

"Long after the hatchet had been slipped out? Well, perhaps so."

"Lem told me you saw it where he left it, Richard. Can you swear to that?"

"Only to seeing some kind of wooden handle, some time before noon."

Her disappointment unspoken, Charlotte watched Cicero shake a long-handled pan over the coals. An intoxicating perfume continued to rise, as dark beans browned further.

"The longer the bag sat there, the more time there would have been for someone else to disturb it," she decided.

"This altercation between Lem and Alex Godwin— that's something you saw, I think."

"So did Sarah Proctor and Jemima Hurd," she replied unhappily.

"Do they know its cause?"

"They must have assumed, as I did, that the two fought over Martha Sloan." Charlotte turned to the young man beside her. Lem seemed uncomfortable, but betrayed nothing more. "Was there something else?" she asked.

"It wasn't just me, you know," Lem answered. "No one liked him! All we did was trade a few words, and a punch or two, I'll admit—but how could I have harmed him, or him me, while we had our coats on? I only meant to show him I *would* fight, if he wanted."

"Some time later?" asked Longfellow. "When you could meet away from the crowd?"

"Exactly."

That was something neither of his questioners had wanted to hear, Lem soon realized. He ducked his head in further embarrassment.

"Did you see him again? Alive?" Longfellow's tone was unchanged, yet he watched the boy more intently, waiting for an answer.

"No. I walked Mattie home so she could finish her chores, and she gave me something to eat—"

"Her sisters were there?"

"A couple of them came in, before I left—"

"What time was that?"

"Around two. Then I went back to the pond, looking for Ned to ask him something . . . but when I didn't see him I decided I'd better go and do my own chores. I walked up and went straight to the barn, and saw to the eggs before milking."

"You didn't go into the house?"

"Hannah was there. And I knew Mrs. Willett was still out—I saw her at the pond before I left."

"You didn't want to be alone with Hannah?"

"After what happened earlier, sir, with Alex, I thought I'd rather not. In case anyone else came up from the ice."

"What about you, Carlotta? Did you see Lem or Alex on the ice during the afternoon?"

"I'm afraid not. I spoke with you and Diana, and Jonathan, and Reverend Rowe—and Rachel Dudley—and then we walked home." She recalled the peculiar feeling she'd had the night before, gazing at the patch of dark firs. With a new shiver she wondered if something had forewarned her. Orpheus, too, had been uneasy. In all likelihood, Alexander Godwin already lay there. Might the boy's death have been prevented, if they'd gone then to investigate? From what she'd heard from Lem, she decided the answer must be no. But she knew she needed to see for herself.

She looked back to Longfellow, hoping he'd suggest they go together to learn whatever more they could.

Cicero took the pan from the fire, and slid the beans onto a pewter plate on the kitchen table.

"But now," asked Longfellow, "what will we do with Lem?"

"What do you mean?" the boy asked, raising frightened eyes.

"I mean that when the village hears of the nature of Godwin's wound, and whose hatchet was found next to him, *and* that the two of you had words yesterday, some might decide they've heard enough. Which is why you will not go back to Mrs. Willett's. If, instead, you are under a selectman's watchful eye, she may find her neighbors less inclined to pay her an unwanted visit."

Charlotte recalled an autumn afternoon three years past, when a part of the village had bustled her up from the mill pond to her farmhouse, looking for someone else they believed she'd taken in to hide—someone they were sure had committed murder, and might do so again. Could they now have the same horrible thought about Lem? Suddenly, she remembered others who would be affected by Alexander Godwin's death.

About to speak, she paused when a grinding noise came from a box on the kitchen table. Cicero took only moments to reduce the beans to a rough powder. "I agree with your point," Charlotte then said, "but first, Richard, might we send Lem off on an errand?"

"An errand?" he asked. "Where would you have him go?"

"To Boar Island. All signs point to a storm, as you predicted. And because it's January, it could be a long one. I don't know if Mrs. Knowles keeps many provisions on hand—"

"An ounce of prevention? Yes, perhaps so. While I haven't met these ladies, I've heard something of their strange situation. But are *you* acquainted with them?"

"I've seen them, on occasion."

"You *are* full of surprises," he answered oddly, causing her to wonder if the suspicion he'd lately shown had been renewed. "Well, if Lem goes off quietly, as you did the other day, I doubt he'll come to any harm."

"If I stay away from thin ice," said Lem, looking to Charlotte.

"I'll give you directions before you go," she assured him.

"It is now, what—?" Longfellow consulted the mantel clock. "Nine-thirty. What would you guess it will take, Mrs. Willett, on skates? An hour each way? Fill their wood box, then, and take care of whatever else they need, Lem. Tell them we'll soon arrange for more regular assistance."

"You could also return Magdalene's cloak, and take some provisions with you, on the flat sled in the barn," Charlotte suggested.

"I will."

"Get Hannah to choose some things from the cellar. She'll know."

"Aren't you going home?" There was a pause. Then he answered his own question. "Oh. Of course. The body."

Longfellow wondered if young love, or several weeks in Boston, might be blamed for this lapse. Though he himself wished Charlotte safely at home, he had little hope that she would go there now.

Cicero had finished making the coffee. He poured it into four cups, near a bowl of crushed sugar. He brought a small pitcher of cream from the fireside, where he'd set it earlier to remove the pantry's chill. And while the others fortified themselves for the unpleasantness that surely lay ahead, he reminded them of something they'd forgotten.

"What," he asked, "of Mrs. Montagu?"

Longfellow's first reply was a sigh. He added, "Keep her in, and others out."

The old man nodded, and sipped the rich, sweet brew he'd made.

When he sat alone a few minutes later, Cicero tried to recall some good of the puffy lad he'd barely known but had disliked, he supposed, no less than others. It was not an easy task. Nor would his next be, he imagined, when a certain young lady arose and found her way downstairs, seeking something to distract her.

THE WALK TO the pond was normally a brief one. Today, it seemed longer to Charlotte than ever before. Cold, raw, and duller than yesterday, this Wednesday appeared unkind to all the world.

She and Longfellow trudged side by side, dark figures against the land's lighter mantle of ice and snow, the taller of the two pulling a sled he'd stopped earlier to take from his stone barn. The sled carried a tarpaulin that would be needed later.

Though it was not the first time they had gone off together to view a body, this time it felt as if something new had come between them. Was it simply a continuing sense of distrust? Or was it the fact that Lem's safety, even his life, might be in jeopardy? As a selectman, it would be Richard's duty to find the truth, as best he could. But what would be the result of that?

Charlotte missed having Orpheus beside her. He'd not been keen to leave her hearth, and small wonder. Though she believed he possessed a curiosity to match her own, what he'd found that morning hadn't pleased him, she was sure. A part of her wished she were seated beside him now, waiting for the storm in comfort while her stout walls, banked by bundled straw, kept out the cold.

As they approached the ice pond, they saw previous activity written all around. But there were no snorting horses, no shouting men, no laughing children, no couples enticing one another, no women offering this or that for the comfort of the rest. Instead there was an emptiness, marked by the wind in the conifers.

Where the day before they'd left open water, the pond was now a solid stretch of black ice. This they avoided, making their way instead to the circle of trees beside the stained snow. Had Alex Godwin gone there for the same reason as the others, during the long afternoon? If so, thought Charlotte, someone might very easily have come up behind him.

Leaving the sled, Longfellow led her into the firs. Once inside she was comforted by the calm, and the smell of resin. Bathed in soft light, the place gave her the impression of having entered a chapel. They'd even disturbed a choir, chickadees gleaning what they could from the scales among the branches. The little birds slid away, and she forced herself to focus on what she'd come for.

There, lying on his chest, was Alexander Godwin. Charlotte recognized the ornate piping on his old coat, and the grouse-feathered hat. His long hair, gathered by a ribbon, had fallen to one side, and at the base of his neck there was, indeed, a dark hole, rather like the gaping mouth of a small fish caught on a line. Nearly an inch wide, it seemed the width of the hatchet's point her father had often used to break the ice in their rain barrel, beneath the back eave.

As a countrywoman, she knew the anatomy of animals used to supply her kitchen—and, that life was quickly extinguished once a neck was wrung, or otherwise damaged. Among her neighbors, the knowledge necessary to kill swiftly and quietly was not uncommon. But who could have committed such a crime in cold blood?

"It hardly seems," she said aloud, "to have been an act of rage." She heard her voice half-swallowed by the soft boughs that surrounded them. Longfellow looked up from a closer examination of the wound to study his companion.

"No," he agreed. With some difficulty, he turned the youth over. The face was white with frost. The frozen eyes remained open, staring horribly.

"I doubt that he put up any sort of fight," Longfellow muttered after he'd examined the entire head, and then the fingers, for scratches and further blood. He tried to open the corpse's mouth, interested in the state of its tongue, but found the jaw frozen shut. He stood with a grimace, and took a step to retrieve the hatchet under a nearby bough. Its point, he saw, was stained to a depth of a few inches.

"Yours?" he asked. She nodded. Then she compared this to other corpses over which they'd stood. Here, at least, was no attempt at masquerade, no possibility of accident or disease.

"I assume it was done just outside," said Longfellow. Then he pointed, and she leaned closer to see a small, sad detail. The buttons that secured the front of Alex's breeches were done up, but not quite correctly. At the top, the last had no place left to go; the first hole had been skipped. She supposed a young man careful of his appearance would hardly have done such a thing unless he'd been surprised, and in a great hurry. Had someone come up behind him with a greeting? Someone he may have had reason to distrust, or even to fear?

"I would also say," said Longfellow, "that he was carried here, so that no one would find him—at least until his assailant was elsewhere." He took a square of cloth from his coat pocket as he continued. "Though I suppose it's barely possible this was done after we all went home . . ."

"I don't think so. Last night, before we left, I had a feeling . . ."

He knew her well enough to stop at this, and wait for more.

". . . a feeling of something not right, here in these trees. Orpheus, too."

"Animals *are* able to smell death at some distance."

"Richard, if he wished to hide his crime, wouldn't he have come back after we all went home, to take the body somewhere we might never find it? That, he did not do."

Longfellow considered this while he tied the sharp and bloody hatchet in the square of cloth, knotting its ends twice together to form a loop.

"He could have felt it unlikely we'd think to connect him with the deed. That, I'm glad to say, suggests someone other than Lem Wainwright—simply because there is much to make him seem guilty."

"That may convince some, though I suspect not all."

Longfellow looked up into the sighing branches. "Godwin, I believe, lived with someone as a boarder."

"With Frances Bowers, Hiram's sister."

"I will talk to her. But it would be better—safer—if you were to leave the rest of this to me."

"If Lem is still in danger—"

"I will see to his interests."

"Haven't you a larger concern? To satisfy the village?"

"My greatest concern will be finding the truth."

"But how will you find it? What do we know so far?" His expression, she saw, had hardened.

"First things first," he told her abruptly. He handed her the hatchet, then bent to pick up Alex Godwin, almost as if he were a sleeping child. He realized at once that instead, the body was little different from a heavy, fresh-cut log.

He took hold of the shoulders of the old coat and pulled backward, slowly parting the boughs. Charlotte waited until they'd snapped back safely. Then she picked up the hat that had been left behind, smoothed its few proud feathers thoughtfully, and followed.

Chapter 11

RICHARD LONGFELLOW PULLED his sled and its covered burden over the compacted snow. They reached the main road, and the village grew larger before them, while the wind continued to rise in cold, biting gusts. It was with intense relief that they came to the trees that marked the beginning of the small, close houses, and then the graveyard.

They turned off the road and wound through several stone markers; moments later, the little party reached the cellar where Alexander might be left alone. They opened its slanting doors, setting them down on either side. Though her companion claimed he needed no assistance, Charlotte helped by lifting the front of the sled, while Longfellow took up the rear. Working in tandem, they prevented the boy's body from bumping down the steps as they lowered it into the ground.

The earthen room and the timbers with which it was lined gave off an aroma of cedar, earth, and mold. In dim light, they set the sled onto a pair of saw horses, but there seemed no need to remove the tarpaulin, nor to light the candle left in a cracked saucer on the dirt floor. Yet feeling that decency required something, they stood a little longer in the quiet gloom. "Shall you come with me to see Rowe?" Longfellow eventually asked. Her eyes, he saw, defied any objection. And so he helped her to climb the first of several steps; once the doors were shut they proceeded past the meeting house to the minister's stone manse, over which hung a web of withered ivy.

Though village women came to help with the upkeep of the house, Christian Rowe was usually alone when one called. But this time, moments after they knocked, they saw the door opened by another.

"Good morning!" Moses Reed cried, immediately extending a hand as if to pull them in out of the harsh weather. Charlotte and Longfellow returned his greeting.

"Is Mr. Rowe here?" Longfellow asked, unwinding his long woolen scarf.

"He's in the kitchen, finishing his breakfast. I'd already moved on, so I leaped up to see who it was. Anything that keeps the blood moving!" the lawyer added with a grin that spread his beard. "But go in to the study fire. I'll see if I can find you some tea. I'll let our host know you're here," were his last words, as he left them.

They soon found chairs, and sat to stare at one another. Each then tried to imagine exactly what Rowe should be told—and how he might take the solemn news.

"Longfellow?" came a query. "And Mrs. Willett! How glad I am to see *you* here, as well. Now, I can thank you again for the sweets you were kind enough to offer me yesterday. A successful day, I think?" the minister asked Longfellow. He received a nod, but nothing more to alter his cheerful mood.

"Do you come on some other business?" Rowe craned

his neck toward Longfellow's bundle of cloth, now resting on the hearth. "Have you brought me something?"

"In a manner of speaking," Longfellow admitted. Then, again, he fell silent.

"I've offered my home to a visitor, as you see. An act of charity, to benefit an old resident." Rowe rubbed his hands together, thinking, Longfellow imagined, of his pockets.

"Business of a sort has brought us. Bad business, I'm afraid, which will benefit no one. An old business with us, too, unfortunately." The selectman stopped, sensing that the preacher had already begun to fear the worst.

"No!" Christian Rowe cried abruptly. "Not again! Not—murder?"

Longfellow gave no reply, but watched Rowe stagger back, his arms reaching until he found a sturdy chair to cling to. "What name, sir?" he demanded.

"Alexander Godwin. He was found this morning, at the edge of my ice pond."

"*Your ice pond? Was he really? . . .*" This information suddenly seemed to restore the preacher. "Was he, indeed?" Absently, he allowed a finger to explore an ear, while he considered further. "Not a member of our church, if he did sometimes attend—but wasn't he the youth who fought only yesterday with young Wainwright?" With something solid to ponder, Rowe pulled a chair next to Mrs. Willett's, and sat.

"Yes," Longfellow admitted.

"Yes, we spoke of it ourselves, didn't we? And I suggested further guidance . . . although you seemed to disregard my concerns."

"Their argument was a brief one," Charlotte assured him. Rowe took her hand in his, and held it.

"I'm very glad *you* were not upset by their behavior,"

he told her. "But I have already discovered the cause of the altercation. It seems it was due to a young woman."

"Is that what you were told?" Charlotte asked.

"By Jemima Hurd, who accused Martha Sloan of being somewhat wanton in her affections. She is a handsome girl, perhaps more suitable for our Lem, after all, than for—" Rowe came to a halt. He realized that the suggestion was no longer worth making, with Alexander Godwin lying dead.

Longfellow answered the minister's next question before it was asked. "We've left him in your cellar, out in the graveyard. I've also sent someone for John Dudley."

Talk of a corpse in his own backyard caused Rowe to consider more carefully the likely impact of the matter. "But murder—you are *absolutely sure*? How, exactly, have you drawn your conclusion?"

"By looking at a hole in the back of his neck, about the size of a shilling. We're certain it was made by a tool found beside him."

"A tool? To me, that would imply an accident, perhaps suffered while he worked on the ice yesterday. Though with so many about—"

"This was no accident. He must have been attacked from behind, struck by an ice hatchet Lem took from Mrs. Willett's barn. The killer left the body in a small wood where it was unlikely to be found for hours, or even days."

Rowe removed his hand from Charlotte's. Had he finally begun to pull the pieces together? She wondered all the more when it seemed his eyes made of new point of avoiding her own. Instead, they went to the cloth bundle on the hearth.

Just as he took a breath to speak once more, Rowe was interrupted by a voice from the doorway.

"Thus," Moses Reed said quietly, "we have a weapon, witnesses to an earlier altercation involving the victim, and a possible motive. But these things are rarely what they seem. Tell me, who found the body?" The lawyer entered, and set the tea service he carried onto a table.

"Lem Wainwright, I'm sorry to say," Longfellow replied.

"Another point for the prosecution." Reed stroked his beard thoughtfully. "Some might say that a man who has committed murder will go back to the scene of his crime . . . but that sort of thing is hardly proof. What was the boy doing when he found the body?"

"Looking for the hatchet he'd lost earlier," Longfellow explained. He mentioned seeing the missing canvas bag himself—and, that it had long rested at the feet of several men at the bonfire, including the village constable.

"Now *that* may take us forward a step. Has the affection reported between Lem and Martha Sloan been put into the form of an engagement?"

"Not yet," Charlotte answered.

"Then I doubt he would go as far as murder to protect his name, or hers. At least a jury may not care to think so. And the scuffle could have been caused by something else entirely. I'll know more when I've talked with the boy—if you wish it," he added, giving Lem's acknowledged sponsors a chance to refuse.

"It could be a good idea," said Charlotte. "Do you think he's in enough danger to need an attorney?"

"At the moment, that's difficult to say."

"If so, would you be able to help him, Mr. Reed?"

"I will try, madam. For your sake as well as for his. Although I've not been asked to stand in court on a case of murder, I've seen one or two tried. It's a challenge I'll gladly accept, should it come to that."

Further speculation was interrupted by rapid knocking.

As he was closest to the front door, Reed went to answer. Moments later, there was a bustle in the entry hall. Then they saw a man with dun-colored hair and a strikingly bulbous nose make his way into the room. John Dudley went straight for the fire. Once he'd reached it he stood with his back nearly covering the hearth, his hands behind him, swaying slightly.

Charlotte could not help noticing, as she looked up, that the constable suffered from a large red carbuncle on his neck, with three or four yellow heads coming up around it. This seemed almost worthy of one of the sly friends of Sir John Falstaff—though which one, she could not recall.

"What's this about a murder?" the constable asked, after he'd sent a bleary eye to each of them.

"You heard already?" asked Longfellow.

"You think it's nothing at all to come walking down the road with a corpse under a sheet of canvas? Several saw you—by now, the news is all over the village. What do you expect *me* to do about it?"

Not known for an ability to converse politely, John Dudley seemed to have outdone himself in rudeness.

"Do, John?" Longfellow answered mildly. "Why, whatever you think best. At least until the selectmen meet to consider this. I presume it will be no earlier than tomorrow. With the look of the weather, it may take longer. Until we give you further instruction, it would seem you and I are of about equal rank here, with Mr. Rowe a close third. But to be sure you have the facts straight, let me say that Godwin was found early this morning, near where we worked on the ice, yesterday afternoon."

Longfellow related the rest.

John Dudley took a long moment to digest the information. He was, it seemed, more than a little fearful of his new responsibility.

"You put him down there?" This was asked bluffly, with a jerk of a thumb toward an east window, and the graveyard.

"That's right."

Dudley reached up in an attempt to scratch at his boil, and drew his hand away as though the area were on fire. With a malevolent eye, he looked to the one person in the room who remained a stranger. He now seemed to find the man familiar. "Who's this, then?" he asked.

"My name, sir, is Reed. I am an attorney, with an office in Boston."

"Reed? The Reed who stole from my father years ago? *That* Reed went off to Boston, thinking himself far too good for the likes of us!"

"Yes, we were neighbors. And I did take some apples that were not mine, as I recall. I once had the ways of an impious and thoughtless boy, I admit. As so many do," he added, considering. "As a matter of fact, Mr. Dudley—John—I seem to have heard that you, too . . ."

"That's enough! We want no lawyers here, dirtying our investigations!" Dudley spat into the fire, his features suddenly pinched by his anger.

"As you wish," the lawyer replied with a tiny smile. "I will retire, then, to begin my own investigations."

"This is not Suffolk County, with your m'lords' pulling strings for you! No, you will have to deal with Middlesex County here, Reed. A good many in this village will have little to say to you!"

"Possibly." The attorney left the room, and they soon heard the opening and closing of the front door.

"Nicely done, constable," Longfellow said dryly.

John Dudley made a show of chuffing on his hands, which must have been warm already.

"What now?" asked the selectman.

"Well . . ."

Apparently, thought Longfellow, the investigation would need someone else to act as its engine.

"How about," he suggested, "going to see Widow Bowers? It was she, I think, who provided a room for Godwin, and allowed him to share her table. She might tell us something of the young man's recent activities. We might also speak with young Martha Sloan, to lay another theory to rest. I'm sure she would have done little to encourage Alex, or any other lad, for I believe she's developed strong feelings for Lem Wainwright."

"You don't suppose, as they're saying, that it was jealousy?" asked the constable.

"Nor do I believe for a moment that Lem is our culprit."

"Where is the lad now?"

"Mrs. Willett sent him on an errand."

"An errand!" The constable turned to Charlotte. "Before I could speak with him? You thought that *wise*, did you?"

"Who knew when you might be roused?" Longfellow countered, subduing his own anger. "Besides, we had to consider the welfare of others. That's why I agreed to sending him off to Boar Island, with instructions to return in a few hours' time. When he does, you'll find him at my house. I'll see he's watched from then on, if you like, until this is cleared up."

"Boar Island, you say?" The constable seemed to shrink back.

"However," said Christian Rowe, wishing to gain some control over matters unfolding in his own house. "I must tell you, John, that I, too, think it unlikely

Wainwright had anything to do with this business. You and I should pursue the *real* villain! I will call for a special meeting of the village, to learn what others know. Until then, we might spy out information together."

"You and I, Reverend?" The suggestion caused the constable to pale.

"It will hardly be the first time I've directed an investigation into a question of murder, *and* found an answer to it."

Rowe's show of audacity left Longfellow speechless. He decided this was just as well, for it gave him time to decide on a plan of his own.

"Dudley," he said at last, "come and take a look at the corpse—but let me show you the weapon first." He lifted the bundle of cloth and untied the pair of knots, then took the hatchet by its shaft. Though the flat blade seemed wicked, it was the darker, pointed end that captured the room's attention.

Wondering what the constable's reaction would be, Charlotte was surprised to see John Dudley take a step backward, and wipe his lips with a trembling hand. His eyes stared around the room. With what seemed a great effort, he swallowed, but said nothing.

"Let's lose no more time," said Longfellow, quickly wrapping the tool again. "If I might, Rowe, I'll leave this in your custody. Come with us if you wish. But I suspect a man of your experience might as well act on his own. Someone, too, should warn the village, if we assume we still have a murderer in our midst. I'm not at all sure they would welcome my suggestions . . ."

"Then while I am out looking for answers, I will advise them myself," said Rowe. "For I am sure, sir, they will listen to me!"

Longfellow now noticed his neighbor, who had been

unusually quiet. "Mrs. Willett? Would you like me to find someone to see you safely home?"

"No, thank you," she replied with a tense smile. "I need to make a few purchases; since I'm not far from Emily's shop, I'll go there first."

"All right, then." Again, he consulted his pocket watch. "It's nearly eleven. Gentlemen, let us be off. The sooner this tragic business is settled, the better!"

Chapter 12

MUCH EARLIER, ACROSS the village bridge, Jack Pennywort made his way into the Blue Boar Tavern. On entering he saw no other customer. Most of the village, after all, took its breakfast cider, ale, or small beer at home. He'd even arrived before Mr. Flint and Mr. Tinder, a thing he was glad to see, for it allowed him to take one of the elders' Windsor chairs at the fireside, where high flames already fought against the growling wind.

Jack had not come far, but it was still enough of a distance, he supposed, to call for a medicinal drink, while he went on with his task. Mr. Longfellow had given him a few pieces of good silver to spend as he liked—though his wife had demanded much of it back for the household. But he'd been assured that the telling of an exciting story would bring its own reward. He hoped so, as he attacked the final chapter of the volume he'd been given the afternoon before.

Not much of it yet made sense to him. Skipping over the blustery preface, he'd decided the place the author described, this *Otranto*, lacked nearly all the charms of his own village. And its duke seemed an ogre, ordering others around as if he owned the place. Jack thought he'd like to see the fellow try this behavior in Bracebridge. Still, Duke Manfred and Mr. Hutchinson, the lieutenant governor, might find they had a few things in common. It seemed the duke had set quite a few of his countrymen looking for ways of getting their own back, as well.

While Jack considered further, Phineas Wise entered from an adjacent kitchen. A Yankee in look and habit, the landlord had already been busy that morning, fashioning a stew from deer trotters, a few turnips, some rubbery parsnips, and other odds and ends he suspected would give the whole a strong flavor. With some ale slop and rinds of old cheese added at the finish, Phineas believed it would satisfy the hungry farmers who would come in to hear the day's news—and to get away from their wives, as Jack must have wished to do quite early this morning. Today, though, the little man had brought with him something quite unusual. A novel, it seemed to be! Would wonders never cease?

"Good morning, Mr. Wise!" Jack said eagerly, holding up a shilling. "A pint of cider to start, please."

The landlord frowned as he took up the coin. He placed it between pointed teeth and bit down gently. Then his face took on a smile, while he slipped the silver into his pocket.

"Gladly, Jack," he replied. "But where did this come from? You weren't working on the ice yesterday?"

"No, but it is from Mr. Longfellow. He gave me a j-j-job to do, reading this b-book for him."

"What's that?" asked Wise. He was sorry to hear Jack's stutter returning. It had improved in the past few years—but perhaps this new responsibility had given him more than he'd bargained for. Extending a long, thin hand, Phineas picked up the leather-bound volume to read the glowing words along its spine.

"It's something like a history," Jack explained. "Written by a man of London. But you'll say he's exercised his imagination along with his pen, when I've told you more."

"Where does the story take place?"

"In the ancient land of S-s-s-sicily."

The landlord gave a groan and rolled his eyes; lately that area of the world had sent them more than a little trouble.

"A dark sort of place," Jack revealed, "where ghosts walk with the living. I suppose they might even have witches there, still."

"Witches!" Wise's curling eyebrows shot up, for he'd been born and raised in Salem. Earlier activities in that seaside town had given even its current inhabitants a bad name. But the spree of hanging had occurred well before New England learned the value of scientific ways of thinking—and, that such unpleasantness greatly disrupts commerce.

Scratching at a stubbly chin, Phineas Wise went off to pour Jack's cider, while a few more customers blew in. Jack bent quietly to finish his work, ignoring the rest.

Within a quarter of an hour, a donation of ale had, indeed, come his way, though its main purpose was to move him out of his comfortable chair and onto a nearby bench. With his book and elbows resting on the rough planks of the table before him, Jack watched Mr. Flint and Mr. Tinder begin their morning. Soon, they began to discuss a few of Otranto's many mysteries.

"Read the prophecy once more, Jack," Mr. Flint requested, pulling anew on his long pipe of white clay. The little man ruffled the pages back to the beginning, and read slowly and carefully.

" 'The castle and lordship of Otranto should pass from the present family, whenever the real owner should be grown too large to inhabit it.' "

"Too large," Flint said thoughtfully. "Round, do you think?" He patted his own girth, situated today beneath a pair of flannel under-vests. "I hardly see—"

"Quite a bit bigger than that, I'd say," Jack answered. "One fellow has a leg said to fill an entire room!"

"A metaphor, then," Mr. Tinder surmised, drinking in smoke more quickly. "Occasionally men become too big for the *comfort* of their fellows. Most especially, when they've been inflated by listening to puff-praise!"

"Yes, indeed," Flint agreed. "Like many in Boston these days, friend and foe alike."

"*And* in London," Tinder added sagely. "In palaces and Parliament. I sometimes wonder if they will run out of room in Britain, and begin to push one another off their little island."

"Do you imagine our lords may become cursed like Otranto, Mr. Tinder, if they will not give over Massachusetts to her rightful heirs, one day?"

"A good many curse them regularly now, I believe," answered Tinder jovially. "And I would not be surprised to see a few more evicted quite handily, as was poor Mr. Hutchinson. The governor already seems to prefer the safety and society of Castle William, out among the lobsters!" Both chuckled at their humorous remarks, though they verged on treason.

Jack did not entirely understand the new drift of the conversation. But he agreed that many in Boston seemed to care little for the interests of the rest of the colony.

Still, he would say no ill against the Bostonian he knew best, who'd moved in among them, and had yesterday paid for today's breakfast. While he went on with his description of the novel's plot, the older men re-loaded their pipes, and continued to smoke in a contented fashion.

"But why," Jack asked eventually, "do you think this helmet fell out of the sky, on top of Prince Conrad? And what got it up in the air in the first place?"

"The wind today is liable to send several things up and down again," said Flint, who watched the trees bending outside. "Mark my words!"

"But it will not move a statue," said Tinder, who thought more deeply on the question. "Could it be, Jack, that there was a war on, nearby? Did Mr. Walpole mention that? Gunpowder could have been used to blow the thing apart. Perhaps this helmet, with its bouncing black feathers, was hit by a cannon ball? I know for a fact such missiles may take the head of a man off quite cleanly, if they come in at the proper angle. Though I've not seen a statue with feathers in *all* my travels."

"It may have something to do with the great arm," Jack said finally.

"Where does that come into it?"

"A little further, after the head has fallen, leaving behind the mangled remains."

"Oof, that's a nasty thought," said another tavern regular. "On an empty stomach, especially." Dick Craft had entered a few moments earlier and planted himself by his old friend Jack, whom he knew to be in funds.

"Now this great arm," Jack went on, "stood up by itself, and hung on to the rail next to the stairs. It was inside some armor—"

"Armor!" Flint repeated with new assurance. "That

could explain a part of it, too. When wet, it tends to lock up, you see. There was one suit—badly damaged by sea salt, it was, years ago, when John Fisher brought it over. Rusted during the crossing. Standing yet at the old house, I suppose. Heard of it from old Mr. Jones—never saw it myself. But what else can you tell us of this Otranto, Jack?" he finished, sucking the dregs in his pipe.

"Well, there's quite a lot about marriage, and how you might trade an old wife for a new one."

"A useful sort of knowledge," Tinder returned. "I believe that is a thing far more difficult to accomplish in the Popish countries, or even in Britain, than here. Assuming of course one has some reason. Marriage here is a civil proposition, while on the other side of the water it is yet the business of the clergy—as is the case with divorce. Now there, separations are favored; but here, most realize the parties might well get up to a great deal of mischief that way, so that we prefer—"

"There is also a young lady who's stabbed, and dies," Jack interrupted.

"Is there?" Flint asked, warming to this new idea. "That is sad, very sad. Most often in books they are only abused, though sometimes it goes on for years, until it seems their woes are worse than Job's! And when they are saved at last, it is seen as a reward for steadfast goodness."

"Not in Otranto," Jack assured him. "Though I couldn't keep track of *all* the women—or the men, come to that. Some are noble, and some are not, but that keeps changing, too. All at once, an old friar is revealed to be the Count of Falconara! And then, it's learned Saint Nicholas has left something buried under a tree—"

"And what is that?"

"It is an enormous sword . . ." Jack paused for a much

needed pull at his tankard, for his head had begun to throb.

"Convenient for the giant hand and great arm," said Tinder, smiling. "It all seems to remind me, at least the way you tell it, Jack, of a Mr. Shandy and his Uncle Toby."

"Then at the very end—"

Dick Craft spoke up in amazement. "What! Have you got there already, Jack? You only started yesterday!"

"Last night," Jack admitted, "I found I'd opened up the wrong cover—then, by turning the whole thing the other way round, I found myself far advanced. I took it as a sign, of sorts. But as I was saying, at the very end there's wind and thunder, and people falling on their faces out of fear, and Saint Nicholas comes out of the clouds and takes up the ghost from the picture gallery. Finally the castle's new owner—for by then Duke Manfred has gone off to a convent—then, the new owner marries, hoping that his wife will help him to, to . . ." (here, Jack read from the final page) "to *indulge the melancholy that had taken possession of his soul.*' And there is the end of it."

"A gloomy ending," said Tinder reprovingly, moving his shoes, which had begun to steam, away from the hearth. "Though it could be the wife was happy, I imagine. Women *often* enjoy a swoon, or a cry. They are such sentimental creatures . . ."

"But why do you think they all stayed in this castle, sir, if living there brought such terrible luck?" asked Jack.

"A good question," said Flint. "When they could have come here, where very little of this sort of thing happens. At least in my experience."

"Except, perhaps, on Boar Island?" asked a young farmer from Lexington, who'd earlier wandered over to listen. He was known to the company, but he was not a confidant, and so could hardly have been surprised when they only stared back. "I've heard," the smiling man went on, "it is a place where odd things often happen. It houses spirits, it's said. Demons, are they? And it is supposed to have wondrous decorations, like this armor you mention, sir. Can you tell me what else might be there?"

"*Never you mind,*" said Phineas Wise, going by with a tray and tankards. No one else ventured anything more. Having been rebuffed enough, the farmer took up his pewter vessel and left them.

"The fewer who know what's on the island, the safer those women will be," Tinder commented belatedly to the customer's back.

"Damned foolish, if you ask me, them living there alone." This conclusion came from Samuel Sloan, who'd crowded in at the table nearest to the fire; moments before, he'd set down linen for the sleeping rooms upstairs, which his daughters had washed. "Far better for us if Old Cat and Mad Maud would come down from there, and go off to live in Boston. Though they're peculiar, they would find plenty of company in that place, I'm sure!"

"It would be safer," Dick Craft agreed.

"Do you mean, Dick, because of the sh—sh—sh—?"

What Jack had begun to ask was swiftly stopped by a kick from Samuel Sloan's boot, given under the table. Jack let out a yelp; Flint and Tinder looked at one another and clicked their tongues. Somewhat chastened, Jack dipped his head, then gave a few sidelong glances to see what damage had been done.

"Don't go too far, Pennywort," Samuel Sloan growled a moment later, after he'd surveyed the other customers. "Or it could be all of our skins, and not just your own hide." Seeing the unfortunate effect of his words—for Jack now seemed about to weep into his third serving of ale—he raised a finger and pointed to the landlord, letting him know who would pay for another. "Only keep what you've learned under your hat, won't you, lad?" he added.

Jack snuffled, and brought forth a smile.

Further comment was interrupted when someone flung open the front door, letting in the wind and a stupendous piece of news.

"There's a body in the reverend's cellar!" The speaker was Amos Flagg, a cobbler who lived by the common.

"What?" came from many throats, as everyone sat up and stared.

"Brought in just now by Mr. Longfellow and Mrs. Willett—both of them in with Reverend Rowe. And who do you think it is?"

"Who?" called Mr. Flint in a high, excited voice, asking for them all.

"It's Alexander Godwin—frozen solid!"

This caused a somewhat lower muttering to begin. Strangely, thought Phineas Wise, who now stood by the ale barrels, one or two even seemed to hide slight smiles. Watching looks pass from man to man, the landlord felt a doubled pang of uneasiness.

"How?" a voice called out.

It seemed that the cobbler had not explored as fully as he'd intended, once he'd gone down and lifted the tarpaulin, to stare into a frost-flecked face with clouded, bulging eyes. He shrugged as he told the little more he knew.

"Can't say for sure. But he was a big, healthy boy, and he wasn't ill, was he? Nearly knocked someone down just yesterday! And he's laid out flat, so I doubt he died of cold. Though he's frostbound *now*."

Before much longer, several men had decided to go

and examine the body more closely; a small party formed at the door, then went out together. But by that time others had gone out quietly on the same mission, through the kitchen in back. More simply sat, and by the looks on their faces, there was a general idea that the young man's death had been no accident.

No one, thought Phineas Wise, had yet mentioned murder. But had they assumed otherwise?

"Mr. Wise," said Jack Pennywort, his voice unsteady, his face unusually pale as he brought his poor foot from under the table.

"Yes, Jack?"

"I think I shall go, now. W-w-will you sell me a b-b-bottle of brandy, to take along? I have another sh-sh-sh—" It seemed he could not bring himself to utter the word, though he set a fresh coin on the table.

The landlord picked up the shilling, studied it intently, and gave it back.

"I think not. Go home, Jack," he said kindly. This only gave the little man further distress, and he began to whimper.

The landlord scratched his stubbled cheek solemnly, and said a silent prayer for them all.

Chapter 13

WHEN THEY LEFT Reverend Rowe's stone house Charlotte watched the minister walk off in one direction, while Longfellow and Constable Dudley took another. She chose a third, glad that she didn't have far to go.

She walked for a few moments toward the river on the main road, then turned into a narrow lane. Beneath bare elms at the corner stood the freshly painted house of Hiram and Emily Bowers. She followed a flagstone path to its Dutch door, recalling that Hiram would be off in Salem, for a brother there had recently fallen ill. Emily had informed her of this, standing before shelves full of odds and ends, when she'd paid a visit to purchase five pounds of dried cherries. Information, after all, was something Emily Bowers handled as often as provisions.

Not everything she heard, of course, was passed on to everyone. Speculating *who* might wish to know *what* was something requiring tact from a woman in her position, Emily herself was often heard to say. While some were eager for every little tidbit, others, including Mrs. Willett, were more particular.

Emily's eyes lit up as Charlotte entered the low room in front of the family's quarters. Clearly, she had something of interest to discuss. She put a hand on Charlotte's arm, and ushered her to one of a pair of padded benches covered in new chintz, next to the hearth. This was lately improved by the addition of an inset stove, which roared a welcome of its own.

"How was the pie?" Emily inquired.

"Once he'd eaten three helpings, Lem paused to tell me it was quite good. I enjoyed it as well."

"I thought so. The best fruit we've seen in some weeks . . ."

Charlotte nodded, readying herself for the match.

"It's not the first time I've heard that young man's name mentioned today," Emily informed her softly, her eyes glittering, like a squirrel's.

"Oh?"

"I see by your face that what I've heard may be true! What has Lem got to do with the death of Alex Godwin?"

"But how—!"

"I don't believe what some are saying, of course— even if the two of them did have a scuffle yesterday. Nothing more than high spirits, I'm sure. And drink, perhaps. A good many took too much, it seems. Two or three ladies have already been in this morning to complain of it. I couldn't go off to the ice with Hiram away, but I did hear that you, Mrs. Willett, and Mr. Longfellow, were there—and that you went back early this morning to haul the body down into Reverend Rowe's cellar! As soon as you went in to speak with him, Amos Flagg went to see who it was, but he wouldn't stay to find out *how* he died. The poor boy! Is there anything more you're at liberty to tell?"

Charlotte supposed there was no point in keeping back the rest, when it would soon be known to all. She wondered what Emily would think when she learned the truth. Taking a deep breath, she decided to find out.

"Oh, shocking!" Emily returned a minute later, though she did not seem to find the situation completely so. "All men, Reverend Rowe so often points out to us, are sinners . . . yet some to a *far* greater extent than others. One thing is sure—John Dudley won't be happy to be constable this day! But what are you going to do?"

"How do you mean?"

"I suppose you could get Henry back; after this, Lem can hardly stay with you. How my heart goes out to him! After all, he is one of us—though the Godwin boy was, too. Still, his family moved away so many years ago. And when he came back, it surely wasn't to be sociable! I hope he spoke more to the old women on the island than he did to the rest of us here."

"Lem has gone there this morning," Charlotte said calmly.

"To the island, Mrs. Willett?" For the first time, Emily Bowers showed real surprise.

"Without Alexander, who is there to assist them?"

"I hadn't thought of that. Who else *would* go up there? Not that it's far—yet who among us would feel welcome? And you know what they've said about the place for generations."

"That it's haunted?"

"As if such things could happen, these days," Emily sniffed. "But some do say they've seen things to make them wonder. Then again, those who live off to the north of the village tend to be less sensible than the rest of us, as you well know. With their country ways."

"Did Alexander see anything unusual, I wonder?" Charlotte murmured, almost as if she thought aloud.

"Not that I know of, dear. And I know he was asked just that by Frances, long ago—I speak of my husband's sister, you know, who took the young man in when she felt she needed something more of a nest egg. She does have that house all to herself. He wouldn't pay much, but at least he was well behaved, for the most part."

"It's difficult to imagine, isn't it, that he could have made such an enemy?"

"Well, I have heard some speak ill of him. He did have an unpleasant way of holding himself, as if he were far above the rest of the world. He came in here occasionally to buy for our Island Ladies, as I like to call them. Not much, for it seems most of what they need is sent down from the north—but when he did come in, Mr. Godwin could not be bothered to pass the time of day. He was *certainly* no gentleman, I thought, for all his airs, and the lace and feathers on his old hats. As he always dressed in cast-offs, you'd think he'd have had *some* humility. But have I said too much?"

"Well . . ." Charlotte began.

"They say he had hopes of having the whole island to himself one day, and not just the pittance they gave him instead of decent wages, which would hardly feed that old horse of his. You didn't know that? Oh yes, old Mrs. Knowles counts her pennies! He even had to beg for money from his family, my sister supposed, to pay her . . . he'd come riding back with the cash, and a few other things young men will spend their money on, which I don't think to offer here—as you know, I buy goods mostly for ladies. But with that great lady worth more than all of the rest of us put together, I ask you! Well, the wealthy are often the last to part with brass *or* silver. In England, I hear, accounts for gentlemen are settled but once a year, if that! I'm glad to say we have far better manners here! Who can live on promises, after all? Though they seemed nearly enough for Alexander. The hot blood of youth, Mrs. Willett—that's what gives me the shivers to think of. Who do *you* think is responsible?"

"I've no idea," Charlotte answered, suspecting Emily had already made a guess.

"None? None at all?"

"Not at the moment. But should I hear anything—"

"Yes, do let me know. How often it's left to the women in this village to set things straight."

"There's something else, Emily—something I've been hoping to ask you."

"Yes, dear?" the proprietress asked, leaning closer.

"Rachel Dudley, I think, has lost several silver spoons."

"Oh, you did hear, then! And that's not all. I didn't know if I should say more . . . but I can hardly believe someone just walked in and took them from a locked cupboard, leaving no sign of a burglary. Things don't vanish on their own, no matter what some claim. And him the new constable!" Emily's tongue busied itself with sounds of disapproval, while she watched for the effect her words might have. Then she gazed toward the door, and in another moment it opened with a jingle. Two women entered.

Sarah Proctor nodded gravely, after she'd pulled back the hood of a heavy blue cloak. Beside her, Jemima Hurd sent them a fleeting smile.

"Good morning, ladies!" Emily called. She rose and offered her seat to the elderly Mrs. Proctor, who, though hardly infirm, took it as her due. Charlotte moved to one side, and Jemima hurried to be near the stove as well, whispering thanks for the privilege.

"We were speaking of Mrs. Dudley's spoons," said Emily in further greeting, holding back the better news of a body in the cellar.

"Most peculiar," Mrs. Proctor proclaimed, "as I've said before."

"And she's not the only one!" added Jemima.

"Oh?" asked Charlotte.

"Oh, yes! First, there was my caudle bowl, which I'd put away until someone else took sick. Now I can't find it anywhere! My husband insists I can't account for anything, since—"

"What?"

"Since the change."

"Ah," came a trio of commiseration.

"At first, I believed him . . . but then last month, Miriam Spender's sugar bowl and creamer went missing. And now Mrs. Pennywort says her children have lost their christening mugs. And a woman in Concord, Mrs. Ames, cousin to Esther Pennywort, told Esther she'd lost a box full of shillings she's been saving for *years* for her daughter's dowry."

"Silver, in each case?" asked Charlotte.

"Most of us have little else in our houses that's of any value," Sarah Proctor stated bluntly. "Who would want our pewter, most of it wretched? Especially that we've recast ourselves."

"Except for that odd man along the north road who buys scraps," Emily reminded her. "But you know, I misplaced an old pewter porringer. Not a very good one, with pits and dents in it; I suppose that was six weeks ago."

"A sneak thief," cried Mrs. Proctor, pointing a finger

to the ceiling. "A horrible thing, coming into houses! He will be caught, when a stolen piece is found for sale. That is what happened the last time something like this occurred here, when I was a girl. Put into the stocks and branded, *he* was! It was enough to make others think."

"And yet, Sarah, I'm not sure we should worry about that today," said Emily Bowers, "after what I heard this morning."

"How do you mean?" asked Mrs. Proctor, her eyes newly suspicious.

"You've not heard?" Emily's smile could hardly be contained.

"How could I? Jemima came to ask my advice, which took well over an hour to give, and only moments ago did we step out to come here. Emily, what has happened? You look as if you've swallowed a toad!"

"There's been a death. And it was *no accident*."

"Mrs. Willett! What is this all about? Tell me, quickly!" Sarah Proctor commanded.

Wondering at her reputation in the village, Charlotte began by relating, once more, the tale of how Lem had found Alex Godwin's body, and her own hatchet taken from the barn. She went on to tell the women of her recent visit with Reverend Rowe, and that Rowe and Richard Longfellow, as well as the lawyer Moses Reed, had begun to investigate.

"So, young Wainwright already has counsel? Hardly a sign of innocence," Mrs. Proctor decided, "especially when it is a Boston lawyer. And I'm sure Jemima and I saw what led up to it. As you did, Mrs. Willett. Fighting, right before our eyes! Rashness, no mistake. At the time, I suspected Godwin must have insinuated himself where he wasn't wanted. Was that it? Or was he guilty of even worse?"

"With who?" asked Jemima, fidgeting at the thought. "Who would have asked him to make such advances?"

"A seducer hardly waits to be invited, Jemima. Especially one with no hope of succeeding otherwise."

Charlotte now regretted her usual lack of interest in local gossip. "Was there some reason Alex had no hope of courting?"

"Beyond the fact that he was a proud ninny, I believe he had no property, no trade, no prospects—and no manners. He may have supposed his family would help him, but since his father allowed him to come back to Bracebridge alone, it would seem unlikely that he planned to leave him a living in Worcester. Or, that he cared what happened to the boy at all!"

"I can't imagine he was a passionate young man," Emily Bowers objected. "According to what my sister told me, he stayed to himself. If he had any visitors, especially young women, I'm sure she would have said so. After all, she would hardly have approved of anything of the sort."

"Boys grow into men, Emily. And when they do, what can one expect but trouble? Lem Wainwright, too, is nearly a man, and may well be responsible for this—whether his motives were admirable, which is possible, or, as I rather suspect, not."

Charlotte flushed at this direct attack on a friend. Catherine Knowles, too, had stated a distrust of men, young and old. Did the pains and changes of old age, she wondered, tend to make one grow more harsh toward the opposite sex? Or was it simply the result of experience?

"Do you think *we* are safe?" Jemima Hurd asked, looking anxiously toward the windows that overlooked the lane.

"No one wants to murder you, Jemima," Sarah Proctor answered. "Not for passion, not for gain. Though if someone has already slipped in and taken your caudle bowl, then you and the rest of us *should* be more careful. Let us all be more watchful of our neighbors, until the perpetrators of these wrongs are discovered. Let us also pass on what we learn to one another—for we can hardly hope for much from our new constable, nor from our inept selectmen!"

"I certainly will," Emily Bowers promised. "And I'll be glad when Hiram returns. I don't like the idea of sleeping alone, though my children are with me. But you, Mrs. Willett! If, as you say, Mr. Longfellow plans to watch Lem until the identity of Alexander's attacker is proven, won't you be alone? Will you be safe? Don't you have several good pieces of silver, and your mother's pewter, as well? I believe you have more than most."

"Orpheus will be there to guard me. And I have stout bars on the doors."

"Take care, my girl," Sarah Proctor advised. "If it was Lem Wainwright, remember he will be nearby. And if it was not Lem, as you seem to think . . . then it must have been another of our acquaintance. *Trust no man*, Mrs. Willett, or you may be sorry for it."

Doubting that she could trust herself in the company of these ladies much longer, Charlotte withdrew and made her way into the open air, hoping to learn more of interest at her next stop, not many doors away.

Chapter 14

As she hurried down the lane, Charlotte noted
that the wind had veered, and that it now carried the
sharp smell of snow. She turned where a new lane crossed
her own, passed a few more houses and deserted gardens,
and eventually came to one that was old and small.

Directly behind the dame school, the home of Jonah
Bigelow and his grandson Ned stood under a tangle of de-
nuded vines, canes, and saplings. In summer it was a quaint
and leafy spot, but today it looked as if the house might be
struggling for breath, within constricting bonds. Yet these
could as well break the force of winter blasts, and keep
those inside a little warmer. First impressions, Charlotte
reminded herself, were sometimes inaccurate.

She mounted a sandstone stoop and stood beneath an
undersized portico of rotting wood, where a descending
current of wind brought smoke curling from the slanting
brick chimney above. At her knock, a voice challenged
the distant wail of the approaching storm, asking her to

enter. She lifted a latch of cracked wood, and went inside.

A man she knew to be near seventy years of age sat next to his fire, in a rocker no doubt as old. Neither appeared artful, nor in any way stylish. But each was pleasing, the chair for its solid comfort, the man for his open countenance.

"What is this?" Jonah asked, attempting to rise, then falling back. A stifled bout of coughing followed. When the old man finally lifted his face, contentment still glistened in his moist eyes. "Young Mrs. Willett! You're very welcome. Sit down, here in Ned's chair." He indicated another seat with a sagging rush bottom but straight, sturdy legs.

Charlotte came in further, after she'd latched the door. Looking about she felt the wonder of childhood, for she'd entered a place she once imagined elves to live in. How many years had it been since she'd come here at her mother's side? And why had she not come since, with more bread and butter, to visit an old man who might find himself longing for company?

"Mr. Bigelow . . ."

"Please, you must call me Jonah. For you're a child no longer, are ye? But it'll be Ned you wish to see. Perhaps you've some small job for him to do? I'm afraid he left early this morning, off after a bird for the larder, so he may not be back for some time. Would you care for tea?"

Charlotte began to search the tiny kitchen at the edge of the room, finding what was needed.

"I'll lift the kettle from the crane. There, now." Jonah set down the steaming iron pot, and poured from it as soon as Charlotte brought cups and a thick brown teapot, with a bowl for the warming water. When Jonah wet the tea, she was impressed by the strength of his arms, if his legs were unusually thin. For some years, the village had watched Ned push his grandfather about while the elder sat in the bow of a handcart, from which he could greet all they met on their errands. She knew they could not afford a horse, though she barely recalled Jonah once riding a pony she'd befriended.

In another moment, Charlotte returned to the fireside with a jug of milk, a pot of sugar, and spoons. "I did come to see Ned," she admitted. "But tell me how you are, Jonah. Yesterday, you were well enough to go out, I was glad to see."

"I grow no worse, though every day a little older. But it's more than some can say! Many's the man I knew here as a youth who's in the ground now. Yesterday was a fine day. Good company, good ale, a sip of something braver," he said with a wink. "Enjoyable things to chew on, too, thanks to our good women. I only wished I could have been some help out on the ice, as I once would have been. Still, I can tell a story or two while Ned plays his fiddle. I suppose that's worth something."

"So do I," she assured him. Feeling less of the day's chill, Charlotte took her cloak from her shoulders. Then she leaned forward, and poured out their tea.

"In fact," said Jonah, "I enjoyed a few old tales myself yesterday, including some I couldn't quite recollect, told by Mr. Tinder and Mr. Flint. Ornamented, perhaps, for the benefit of the young men around the fire. One day, when we're no more than history ourselves, I hope they'll recall the old folk, dead and gone."

Charlotte decided her questions could wait. "Tell me, Jonah, wasn't it iron-making you were engaged in?" She saw a shadow pass over the old man's face. After that, he appeared to resign himself.

"Something I've not often been asked by a young lass!

We used to make ingots not far from here, out of bog iron long gone—that which supplied smiths, ferriers, and even some who cast pots, like this old veteran of many a campaign." He bent to return the black kettle to its crane, and went on.

"Back then the land was thick with trees, you know, which were took down to make the charcoal. Every year they cut miles of it down, and other damned souls burned the logs under great piles of sod—mountains that glowed for a week and more, day and night, covered to keep the air out. Very bad work that was, and many died of it, I'm sorry to say, falling in while seeing to the state of things on top, always keeping the blanket tight. A quick way to go, it may have been—but not a pleasant one to think on." He took a sip of his tea.

Charlotte imagined the gruesome work for herself, while she waited to hear more. Jonah's hands, she noted, shook as he curled them around his cup. "What did you do, Jonah?" she finally asked.

"I, and many another, took the baked wood and used it to smelt out iron from ore. In beehives, as we called 'em. Great furnaces they were, with bellows taking the heat so high, the Devil might have felt at home inside! Once the ore melted, we'd throw in lime, and skim off what came to the top. The iron we drew off below. Twice a day it flowed down to molds on a sand floor. Sows and pigs, that's what came out of our beehives. Sold so others could melt 'em down and re-cast the iron, or more likely beat it into plate. Nowadays, better ore is mined from caverns underground, and I thank God none of those is near to our village. For men who do such work burn out, like the furnaces. A furnace is often rebuilt. But a man is not something to be torn down and raised back up again.

Once my lungs were afflicted, I was never much good for anything else. To be sure, the making of iron is a good business. But for some, at least, it's an unprofitable one."

Charlotte was sorry to have reminded him of the cause of his infirmity. After gazing quietly into the fire, she poured a second cup of tea for them both. Jonah accepted his with a smile.

"Ned, now, won't fall into the same troubles as I did. I doubt he'd be fool enough to do the work, even if it was offered him . . ."

Perhaps sensing her silence held less than approval, Jonah was quick to add something more. "The boy takes good care of me, which is more than many a grandson will do."

"I wonder if I should ask—is it true you and Ned aren't quite blood relations?"

"That is something we rarely mention, lass. But it's true enough Ned is my wife's nephew. I suppose Moses Reed told you, when he brought you to the ice yesterday. He has a sharp eye, and a mind that's nimble," said Jonah. "And a good memory."

"You were once neighbors, I think?"

"Many years ago. My wife was quite fond of him— called him 'little Moses, of the Reeds.' "

"Jonah," Charlotte asked while the old man still chuckled, "I'd like to hear another old story, if you wouldn't mind. Can you tell me something about Boar Island? Do you recall when the house was built?"

This time it was Jonah who looked away toward the fire. Regretting her curiosity, Charlotte wondered what unhappy memories her new question might have revived. A short convulsion of coughing followed. After that, his eyes came back to hers.

"I do remember something of that. I was, oh, twenty-two then. It's a fact I often seem to recall those days better than what happens now!"

"I've sometimes wondered why, when such a great house was erected, it had so little effect on our village. Not many here have ever visited the island, have they?" she prodded gently.

"John Fisher," Jonah began in earnest, "first bought the isle, then sent across the sea for a ship full of masons and carpenters. That would have been in 1718—fifty years ago. And he brought with him a master builder. He and Fisher knew other men who'd settled to the north of us, across the Merrimac. It was their quarries that supplied the rock they floated in on barges. Once the house was begun, Fisher welcomed parties made up of these men and other sporting gentlemen he was acquainted with, not a few from his homeland. He only sent for his wife and daughter some time later, when the place was nearly finished. And the hunting parties continued, for the first boars had multiplied, once they'd driven out whatever else lived wild there."

"Why were so few from Bracebridge invited to visit the island?"

"Our minister at the time was an old Puritan, a sour apple by the name of Dr. Pruitt. He had no liking for the place, or what he heard went on there. Hunting for sport—men dancing with many young ladies—none of them taking a proper interest in religion, though Lutherans, I think some were—all of this, he told us at meeting, was sinful. He forbid us from having anything to do with the builders, and as Fisher had his own friends up in Nova Scotia, it was them that cleared his goods, and sent them on to Salem—so he had no need of us, nor Boston, either! We did see the house going up, and some of us might have gone to take a peek or two. But we mainly stayed away. All but James Godwin. It was Godwin who sold Fisher his liquor, at a good profit, which I suppose Dr. Pruitt might have envied. Then around twenty years ago, Fisher went to meet his maker. After that only Alaric Jones went to the isle, to do chores for the two women who stayed on. The rest of the world forgot them, or at least left them alone."

Charlotte had further questions, but before she could ask another, Jonah delivered a query of his own.

"What brought you here today, Mrs. Willett? Was it to ask Ned for his help, as I guessed earlier? Or was it something quite different?"

"You've not been out this morning?"

"I may still walk a bit, but not for long. With Ned gone, I usually stay indoors. A cruel wind, too, has come upon us."

"Something worse came last night, Jonah." Charlotte repeated the tale of what Lem had discovered, and what she and Richard Longfellow had brought back to the village. When she was through, Jonah Bigelow continued to watch her intently, his faded eyes unblinking.

"That hatchet," Charlotte added, "is what has brought me here. Yesterday it rested near Ned's feet, not far from your own. Can you recall? Did someone else come and take the canvas bag, or remove the hatchet from it, while you sat there?"

"A woolen scarf on top, you say," he answered slowly. "I did see that, for I recall thinking it would be warm. I asked myself who'd left it. But then, having a nip of something to warm myself, and perhaps another after that, I lost track of things. This hatchet, now, I wasn't aware of. You might ask Mr. Flint or Mr. Tinder. Or John Dudley. Though I doubt any would tell you more."

"And Ned?"

"Ned seems your best hope. He rarely takes anything to drink beyond small beer, for it worsens his playing, you see. I'm sure he never got to be as bad as we were—and later, he had no trouble helping me home."

"When was that?"

"Oh, some time after two. Most were still enjoying themselves, but it seemed time for me to go."

Seeing her disappointment, Jonah added a comforting word. "You needn't worry about Lem Wainwright. He's a good lad. Each time he's been here lately, he's been cheerful as can be."

"He comes here?" she asked abruptly.

"As men will seek out others, to discuss this and that, you know. Lately, it's most often been to talk about a pretty miss. I once thought Ned might be interested in Mattie Sloan—but it seems it's Lem she's chosen. A good wife she'll make him too, once he's old enough to ask."

Charlotte suddenly heard the wind she'd forgotten—felt it, too, as the door swung open and Ned Bigelow came inside. He glimpsed two figures out of the corner of his eye and gave a start, peering into the gloom to see who sat next to his grandfather.

"Mrs. Willett?" he asked, before he was entirely sure.

"That's right," Jonah said quickly, "come to see you, and ask a question. I warned her you might be gone a while, looking for a bird for our dinner."

Ned took off his hat and slipped out of his coat. While still wearing a mitten on his right hand, he reached down to unbuckle his leather overshoes. He cast these aside as well, and took a small crock from a shelf. Then he came to sit easily on the edge of the brick hearth, his back against the wall. Charlotte again noticed his intelligent eyes, unkempt hair, and barely bearded cheeks that glowed from the wind. Imagining that at this moment he did look something like a grasshopper, she smiled.

"Anything you would like to know, you've only to ask," he told her. For a moment, he appeared to admire the colored yarn of his mitten. He took it off, and revealed what seemed to be a burn on his sooty hand.

"What's that, son?" asked his grandfather, leaning forward.

"Nothing much. The cock of the fowler slipped while I was adding powder, and the flash caught me."

"That ointment will soothe it," Jonah assured him, sitting back again as he watched Ned apply what looked like green grease to the webbed area between his left thumb and forefinger.

"But please, Mrs. Willett, go on," Ned requested, making light of his injury. "You came with a question for me?"

"I've come to ask about a canvas bag. Lem left it near your feet yesterday. Do you remember?"

"Yes, of course. Has he lost it? Maybe at day's end someone picked it up by mistake."

"Someone took something from it, at least. An ice hatchet." The young man waited. Seeing his lack of surprise, Charlotte decided that Ned knew nothing of the news the rest of the village hummed with. Out on the marshes, he would not have heard.

"You don't know about Alex Godwin?" she asked.

"What of him?" The young man's tone was suddenly cool.

"He's dead, I'm afraid."

Ned looked swiftly to his grandfather.

Yet again, Charlotte began to relate how Lem had found the body, while looking for what had already been stolen by a murderer. She mentioned that Lem and Alex had earlier been seen arguing, hoping Ned would know the reason. By the time she finished, the young man had regained his feet.

"I suppose he was angry with Godwin, Mrs. Willett, and probably for good reason. Alex enjoyed irritating people—he even told stories that weren't true, just to make others as angry as he often was. If he said something malicious about Mattie, then Lem had a right, it seems to me, to try and stop him. Yet it *must* have been someone else who killed him."

"Have you someone in mind?" she asked.

"Not I! But it wasn't Lem. If anyone thinks *that* . . . then I suppose I might come up with a name or two. The 'Little Lord' insulted most of us, and tempers wear thin, once things have been traded back and forth. But I find it hard to think anyone we know would have murdered him."

"Mr. Longfellow, Dudley, and the preacher are investigating Godwin's death," said Jonah. "With the Boston lawyer, Moses Reed," he added.

"Where do they plan to start?" asked Ned.

"When I left the constable and Mr. Longfellow, they were going off to visit Frances Bowers, and then the Sloans," Charlotte answered.

"I suppose we can expect them to visit us soon after," said Ned.

"I have no right to ask anything else . . . but if you remember something more—?"

"I've long been Lem's friend," Ned replied firmly. "That won't change. I'll do whatever I can. Where is he now?"

"He's probably still on Boar Island, where he went this morning."

Once more, Ned looked to his grandfather.

"No doubt he went to see if the women there need any help," said Jonah. "For they'll be alone, now."

"Of course. But there's good reason to stay away from the place, Mrs. Willett."

"So I hear! I was there only two days ago—"

"You've been to the island? Did you find anything unusual?" Ned asked with interest.

"Only a spoon." She had spoken without thinking. The two men waited for her to say more. "A lost spoon, which I've returned to its owner," she added. "No ghosts or goblins," she concluded with a smile.

"You may think such warnings come only from simple folk," Jonah replied soberly. "Yet odd tales have been told about that place for a long, long while. Once it was called the Devil's Isle—and no one dared to live there before John Fisher came. Is that not a little strange, when it's surrounded by good hunting and fishing, and water meadows? It is because *something* goes on there—something none of us can explain. And such things will continue to occur, I think, long after we're gone."

Jonah Bigelow sat back and rocked, regarding his guest seriously.

"I promise I'll keep what you say in mind," she said to soothe him. "But I must start for home, before the storm truly arrives. Thank you for tea, and your stories."

"Will you come back to visit us again, lass? I should like to hear what you discover about poor Godwin. And I still have plenty of other stories to tell."

"I would be very glad to come."

"Good! And Ned knows even more about the distant world than his grandfather, reading so many books and newspapers. The islands to the south are his passion now. He will tell you all that's said of the pirates of the Bahamas—or our colony at Kingston—or trade with Tobago, even—if you'd like to hear of such things."

"I would," she answered honestly, for she'd wondered what Ned learned from his varied sources, surely different from the volumes in her father's library.

Yet now, she thought, she had no time to hear exciting tales of distant lands. For without a doubt, they had more than enough excitement of their own to deal with, in Bracebridge.

Chapter 15

FACING A BITING wind, Charlotte trudged up the Boston-Worcester road, with only her thoughts to temper the difficult going.

She'd heard that Alex Godwin was less than a pleasant soul; she now was sure he'd enjoyed few friends. What had truly surprised her was that Lem often visited Ned and Jonah Bigelow. She knew he went off to see others some evenings, but he'd rarely said, lately, where it was that he went. She imagined Ned, unlike Alex Godwin, had many friends, for he had an enjoyable way about him—a desire, and an ability, to please. But she supposed his friends might be quiet ones. Some would wish to avoid having fingers wagged at them by village scolds. Could it be that Lem put her in this category? She thought not, and asked herself again why he would want to keep his visits to the odd little house a secret. Perhaps it was because of Hannah. The displeasure of Mattie's mother was something he would not care to risk, while he tried to win her daughter.

Jonah's story of the furnaces had been interesting. Again, she considered how much the present owed to the past, and how often this debt remained unpaid. Life had given little reward to Jonah, it seemed. Some, like Sarah Proctor, organized assistance for widowed or abandoned women and their children. But Jonah Bigelow, she supposed, made do with what he'd saved, and possibly what he'd invested somewhere. It could also be that relatives to the west, grateful for the care he'd given Ned, continued to help them. It was not her place to ask, though perhaps when she next stopped in, she might see if there was something else she could do.

A pair of high voices broke into her thoughts, for they called out her name. Turning her back to the wind, Charlotte saw a horse that carried two children somewhat precariously, on a makeshift saddle of rope and blankets strapped to its bowed back. The Dudley children, Winthrop and Anne, waved their arms, trying to attract her attention.

She walked back to meet them, and soon felt the nuzzle of a moist, warm mouth against her own.

"Whoa, mare!" cried Win, a youth of thirteen. Still holding the reins, he slipped down from the saddle leaving Anne, four years his junior, on top. "Mrs. Willett!" he cried, moving very close, then stepping back to make a small bow. "I have a message from my mother. I'm glad I found you, before we had to go all the way up the hill. We borrowed a horse from our neighbor, but she's not very willing and would rather go home!"

"As we should all be thinking of doing, Win," said Charlotte, blocking the wind from him as best she could. "Is something wrong?"

"It's only that our father—well, Mother's not happy. About her spoons."

"Oh, I see."

"He wouldn't go and look for them, after somebody came and took them away." The boy stopped and began to shuffle his feet, staring down at them until his nose began to run. He quickly brought up a mitten to absorb some of the moisture. "But now they're back."

"What? *All* of them?"

"Yes. Mother wanted me to tell you that, and to bring you this." He hopped back to his sister, who took something from beneath her cloak where it had been providing her slight body with an extra layer of warmth. "Hello, Mrs. Willett!" she called down, her voice quivering from the cold.

"Good day, Anne!" Charlotte called back. "What is it you've brought me?"

At first she imagined it would be a small gift, something to thank her for returning the spoon. Then she saw that it was the canvas bag she'd been seeking. It passed from Anne's mittened hands to Win's, and then to her own. Inside lay the scarf with a snowflake pattern—the one she'd knitted herself.

"Mother says she recognized whose it was as soon as she saw my father brought it home with him last night," Win said. "And she said instead of returning it when she came to visit, she'd send it now. She also wanted us to find my father, and tell him he needs to come home."

"He's with Mr. Longfellow," Charlotte told them. "Try the Sloan house. If he's not there yet, you might leave a message. But you and Anne should then go home. Look—!"

Fat flakes suddenly filled the air.

"*Come on, Win,*" his sister cried, bouncing on the strange saddle. "Good-bye, Mrs. Willett!"

"Good-bye, Anne. Tell your mother that I look forward

to seeing her! You, too, if you'd like to come for tea. Thank
her for the return of the bag!"

"I will," came the faint voice, from inside the girl's
cloak.

"There's one more message!" the boy exclaimed, turning back from the horse, who'd already made a dancing
turn toward the west.

"What's that?" asked Charlotte.

"She said—she said my father told her not to say anything more about the spoons, or what happened to them.
And he says he knows who took them, too."

"Who?"

"Some imp of Satan, my father says. They've long
lived across from us on the isle. Now they're doing the
Devil's work, trying to make it seem my father's not doing
his job. That's why they came across to take the spoons,
probably by magic, and put them back the same way. To
make him look foolish while he's constable."

"What does your mother say to that, Win?"

"She says she isn't sure. But at least she's not as angry
as she was before. She will be, though, if I don't bring
Anne home, now that the snow's started. Will you hold
the reins?"

The boy held out the long leather straps. He put his foot
in a loop of rope and slowly hoisted himself up, while his
bulky winter clothing fought against him. At last he settled
himself in front of his sister, and reached down for the reins.
Within moments, the horse started eagerly for the river
bridge and the north road beyond.

"Thank you!" Charlotte called after them, holding up
the bag. The children did not seem to hear. Very soon they
were lost in the thickly falling snowflakes. Waiting no
longer, she clutched her cloak, bent her head, and made
her own way toward home.

Suddenly, halfway up the hill, the wind slowed, and for a while the snow fell like powder about Charlotte's head. Passing the Bracebridge Inn, she looked closely, but saw no one out. Yet when she looked left toward Richard Longfellow's front lawn, she saw a woman walking toward her.

The hooded cloak of black sealskin told her it must be Diana, picking her way carefully over slush that had long ago frozen into peaks and valleys; now, these were receiving a new and treacherous coating of pure white. Even though Diana extended her arms for balance, it seemed likely she could lose her footing at any moment.

It was a relief to them both when the young woman finally gained the road. She reached through her cloak, and her neighbor's, to clutch Charlotte's arm. They stood together a moment, looking with wonder at the sky. It was a greenish-gray; white flakes caught all the light that remained, falling in a dizzying display against the bleak background.

"Richard had already gone off when I awoke," Diana complained petulantly. "And no one else has been to see me all day! Cicero said you were away, but he wouldn't tell me where—and then he hid my shoes. It took me an hour to find the boots I'm wearing, which I'm sorry to say are *his*—"

"Come with me, then. He can guess what's become of you," Charlotte added, having already seen someone looking out of a tall window across the yard. "I would appreciate some advice, since I've heard a great deal today."

"Is Hannah not there?"

"Before I left this morning, Henry came up to tell me his mother's sciatica is troubling her again."

"Then I'll gladly come and keep you company. I will be happy to hear *anything* new. What's going on down there?"

she asked, looking briefly over her shoulder. "Clearly, it's something that interests both you and my brother. Is it left over from yesterday's fête?"

"In a way," Charlotte answered. The storm took her next words, and flung them far down the hill toward Bracebridge. Holding on to the young woman at her side, she hurried them both along through curtains of snow.

Chapter 16

THE TALL CLOCK at the bottom of the stairs told them it was a little after two, when they entered the front door of the old farmhouse. It was already dark inside, but at least they didn't find themselves alone. Orpheus greeted them happily, and Charlotte bent to stroke him, rewarding his patience before she let him out into the snow.

In the kitchen she knelt to fan the embers of the morning's fire, then added fresh sticks of dry wood from which smoke immediately began to curl. Next came a pair of stout logs. Soon the hearth gave off not only a steady heat, but a welcome, flickering light. To cheer them further, Charlotte went to the pantry and brought back four joined tapers, cut apart their wicks, then inserted them into brass candlesticks. When she'd placed them around the room, glimmers came back from the window panes and a small hanging mirror, and from silver, pewter, and copper objects on the shelves.

Upstairs she found a pair of slippers. She brought these down and offered them to Diana, who had already removed the boots she wore. Charlotte put on a pair of house shoes. "Tea?" she asked.

"Thank you, no. I've had nothing to do but drink tea *all day*, and it's ruined my nerves."

"Some sharp cider, then."

Going off once more, Charlotte took a candle down the cellar steps, and returned with a jug. Bubbles at the top told her it would be just the thing. She poured two glasses, then went to let Orpheus inside. With duties and comforts taken care of, the women settled to talk.

Charlotte began with the too-familiar tale of the morning's activities.

"I *knew* something had happened!" Diana cried after hearing the worst. "I never saw this Godwin boy, did I? At least I never met him, though he was there yesterday. Have they told his family?"

"The Godwins moved to Worcester many years ago. From what I gather, Alex has lately had only a little contact with them. Someone will go and tell them as soon as the storm subsides, I'm sure—if no one's gone already."

"I'm very sorry for them. But there won't be much anyone can do."

Charlotte sensed Diana had gained new compassion as a result of her own loss. Yet something else seemed to carry her on with a nervous intensity.

"That's not exactly right, since it *was* clearly murder. What is Richard doing about it?"

"He's gone with Constable Dudley, to talk to the woman who allowed Alex a room in her house. Then they meant to visit the Sloans, to speak with Martha."

"The one Lem missed so last summer, while he was in Boston?"

"The same."

"How is she involved? They can't believe a *woman* would have killed in such a brutal way?"

"I think they would like to be sure Martha gave Lem no cause for jealousy."

"Oh. And did she?"

"I doubt it."

"So, nothing really ties Lem to this awful deed, except the hatchet."

"Left in this . . ." Charlotte lifted the canvas bag from the floor, where she'd set it when she refreshed the fire. Now she looked at it more carefully, to make sure nothing but the scarf was inside. "It's said it was taken home in error last night—by John Dudley, our new constable."

"*There* is a man I hardly like. Every time Dudley has been pointed out to me, he's been drunk. What is his wife's name?"

"Rachel."

"She lost a son a few years ago, didn't she?"

"That's true."

"Having children can be a terrible thing. It could be, Charlotte, that you were fortunate to have none of your own."

"I've wished it were otherwise."

"Oh, of course. You and Aaron could never—"

Charlotte reconsidered Diana's new compassion, before she replied.

"We had little time. Life, like death, seems to come only when nature agrees—"

"Unless it is a case of murder, like what happened to this Godwin boy. *His* death was not 'natural.' Nor was it 'the will of God'—something we must expect, and prepare for—not our fault, *for there was nothing we could have done about it!* But was Charlie's death so very different?

I'm not sure when I will be able to forgive whoever, or whatever, took him from us!"

Tears sprang into Diana's eyes while Charlotte sat quietly, startled by the rage that had finally flashed out. Diana's anger, it seemed, had been set against Heaven itself.

She recalled the young woman as she'd once been: last summer, on the evening of Signor Lahte's recital, regal and confident at the side of a dashing husband in her brother's Boston home—before that, fighting bravely against the smallpox, while Edmund watched—even earlier, playful but determined, setting her sights on the mysterious King's man she now missed, one suspected, more than she would say. Despite her bravery, she'd been deeply wounded.

"Was it all for nothing?" Diana asked, her lips trembling. "At least in the case of this Godwin boy, he must have died for *something*! But our child harmed no one. He was a boy we cherished, and spent *weeks* praying for . . ."

She sank back, her eyes blazing defiantly. Charlotte asked herself if she should try to soothe, or if Richard's approach wasn't a better one, after all.

"Was it for nothing?" she returned. "You will have to take that up with God or the Devil, when you happen to see one or the other. But are you saying Alex Godwin may have deserved to die? That is unfair, Diana—he was little more than a child himself."

Diana seemed startled. She forced herself to reconsider.

"You're right, of course. Well, it *does* seem divine justice is rather limited, these days. Perhaps you will let me help you discover a more worldly sort. You do plan to solve this murder?"

"I don't really know how, or if—"

"Bracebridge has need of a Nemesis," Diana concluded

darkly, recalling one of her brother's stories. "We must both do what we can. This time, at least, we'll have the advice of an attorney. Charlotte—you don't suppose Lem could possibly have done this thing, do you?"

"I see no reason why he would have."

"Not for love? Or jealousy?"

"I don't think so. Nor, I suppose, do you."

"He is nearly a man."

"One with a good deal of sense, and a strong conscience. I've never known him to hurt anyone. At least, not intentionally."

Had Diana, too, begun to see men as likely to bring trouble, before anything else? If so—poor Edmund!

"We'll forget about Lem, then," Diana decided charitably. "Who else is capable of it?"

"Of murder?" This was something Charlotte felt it would be better not to ask, for she supposed she knew the answer. "We might ask, instead, who had the opportunity. That might narrow things down a little."

"But nearly everyone in the village was there by the ice yesterday! And since you found the boy this morning, we can't know when, exactly, it was done. It's a shame no one missed him. Was he usually by himself?"

"It seems so. The only thing he did regularly, that I know of, was visit Boar Island."

"Tell me again who lives there."

Charlotte began to explain, and found herself repeating the story of her adventure two days before. Diana gave a scream when she heard of Charlotte's fall into the icy marsh—yet there was a new respect in her eyes while she listened to the rest.

"And you found them *entirely* alone?" she asked at the end, unable to believe something so different from her own experience in Boston.

"They'll remain that way until someone can be found to work for them again. That's why we sent Lem off this morning. I'd hoped he'd be back by now," she added uneasily, looking out to see snow building up in the barnyard. She thought, too, of the cows. One way or another, they'd have to be milked soon. Perhaps she and Diana? . . . That gave her a welcome moment of amusement.

"Here's something else I find curious," she said at length. She described the return of the spoon to Rachel Dudley, and the message she'd received from the children only an hour before, saying that the rest of the missing silver had now been found. In the silence that followed, each came to the same conclusion.

"It *must* have been the husband," said Diana, with a look of disdain. "A locked cabinet, and nothing else in the house taken? The children are hardly old enough to have become such villains. He probably needed money, and traded the spoons for silver coins. Then, seeing what a fuss he'd raised, he bought them back, and returned them. The Devil, indeed! These are hardly the Dark Ages—even here in Bracebridge."

"It could be he said that for the children, so they'd not see his hand in it. Rachel blames him, I'm sure."

"His children might as well know what he is. And the rest of the village, I should think. This is the man who's to investigate the latest outrage to occur here? What a joke it all is!"

Diana's laugh signaled a return of her usual humor, but its edge seemed uncomfortably cutting. Perhaps, thought Charlotte, another glass of fermented cider would do no harm. She rose to pour it.

"I wonder," she then said, "what business Dudley could have had on the island."

"I wonder," Diana countered, "why he took this bag of

yours, which he must have known wasn't his. Though I don't suppose it still held the hatchet, or he would not have sent it back."

"But he didn't, did he?" Charlotte asked. "Rachel did."

"Yes, that's true—"

Their thoughts were interrupted by sounds outside. With a rush of relief, Charlotte put down her glass. She walked from the kitchen to the front room, imagining Lem had come from the main road, as she'd done earlier. But before she could cross to the door, it seemed to blow open on its own. Covered with snow, Lem lurched in, pulling the loaded sled. Someone else, white-headed as well, came behind him.

"For pity's sake—!" Charlotte began, as the boards of the sled scraped across the polished floorboards. Then she realized its burden strongly resembled one she and Richard Longfellow had pulled down the hill that morning. Thankfully, this one had a small section of its face exposed, for breathing.

"Sorry! Couldn't be helped—" This came from under a swath of scarf. Lem turned and made sure the door was shut, with the woman who had followed him on the right side of it. And Magdalene Knowles stood looking down at the bundle on the sled, which still had not moved.

Chapter 17

I<small>T'S OLD MRS</small>. Knowles," said Lem. Charlotte knelt quickly and pulled the wool away from the pinched face, then put an ear by the partly opened mouth. She heard and felt short, sharp breathing.

"What happened?" she asked. Lem had by now removed his hat and scarf, and stood wondering what to do next.

"She's burned—badly. Her skirts caught fire while no one was with her. By the time I heard her screams, it was nearly too late. It might be yet," he said in a whisper, for Charlotte had risen to stand beside him.

Diana opened the kitchen door, and gaped at what she saw.

"We'll carry her into the kitchen," Charlotte decided. "Then run upstairs, Lem, and build a fire in my bedroom—it's the warmest. Diana and I will see to the rest." She helped Lem lift the slight body of Mrs. Knowles by the blankets surrounding her.

They soon put the bundle down again, beside the

kitchen fire. The change seemed to awaken Catherine; she turned white eyes toward the flames, then raised an arm before her face, as if to save it from the heat. Charlotte took the woman's frail arms, and leaned forward to assure her.

"You're safe here! Catherine, it's Charlotte Willett. You've come to my house. You must stay warm by the fire, while we see to your—"

She quickly swallowed her next words, for on lifting the blankets she'd seen beyond the remains of ancient skirts, matted on top with grease from a succession of meals, below by oils from a body rarely washed. The smell of burned flesh was far worse than the other. Some of that flesh was blistered; more was mottled and weeping, with here and there some red that had been newly torn by writhing, and bits of white where bone showed through.

Lem stood spellbound. Charlotte signaled for him to help Magdalene into a chair across the room. This he did before he left them, his boots ringing on the stairs.

Charlotte knew she and Diana would have to cut away what remained of the skirts, and cleanse as best they could what had suffered beneath them. Only then would they be able to apply a salve and bandages. Fortunately, Catherine's face had been spared. They could look without revulsion at her nearly sightless eyes as they spoke to her. But for how long?

Charlotte went to a chest and removed discarded linen sheets already cut for bandages, as well as a crock of goose fat she'd simmered with house leeks, comfrey, feverfew, and lavender. To her amazement, when she returned to the fire she found that Diana had begun to work efficiently, exposing more and more of the withered body, easing off bits of wool with warm water from the kettle, poured into a bowl.

The clock by the stairs struck three times, and then they heard knocking on the front door. It went unanswered. In a minute more, a tapping came from outside the kitchen. Orpheus, who had positioned himself at Magdalene's side, let out a growl when it opened.

Astonished by what he'd already glimpsed through the window, Moses Reed entered, taking in the activity at the hearth. When he turned to close the door he saw Magdalene in the dark corner.

Charlotte thought she heard the attorney call the woman's name. Turning, she saw him bend and offer his hand. It was good to see someone talking to her, if it was also a little strange. But she had no time to think further on their apparent acquaintance.

"Mr. Reed?" she called. He came swiftly to her side. "It's Mrs. Knowles, from Boar Island. She suffered an accident there. She's badly burned, as you can see."

"But how did they get here?"

"Lem brought them. I sent him upstairs to prepare a fire in a bedroom."

"The boy was on the island when this occurred?"

"Yes."

"I see," he answered with a deep frown. "I'd assumed . . ."

"We sent him to learn if anything might be done for Mrs. Knowles and her companion."

"No—no—no!" Hearing her name, Catherine had become more aware of her situation. Her chest labored, and she began to gasp.

"What can I do?" asked Charlotte, leaning closer.

"Nothing," the old woman managed in a whisper. It

seemed she suffered from fluid rising in her lungs—perhaps she was even drowning. Diana positioned a pillow beneath the thin shoulders. Breathing more quietly, Catherine formed a few words with great effort.

"I stood—but saw nothing—" Then came a desperate cry, as if she were reliving her fall into the fire.

"I have something to calm her," Charlotte said softly to Moses Reed.

"Opium, I hope?"

"Given to me by Noah Willett."

"Ah, yes. The sea captain."

"It should bring her sleep, at least. Under the circumstances, I think we need not worry about anything else."

"I would agree," said Reed. They watched Diana apply salve to a piece of linen, and set it gently in place.

"There seems little chance she'll last the night," Reed added.

"But we'll try, with what we have on hand. We must."

"Call me if she speaks again. I'll go and talk with Lem."

The lawyer left them. Soon, over the whistling wind, Charlotte and Diana again heard the sound of boots stomping. Without further preamble, the door opened. This time, Orpheus let out a single bark.

Richard Longfellow came in with a blast of cold. Behind him trailed Christian Rowe. No doubt they'd expected to find warmth and calm, once they'd escaped from the swirling menace of the storm. What they saw made them stop quite suddenly, and stare.

"Carlotta?" asked Longfellow.

"It's Catherine Knowles. That is Magdalene Knowles

behind you. Lem brought them here after an accident," she added quietly, so that Longfellow had to bend close to hear.

"Dear God!" he then exclaimed, his face contorting. "Where is he?" he asked, after he'd pulled back.

"Upstairs, warming a bedroom."

"Constable Dudley left us to stop at the inn, but he's on his way here to speak to the boy," Christian Rowe announced. Charlotte's glance showed she believed this to be a thing of little importance at the moment.

"Have you seen burns this severe before?" Again she nearly whispered to Longfellow, supposing that Magdalene and Rowe would not hear her.

"No. But I don't see how she can survive them."

"Nor do I."

"You say that is Mrs. Knowles there?" Rowe inquired, after he'd made himself more presentable in the small mirror.

"She's in great discomfort," Charlotte replied, hoping he would take the hint.

Rowe held himself aloof. He had little use for illness, which he suspected lay before him. Always, it was a thing he found others to attend to.

"This lady has never made herself known to me, and I think she has little time for religion, or for our village. Nor have I met Miss Knowles, though of course I have heard of her situation. Madam, how do *you* do?"

Magdalene, still encased in her cloak, blinked and drew back further.

Longfellow supposed Rowe had been offended. He wondered himself if Magdalene might be mute. Perhaps she was merely stunned, or tired. Certainly the lady had good cause, for she must have walked several miles that morning.

He went and knelt before the perplexed woman, holding out his hands. She stared briefly into his eyes, as she'd done with the attorney. Then she looked down to her feet, and he took it upon himself to unlace her boots. She waited like a child, and finally stood to allow him to take her cloak.

"Would you like something to drink?" he asked. "Are you hungry?" She shook her head to this, but then said her first words since she'd entered the house.

"May I have a cup of tea?"

"Of course. Rowe, what do you suppose Lem and Reed are doing upstairs?" The minister wondered himself, and left them.

"Now," said Longfellow, "there is the can of tea, Miss Knowles, and here is the pot. I presume you know what to do with them. I will watch, and talk with you a little, if I may. It was a long walk here, was it not? Are you tired? Would you prefer to lie down upstairs?"

"I often walk," Magdalene answered. Longfellow decided that she had received much benefit from it. "I am not tired." Neither was she bent or weak, he saw. In body, she seemed a healthy woman.

"There," said Diana, rising wearily to her feet. "At least all of it is covered. I'll take the teapot, Richard, and see to Miss Knowles."

Amazed, her brother allowed her to take the vessel he still held. It appeared that Diana's brief encounter with motherhood had changed her significantly—and her time as a nurse, he reminded himself with a twinge. Having something of importance to do now might be balm for her own bruised spirit.

Looking through a window at the snow, he observed that the light was nearly gone. Considering the worsening weather, he then asked himself if the constable would appear, after all.

He soon had his answer.

Chapter 18

POUNDING RATHER THAN knocking, John Dudley startled them all. Orpheus let out a volley of growls; Longfellow lunged for the door, and let the constable in.

For once, he was nearly sober. Still, when Dudley caught sight of a body lying by the fire, he became less sure of himself. His eyes went to the ceiling as he heard boots creaking across the floorboards.

"The boy's up there?" he asked Longfellow.

"With Moses Reed, and Reverend Rowe. I presume they are asking him questions of their own."

Dudley grumbled, and looked for the way out of the kitchen.

"Not so fast," Longfellow ordered. "First, I need your help with Mrs. Knowles. From Boar Island. One of your near neighbors, I think."

"How is *she* here?" Dudley blurted.

"There's been an accident. Now, she needs to be taken up to a bed. If you'll lift an end of that blanket, I'll take the other. Careful, man! She's been badly burned."

"How?"

"It appears she fell, or stepped too near the flames at one of her own hearths. An old story, I'm afraid. Perhaps Magdalene Knowles, standing behind you, will be able to tell us more. Or Lem, more likely. Lift—gently, now!"

Together, they took the old woman, who moaned at the inevitable jostling, across the kitchen and up the stairs. Once they'd reached the upper hall, the two took their burden to the middle bedroom where they found a good fire prepared.

Lem and Moses Reed sat on the bed, their heads close together. The minister, meanwhile, used the opportunity to look around him. Longfellow reminded himself that this was Mrs. Willett's winter bedroom, which she currently occupied. A strong reaction to its invasion nearly overwhelmed him, until he heard his sister behind him.

Diana expressed her own shock at the fact that the bedclothes had not been folded back. She prepared the bed in her own way; then they eased the light body onto the smooth sheets, and it was covered.

Catherine's white eyes seemed to have darkened. Longfellow concluded that Charlotte must have opened her store of opium gum kept for emergencies. In another moment, Mrs. Knowles sighed. Her features relaxed, and it appeared she might be dreaming.

Charlotte and Magdalene entered, making the place altogether too crowded.

"We'll withdraw, gentlemen, and go below," Longfellow said firmly.

"But I shall stay," Moses Reed countered. "For reasons you'll understand shortly. It is of some importance, sir," he added, as if begging a favor.

"Of course," Longfellow assented. "The rest of us will

go, then. We still have much to discuss. Now, perhaps, more than before."

"You come with me, young man," the constable said gruffly, taking Lem's arm and pulling him out before the others.

"I'm glad that's over," said Diana as she went to shut the door. "These two ladies will benefit from quiet as much as anything else," she added significantly to Reed, who bowed his head and waited.

Taking a cup from the tray Charlotte had carried up with her, Diana seemed about to offer its contents to her patient. Then her green eyes widened, and she herself took on an ill appearance.

"Her lips!" she whispered desperately. "They're blue, the way it was with Charlie!"

Her friend reached to take her trembling hand. The color of life had begun to ebb from Catherine's face, and Charlotte doubted it would rise again. Magdalene moved forward to stand over the person she knew best in the world. It seemed she meant to speak. Instead, she bent to kiss the brow of the woman so long her mistress, her care-taker, perhaps even her friend.

When she turned away at last, the younger of the island's women looked directly into the face of Moses Reed, for he'd come to stand quietly beside her. Magdalene seemed to feel some new confusion. Charlotte supposed her reaction was quite different from their earlier aware-ness of one another, in the corner downstairs. Were they, in fact, acquainted, as she'd first assumed? Magdalene's expression dimmed, and she went to sit in one of the room's two chairs, choosing the one most distant from the rest.

"It cannot be long," said the lawyer. "Mrs. Knowles? Is

there anything you wish to tell us? Anything of importance?" They saw a flutter of her eyelids, a slight roll of her head. "It may make a great difference."

The old woman's eyes focused, one of her arms moved, and then Charlotte imagined the claw beneath fresh bandages would have pointed to her, had it been free. Carefully, she sat on the edge of the bed and leaned closer. On his own side, Moses Reed did the same.

Catherine's mouth began to move. "Pushed!" she finally expelled in a gasp. Charlotte sat back, struck as much by the thought as by the fetid breath that had delivered it. "Pushed," Mrs. Knowles insisted once more.

"No!" Reed exclaimed. It seemed he'd not received the information he'd hoped for. And yet, was it entirely unexpected? Charlotte considered a new suspicion, while they waited to hear more.

"Who?" Reed finally asked, after many seconds had gone by. During that time Catherine seemed to have retreated into dreams. Then, marshaling the last of her strength, she attempted to speak again.

"You, madam, you . . . find out if the boy was . . ."

It was nearly too much; she clenched her body in a final attempt.

"If . . . the boy . . ." A bubble of red came to her lips, then another, and another, until they appeared to be a rosy cluster of honeycomb.

"What does it mean?" asked Charlotte. "Find out what? And which boy?" It was no use asking further.

Moses Reed regarded her soberly. "A dying wish, Mrs. Willett. Did you know her well?"

"I saw Mrs. Knowles two days ago, for the first time in many years. For the third time, I think, in all my life!"

"You must have made an impression," he replied.

"Do you suppose she *could* have been pushed, as she said?"

"Many things could have happened. That, I think, is only one possibility. She could as easily have been in a delirium at the end, due to the opium. Perhaps she only stumbled at the side of her hearth. Her eyes were clouded, and perhaps she could not see something at her feet. The fire could have taken her with no further help. I've observed the results of such a thing before."

It was, Charlotte agreed silently, an all too common occurrence.

"However," the attorney went on, "as Mrs. Knowles *believed* she was pushed, she may have supposed Lem was behind her, though she could not be sure. I find his involvement difficult to imagine. Do you know of any reason he might have done such a thing?"

"None! She *must* have been mistaken!"

"Or, she could have meant someone else. But who?" he asked, looking away suddenly.

"No one else was there, that we know of. Except, of course—"

She, too, then looked to Magdalene, who sat quietly. Diana stood at her side, staring from a window. Neither seemed aware of what had just occurred.

"Let's not speculate," Reed said swiftly. "Let us, instead, ask both of them what, exactly, they saw today. Lem, I think, will go back with Mr. Longfellow this evening. If I'm offered a bed there myself, I'll have a chance to ask your young man a few things more. You may find an opportunity to question Miss Knowles, if she is to stay here."

"It would be quieter for her, I suppose."

"Given time to recover, she may recall something. She's not entirely without sense."

"Do you know her, Mr. Reed?"

"We have met before."

"What you suggest does seem the best plan."

"I would also ask that you say nothing to any of the others yet, about what Mrs. Knowles may have felt, or imagined. At least until we've obtained more facts."

"Yes, I agree."

"If you'd like, I'll see to moving her into an unheated room."

"The one at the top of the stairs is the coolest."

"I'll go down and speak with Mr. Longfellow."

Moses Reed moved away from the bed, but went first to the north window where he spoke to the two women.

"Her suffering was brief. It is over."

Diana nodded, but made no other reply.

"Miss Knowles? Mrs. Willett will care for you here, tonight. Have no fear. Rest. Later, you may begin to think of what you would like to do."

Magdalene, too, said nothing.

The lawyer sighed. "Mrs. Montagu, if you and your brother have no objection, I would prefer to stay near Lem, this evening."

"I'm sure that will be fine." Diana rose. Giving no more than a glance to the woman she'd tended, she made her way to the door. "A word, Charlotte?" she called back.

Passing them in the hall a moment later, Moses Reed went quietly down the stairs.

"You know," Diana then said, "that my ears are nearly as good as your own, Charlotte. And the room is not a large one."

"You heard?"

"Most, I think. At least at the end, when I held my breath. I listened for Magdalene's, too. Either she is very cold, or she didn't understand. Or perhaps her hearing is not as acute as ours. But I rather think it is the first."

"Mrs. Knowles has told me that Magdalene was born a natural child."

"Do you mean to say that her father—?"

"No, not that. She has always had an affliction. Magdalene is not as we are, as you've probably seen; there are things she's unable to grasp. She is, in some ways, simple."

"Well, do be careful. The old woman may have been right in blaming *someone*."

"What would you have me do?"

"Be safe. Lock your bedroom door tonight."

For the first time, it occurred to Charlotte that she would offer Magdalene the far room, while Catherine would soon lie in the first along the hall. That left her own bed, here. More than one life had ended in it, she told herself. Those of her parents, in fact. And before that? It was not sensible to be squeamish about such things. Most slept in beds passed down to them.

"I'll give Magdalene something to help her sleep," Charlotte decided, suspecting that she herself would choose the kitchen, after all. "If she'll agree to it."

"Good. Take none yourself."

"But I really can't imagine—"

"Well, I can. We'll need further proof, of course, before accusing anyone. But not that kind of proof!"

"Go and sleep well, yourself. You and Cicero will have your hands full."

"Rowe and that awful constable can't stay for long.

The snow shows no sign of letting up, and you know what that can mean. May the Lord protect anyone out on the roads on a night like this!"

Had she known that one traveler, in particular, was not far away on the road from Boston, Diana would have prayed all the harder.

Chapter 19

EDMUND MONTAGU REINED in his horse for perhaps the hundredth time, wondering how he had ever gotten himself into such a situation.

Once he regained the road, he would find the village of Bracebridge. The builders had made enough cuts through the low hills to indicate where it might be, but he'd seen none of them for half an hour due to the snow—now, the increasing gloom had turned to night.

There was no point in going back. The wind continued to hurl sheets of icy snow at his horse's tail. Because his lantern illuminated nothing more than what whirled around him, he'd begun to feel as though he walked through an endless box, whose dull sides never changed.

If his horse had known where they were going, perhaps it could have been trusted. But home for his mount was back in Boston, which they'd left hours before. It was all he could do to keep the poor beast going forward. Before long, it would be impossible.

He had the idea of simply finding the shelter of some

trees, and staying where he was for the night. But as it could be no more than five o'clock, it would be a very long time before dawn. And he'd seen storms in this wretched country last for days. Only the year before, he'd been forced to walk through knee-deep snow one morning through the streets of Boston! It was difficult to believe, after one had lived through the intense heat of a Massachusetts summer; storms here could be devastating, and might quickly kill one who wandered, unprepared.

As the wind continued to howl, the horse under him began to shudder, and Edmund's feet no longer felt the stirrups. This, he knew, was the beginning of a bad end. He had only one choice more. Slowly he got down from his horse, and began to walk.

By stamping his feet against the ground, he felt, at least, a little pain. He also felt new sympathy for ordinary soldiers, who regularly found themselves in foul weather. He'd spent most of his early years in the King's service within the cities of England, helping men out of trouble. In the past he'd aided scores, allowing them to make amends to those they'd wronged, and to free themselves from ruinous situations. Not all, of course, could be saved. Some had been abandoned—young men with unusual vices, or those born with too little sense.

He heard himself laugh in spite of his growing fear. Could it be that he'd fallen at last, as they had, into a pit of his own making? Lately he'd woven together a net of men who ranged far from Boston, to inform him of what went on throughout the colony. But none of these could help him now; none could even tell him if he trod hard-packed earth, or gentler field. And that was the thing of vital importance. Without the road, he might go searching for a bed forever.

Forever? No, surely not. In fact it should not take long

at all. Another hour or two at most, and a hard bed would be his—an exceedingly cold and lonely one.

If only Fate would bring him within sight of another light—a house, or an approaching horse or carriage. Otherwise he would fall and be buried, until the sun resurrected him in the spring. What would his wife do then? Worse, what would she do before, wondering how much more she'd lost?

Diana! He should have gone after her days ago. Too late he'd come running, having been given only a scrap of a reason—even though he'd been warned the weather would change for the worse. He'd supposed he knew better than the colonials who advised him. Was he not, after all, an Englishman born and bred, unlike country fellows of limited skill, imagination, intelligence, and passion?

Who would have the last laugh now? His intolerance, his own stubbornness, had gotten him into this trouble. Were they also the reason he'd not listened to Diana? Had he tried as hard as he might have, to console her? No, that had been the fault of pride, and a fear of showing weakness in his own despair, after the loss of his son. Yet even that was not entirely true. How could he ever explain the rest?

Charles, he'd been called, for his father's father. Little Charlie had cried at first. Then, nearly silent, he'd faded as swiftly as a flower.

Again, Edmund cursed the men of Boston for the pain they'd caused, for he had no one else to blame. They'd taken government into their own hands, against Royal orders. Could he in all conscience have gone off to Bracebridge earlier, leaving a dangerous mob with no check, seeking only the comfort of his wife? Governor Bernard would hardly have approved.

Yet if only he had it to do over. If only he were given

another chance! A year at Diana's side had been worth more to him than all the rest. With time, he could surely make her happy again, and give her another child. At that moment, Edmund Montagu imagined the snow suddenly lessened. In the next, a ghostly line spread before him. It seemed to be a planting of trees. Stepping beneath its low branches, he found himself facing something like a hedge, which gave him a new difficulty. Once he and his horse had pulled themselves through the interwoven branches, he found they acted as a lee, slowing the wind. He paused to rest and think.

It looked familiar. But could it be? Hope made him almost joyful. Holding up his lantern, he examined branches that had scratched at him, catching his long cape with cruel spines. It was, indeed, a hawthorn!

At last he knew where he was, though he should have been at one end of the line, rather than somewhere in the middle. This was better than he could have hoped! For it was the same hedge he'd examined during the past summer, when a traveler had been found dead on the ground nearby. Now, he suspected this need not be his own fate, after all.

The line ran north and south, abutting the main road. For this reason, the captain turned to his left. He soon came upon the ditch he'd expected. Calling out to the horse, he continued to pull at its reins, encouraging a faster pace, staying in the frozen ditch so that there would be little to fear for the last two miles.

Soon he would reach his wife, and then he would cover her with kisses. A few hours after that, he imagined he would be glad to fall asleep, finally, in her arms.

Chapter 20

RICHARD LONGFELLOW STOOD with his back to a snow-splashed window, his eyes playing over those who sat in his study, close to the blazing fire. Each had in hand a glass of brandy to further ward off the effects of the cold. John Dudley had already been given another; Moses Reed nursed his first, appreciating its bouquet.

Upstairs, Diana refreshed herself by a fire Cicero had kept burning while awaiting her return from Mrs. Willett's farmhouse. He and Lem were now creating some sort of supper in the kitchen. Happily, Reverend Rowe had stayed only briefly, to complain that he'd learned nothing helpful from his foolish flock. Then he'd hurried home.

Longfellow asked himself what he had accomplished that afternoon. For one thing, he'd been able to persuade the constable that a close watch on Lem, rather than an arrest, would be sufficient. This had been easier than he'd imagined. But it seemed Dudley was incapable of deciding more. Hardly surprising—though another occurrence was. Returning to the study after seeing the minister out,

Longfellow found Dudley and Lem close together, speaking quietly to keep Moses Reed from hearing whatever it was they discussed. The constable stepped back abruptly, his expression of innocence seeming highly improbable. Neither offered a word of explanation; both, Longfellow suspected, shared some secret. His frustration increased as he recalled other times he'd come upon similar scenes in recent months.

Lem had been eager enough to ask how things were with Martha Sloan. He'd eased the boy's mind on that account, at least. She was anxious enough to fear what the future might hold for her prospective mate. Godwin, she swore, had been nothing to her at all, and both young men knew it. Why they'd decided to fight on the day of Alex's death, she had no idea.

Later, while John Dudley did little more than play with his boil, Longfellow had questioned Frances Bowers. Again, he'd been disappointed. She'd rarely spoken to Alex of anything important, it seemed, and never at length. Apparently, he always ate quickly and in silence, well before she sat down to her own supper, so that Miss Bowers had not even shared a table with the young man— an arrangement that had suited them both for nearly a year!

Leaving the lady, Longfellow had suggested they inquire about the missing canvas bag and the found hatchet, starting with a visit to the Bigelows. Dudley rejected the idea, insisting instead that they go immediately up the hill to speak with Lem—though they could easily have seen Jonah and Ned on the way. In fact the constable had left them to go into the inn, no doubt for a bumper of courage. Some time later, before he'd left Charlotte with Magdalene Knowles, she'd told him quietly that the seed bag had been sent back to her—and, that it had been taken off accidentally by none other than Dudley himself! No doubt the constable had been in his cups the day before. But why, today, had he neglected to mention what he'd done? Longfellow asked himself if something else might have taken place by the bonfire.

And then, he recalled that when Moses Reed came down to inform them the old woman was dead, Dudley had hurried to say the second death could in no way be related to the first. Reed seemed not entirely to agree, but he'd said no more. Perhaps the lawyer thought otherwise? If so, what did *he* know that he wasn't saying?

After he'd simmered for another minute, Longfellow forced himself to ask fairly if he might not be imagining things. Yet it did appear that everyone kept him in the dark about certain events. Perhaps even Charlotte had done so. Above all, it hurt him to suspect that this might be true. But she was a villager by birth, something which carried a level of acceptance here that he'd not been granted—and probably never would be.

At any rate, before much longer he would confront them all with what he'd discovered on his own. As a selectman, it had been his duty to investigate. As a man ignored, it had been his pleasure. Now, he was reasonably sure he knew what at least some in the village had been up to. And at the proper moment, he was certain he'd find a few eager to turn about and give more evidence, by which the others might be discomfited, at the very least!

Returning to the problem at hand, Longfellow began to sift through what Lem had told them of his trip to Boar Island, while Catherine Knowles lay dying. He'd first informed the two women of Alex's death. Both were surprised, but beyond looking long at one another they'd shown no regret, at least in front of their visitor. Catherine had instructed Lem that he would find a woodpile on the western side of the house. There he'd discovered a great many sawn logs made from windfalls. He'd taken up an ax and set to work splitting some of the dry stuff for kindling and cooking. Meanwhile, he had a clear view of the path that led from the front door, and he'd soon seen Magdalene go out walking.

For half an hour, he continued to work alone. Startled when the old woman screamed, he ran back into the house. He recalled his own ringing footsteps, but no others. When he found her, Catherine was on her hands and knees by the hearth, her lower clothing aflame. Keeping his wits, the boy had rolled her back and forth across the hearth rug, then poured a pot of tea on a few parts that continued to smoke. After that—

Moses Reed cleared his throat to attract the attention of the others, and picked up their earlier conversation. "What do you think the village will say, Dudley, of two recent deaths here?"

"The village?" the constable asked blankly. Like Longfellow, he'd been gathering his own wool.

"We have one man obviously murdered, but not enough proof to lead us to arrest anyone. Unsettling, yet these things take time. What I fear is this: matters can quickly get out of hand when people take it upon themselves to decide the truth, without the weight of oath, judge, or jury. What do you think will be said about Lem Wainwright's involvement in Godwin's death? He is, as you know, my client, and my responsibility."

"Yes, yes," John Dudley said, somewhat nervously. "I think they'll agree with me there's no sense in blaming Lem—even though he did leave the hatchet where someone else could pick it up and do this filthy deed. But he has told me he did not do it, and I believe him."

"Then you think Lem is in no danger?"

"Danger? No. Of course, someone murdered Godwin—we're certain of *that*. But there's no reason to suspect anyone from Bracebridge. No, more likely whoever it was came down the road and saw the rest of us by the ice. The worst sort of man is drawn to such gatherings—pickpockets, especially. It could be this stranger first took up the hatchet to steal it. Once taken, though—if Godwin insulted him in any way, as he often did—then, matters might have gone another way. That, I think, is what the village will say, sir. I've little doubt it's the truth."

"Do you suppose," asked Reed slowly, "any might wonder if someone here made it *appear* Lem was responsible for Godwin's death?"

"Would it be in the interest of young Wainwright, if such a suggestion was to be thrown about?" Dudley returned. "Better, I'd say, to ask around Worcester, where Godwin spent most of his years. To see if someone there might have had revenge in mind."

"Perhaps we should stay with your earlier fabrication—that of a complete stranger."

Now Dudley scowled, his dislike of the attorney returning.

"This second death, then," Reed continued, "which Lem seems nearly to have witnessed. Will the village take it for an accident? You seem to have decided, John, on very little evidence, that it was no more than mischance."

"Well, it would seem Catherine Knowles did no more than what others have done! She was old and feeble, and could hardly see. However, some may say 'Mad Maud' is now free of the old woman, and is off that cursed island. Not that I'll be among those to suggest she had anything to do with what happened. But it was a strange thing after all, the two of them living there alone. If they *were* alone. I believe they may have had company—unquiet spirits, and other unnatural things that have kept most men away."

"Some will be more interested," said Longfellow, "in learning where the money goes, now that Mrs. Knowles is dead. Isn't it said she controlled a fortune?"

"As it happens, I know the answer to that particular question," said Moses Reed. Longfellow rose to pour another round of brandy.

"Do you, Mr. Reed?" he asked, when no further information was offered.

"I should. I've acted as attorney for Mrs. Knowles for many years."

"I wasn't aware of that."

"Few are."

"Will you tell us more?"

"At the moment, I'm afraid I can't say much. First I must speak with the family—at least with Magdalene Knowles. Though there are some things, I suppose, that I might reveal to you now."

"Gentlemen, may I join you?" asked a new voice. The men looked to the door and saw Diana Montagu sweep toward them.

In fact, she had been waiting for some time in the passage, wondering if she would hear something of interest within.

"We're discussing legal matters, Diana," said Longfellow. "Which you'll probably find tedious."

"I think not. Please, continue."

Moses Reed made no objection. Constable Dudley, Diana thought, actually blushed at her approach. He reached to a table and picked up his hat, looking as if he might run away. But it seemed he only wished to mangle the thing further.

"Sit, then," said her brother, setting a chair near, but not too near, the fire.

"When I came here two days ago," Moses Reed went on moments later, stroking his beard, "it was for two reasons: First, I wished to discuss a small legacy with Mrs. Willett, as I believe you already know. Second, I also hoped to see Catherine Knowles, or at least to send a message to her, and wait for a word in return. I needed to clarify certain matters relating to her late husband, Peter Knowles."

"Oh, yes!" said Diana, suddenly sitting forward. "I knew I'd heard something about a family named Knowles. But I hardly thought this could be the same, for they live in Philadelphia. Yet I'm sure a Peter Knowles was mentioned by my friend Mrs. Cooper."

"It is a wealthy family," Reed went on, "and an old one with several branches. Peter Knowles, the patriarch of one, has just died."

"I'd assumed he'd done so long ago," said Longfellow. "Then husband and wife lived apart?"

"For reasons that had to do with an unfortunate bent in the husband. After the marriage it became clear that his mind was weak, or worse—not entirely unlike the case of Magdalene Knowles, his unfortunate sister."

"You've known them long?" Longfellow asked.

"I met Peter Knowles a year or two before he returned to his family in Philadelphia, now some twenty years ago. I can also tell you that while he lived, Catherine Knowles gave up her right to his support, in exchange for complete control of the fortune left by her father—including the island. That, perhaps, was not in her best interests. I found she had little understanding of business, and refused to invest wisely. But under the new arrangement, she retained a right to a widow's portion, a third of her husband's estate. At his recent death this became hers, as well."

"She will hardly need it now," said Longfellow. "But then there's Magdalene to consider. Yet I don't imagine she can inherit, if she's not of sound mind. Still, if her brother did so? . . ."

"Because he was a male, the best light was put on Peter's doubtful condition by the immediate family, so that they might not lose the fortune to another part of the line. With Magdalene, there was no reason to ignore the obvious. Catherine made a small provision for her future and instructed me to set it aside, which I've done. For years, she refused to bequeath the rest to anyone."

"Was that wise?" asked Longfellow.

"Hardly. She was a woman who rarely listened to good advice! Then, a little more than a year ago, a will was made in favor of a sole individual . . ."

"Whose name you won't give us just yet," Longfellow finished for him.

"This I can tell you—seven weeks ago I received another packet from Catherine Knowles. It contained a *new* will. Like the last, it was barely legible—but that came as no surprise, for I knew she could hardly see. Her signature, too, had greatly deteriorated, but it is one I've grown used to. And it was signed by a witness: Alexander Godwin. I decided that if Catherine signed it again in my presence, I would be more comfortable. However, after discussing it with a colleague, I believed it would stand."

"Seven weeks ago?" Longfellow interrupted.

"We have all been busy in Boston lately, with many insisting their business be concluded before the revenue stamps arrived."

"Of course," said Longfellow. "But will you tell us who the final will names as her heir?"

"Soon . . . very soon," the lawyer replied. His smile did not seem altogether happy. "There are things I must learn first. The interests of others are bound to be involved."

"Perhaps we can help. You realize this situation could have a bearing on a murder," Longfellow added, watching the lawyer's face carefully.

"Soon," Reed repeated gently. "It's all that I'll promise, at the moment."

"But the second will," said Diana. "Do you suspect Catherine Knowles might *not* have sent it to you?"

"I think that she did, Mrs. Montagu; but I would like to question Magdalene on this point, as well. When she is ready."

Longfellow rose and walked to the tall window that faced west, toward the village. Tonight no light was visible, but by the reflected glow from the house he could see snow eddying as it came over the rooftop, and around the corners. To the east, he imagined, it would be even worse.

"This is all very interesting," he said finally, "but I suspect we'll get no further tonight. And there is no improvement in the weather," he added to John Dudley. The constable leaped to his feet.

"I must be going. I may have to stay in the village after all."

"As I've offered Mr. Reed a bed here, you might take his, John, at Reverend Rowe's."

"Or I might make my way to the Blue Boar. That would save the preacher trouble."

"And make Phineas Wise glad, I'm sure," Longfellow returned. "I'll see you out."

Moses Reed stayed with Diana, although he respected her silence with his own. When his host returned, the attorney left sister and brother to sit together, saying he would speak with Lem in the kitchen and give him the latest news.

"Someone will pay for Godwin's murder, I suppose?" Diana then asked, her voice weary.

"If we can find him," said Longfellow. He, too, found the thought an unpleasant one.

"Richard, I hoped earlier that I could be of some help to you, in seeking some sort of justice. But after all that I've seen today, it seems to me I've had too much of death lately. All that I truly wish—"

"I know, Diana. I know. It's anything but easy. Yet whatever happens next, we'll face it together. Until something better comes along."

"I hope it won't be long. If only Edmund—"

She suddenly seemed to fade, as she'd often done in the last week. He was about to say more to distract her, when his eyes shifted.

Had something moved, out in the snow?

There, through the dark window, he saw the ghost of someone coming along, making a path through the new drifts. Who could have come out of his barn on a night like this?

"Diana," Longfellow said with a twisting smile, "I think we're in for another surprise."

"Oh, what now?" she asked, trying to restrain her tears.

She might soon shed a bucketful if she wished, her brother told himself. "I'll be back in a moment," he added aloud, leaving her.

Diana sank back into her chair once more, and drew a handkerchief from her bodice. Down the corridor, she heard the front door open. From the entry hall came a muttering of voices and her brother's ringing laughter, which jarred her. Neither did whoever had entered share his mirth—but that did not stop it. Another peal broke out, and then she heard Richard's heels clicking as he came toward the study. Behind him, someone shuffled feet that were far heavier.

Longfellow entered and stood to one side.

"You have a visitor, madam," he said, extending a hand. What she saw next frightened her, for it was more a bundle than a man, covered by a cracking layer of snow. He flung his cloak open, and threw off his hat.

"Edmund!" she cried, running into her husband's quivering arms.

"My love," he said with something that sounded like a sob, though Longfellow assumed the captain's voice had merely been muffled by his wife's neck, onto which his lips had fallen.

"Now it is my turn to go," said Richard Longfellow, relieved to do so. Quietly, he shut the door on their renewed happiness, and went to see how affairs progressed in the kitchen.

Chapter 21

THE FIRE IN the farmhouse kitchen had fallen to a comfortable glow, as occasional tongues of flame rose above the red remains of logs. Together for several hours, the two women at the hearth enjoyed a companionable silence.

Earlier, they had spoken while Charlotte prepared a supper of eggs and cod, to be followed by a pudding of apples and currants. Magdalene Knowles had walked along the walls, softly touching the china teapot on the sideboard, a polished silver tray, the glazed crock containing dried beans. At last she'd seated herself to stare at the long hunting gun that hung above the fire. Occasionally, she reached a hand to Orpheus, who kept one eye open.

Now Charlotte sat as well. She recalled Diana's warning, then Magdalene's responses to her own brief questions. These had been answered with the directness of a child. Seeking to establish the extent of the woman's understanding, she'd learned that her guest was anything but stupid, whenever her attention could be captured and held. However, it soon seemed to return to a place within her—something Charlotte supposed was not surprising, when one considered Magdalene's life had been more solitary than if she'd lived within a convent's walls.

"Do you have a favorite kind of work?" she asked, after speaking of her own delight in her plantings.

"I ply my needle, to keep our clothes. We have no garden."

Of course, thought Charlotte, for where would they have put one? Magdalene had said, though, that she enjoyed walking about the island, so she must have watched many things grow. Did she also know the place had an odd reputation? Surely, she must have seen the boars. Had she no fear of them? Later, perhaps, she might ask.

"Would you like to help me in my garden one day?" she tried. Magdalene seemed unable to imagine such a thing. It would be a pleasure, in a few months' time, to show her Longfellow's roses.

Charlotte next decided that she must inquire, after all, about that morning.

Magdalene showed no reluctance. She described Lem as he'd appeared at the front door. She had taken him to Catherine, as she'd recently taken Charlotte in. He told them Alexander was dead. Catherine then put him to work. Magdalene went out for a walk as she did each day. She knew nothing more of what went on in the house until she approached it again, and heard Lem calling her. By then he had wrapped Catherine in blankets, and told her to gather a few things of her own, which might serve as the old lady's pillow. He told her they would walk over the ice to the village. It was something she'd often longed to do, but could not.

When asked why that was, her guest became evasive for the first time. Was it, Charlotte asked, because Mrs.

Knowles would not allow it? Magdalene nodded, and added something more.

"How could I go? I had to wait for him." This she would not clarify. Charlotte decided to ask nothing else until she could make more sense of what she already knew.

Only Lem and Magdalene had been on the island when Catherine fell into the fire. If it had been no more than that, there would be nothing else to do about it. But the woman had accused someone of pushing her. Such an action would have amounted to murder. Who could have wished her dead?

Catherine surely possessed a heightened sense of her own importance in the world; no doubt she'd also formed strong opinions about a number of things. Her outward manner had not been pleasant—yet her description of her marriage gave some indication of why she had become embittered. Perhaps it had done more than that? Had Catherine been entirely sane before she died? Since she'd lived with no restraints, and with only one companion of limited abilities, it would hardly have been noticed, had her mind become unbalanced.

The same, she supposed, could be said of Magdalene.

Still, Catherine could have stumbled, causing her own death. Dying, though, she had spoken as if she were *sure*. Had she been pushed after all? Who could have done it? Not Lem, of course—and no one would imagine he'd had a motive. Even if Old Cat had baited him, as she'd enjoyed teasing Alexander Godwin. Even if Lem had taken offense and lost his temper, and then—?

Could Magdalene have been capable of such a thing? It was true she'd had a long and difficult servitude. Might she have been overcome, in the end, by an urge to give one savage thrust? Had she the ability to plan? What if she'd somehow come back into the house quietly, meaning to blame someone else for the old woman's death once she'd accomplished it herself? Could Magdalene be clever? No—a woman able to plan would have left Boar Island long before this! Today, she'd not found it difficult to walk to the village.

You, madam, you . . . find out if the boy was . . . if . . . the boy . . .

Alex Godwin was dead. What other boy was there but Lem? Catherine had not been off the island for years. Who else, Charlotte wondered, might have gone there lately, and especially this morning?

Once again she considered the spoon, and the canvas bag taken up by Constable Dudley, after Lem had put it down by the fire. Might Dudley have carried it off for a reason? As soon as he returned home, the spoons were discovered in their usual place in Rachel Dudley's locked cupboard. If, as Charlotte already suspected, Dudley had first taken the spoons himself, and then lost the one she'd found, he must have decided the best thing to do would be to retrieve the rest. Had someone near the bonfire slipped them into the bag, then, with a nod to alert him?

But it wasn't only the spoons—a good deal of silver, and some pewter too, had gone missing in the last several weeks, in Bracebridge and beyond. What had become of it all? Had it been taken to Boston? If so, why had she found a piece of it on Boar Island?

Lem had told her he'd once been to the island, but he'd discouraged her from returning—as had Ned and Jonah. Hadn't he withheld something else from her lately? For one thing, there was the fact that he was fond of visiting the Bigelows.

Lem had also said there was a house in a hidden part of the island. Hannah had mentioned fires in the night, and phantom torches bobbing along the shoreline. Recently, these occurrences seemed to have increased.

What else might happen to a set of spoons, once they were sold? A caudle bowl, part of a silver tea set, a box full of shillings? Melt them down, add some pewter from an old porringer, a dented mug or two, and what would you have then? Something less than silver. And yet, perhaps something more?

Was *this* what some men in Bracebridge had been doing lately, keeping it to themselves? Hadn't their wives seen something unusual going on, without being able to put a finger on it? Could Longfellow know? Was that why he'd been avoiding her? And what if Lem and Ned, too—? Did they sometimes meet on Boar Island, a place Alex Godwin visited regularly? She'd supposed he only went up the path to the stone house, and back down again. But what if Alex had begun to suspect something else was happening on another part of the island? Might he have told Catherine Knowles of his suspicions? Or had someone decided to prevent him from doing so?

Her head reeling, Charlotte looked to Magdalene. She had taken daily walks about the place. Might she have known what went on? She must have! But had she the sense to realize it was not only unusual, but against the law? It seemed she'd told Catherine Knowles nothing about it. Did she enjoy keeping secrets?

Magdalene raised her eyes from the fire, sensing something new in the air. And Charlotte began to pose a new series of questions.

"Magdalene, do you recall seeing men on your island?"

"Once, many came. They sang . . . danced . . . fought. They came to kill the boars. Then they went away."

"But recently?"

"There was one . . ."

"Within the past year?"

"One who came for me. He promised to return."

For years, according to Catherine Knowles, Magdalene had waited patiently at the cliff's edge for a lover. Had there been such a man, long ago?

"Magdalene, what was his name?"

"She won't allow it! I can never speak of him. When he looked at me, when he touched me, then, how his eyes would dance! But I know . . . I'll see him no more. His eyes—his eyes are now my son's."

"You have a son!"

Magdalene turned, her own eyes wide. "*He* has come back to me," she insisted. "But please, you mustn't say. She would send him away."

"Magdalene, you do know . . . that Catherine Knowles is dead?"

"But now that I am here, how will he know where to find me?"

Magdalene sank back. She shook her head slowly, as if she felt the return of a familiar, coursing pain.

Charlotte became aware of a drop in the wind's savage roar. Now it almost sobbed along the eaves. Enticingly, it began to whisper . . .

Some time later, she looked up to see Magdalene watching the flicker of the fire, her eyes staring, her hands folded in her lap. Loss, thought Charlotte, was something about which she herself knew a great deal. And yet, her own had been nothing like this.

Nothing at all.

Chapter 22

To the relief of all but the youngest in the village, by the next morning the storm had blown itself out, leaving behind only a west wind to cut through the sharp sunlight. Drifts of snow had made a sort of white washboard across much of the village, including its lanes and the two main roads.

As the villagers emerged from their burdened houses, they found a world fresh and clean, through which teams of oxen pulled heavy sledges to compact the snow. Everyone, it seemed, was eager to be out, wishing to trade stories, and suspicions that had been born in the night. To this end not a few bundled themselves up and headed for the Blue Boar across the village bridge. Others took a different direction, stomping uphill and then through the welcoming door of the Bracebridge Inn, proceeding to the taproom to find an audience that was more civilized than the one found in the rival tavern.

Still others, mostly women and girls, made their way to nearby houses where they found chattering companions;

together, they then ventured further afield, frequently stopping at the shop of Emily Bowers.

A lone woman and her dog had the best view of the dazzling new blanket that lay over the broad marshes and the town, below a wind-whipped sky. All of this she admired, as her skirts plowed a path from her farmhouse down to the lower abode of Richard Longfellow.

Though covered from head to toe, Charlotte shied at a gust that raised crystals of ice in a fierce flurry, then spawned smaller devils that skittered off across the buried herb beds. While the air was exhilarating, she began to wish she'd taken the road after all, as she encountered a drift that came up to her waist. She might have led one of the cows out of the barn after milking, and walked behind with a switch—but that had seemed less than kind. She smiled, too, at the thought of reaching Richard Longfellow's door with an unexpected guest, its bell clanging to warn of their arrival.

Even Orpheus, who'd started by frolicking at her side, had now decided to follow her, easing his steps and avoiding the biting wind. Somehow she hadn't felt comfortable with the thought of leaving him with Magdalene, though she doubted her guest would rise before her return. More than once, she'd awakened in the long night to hear the other woman pacing the floorboards above. Magdalene might well need extra sleep, after the frightful day she'd endured.

Reaching Longfellow's back door, Charlotte opened it to step into a cool kitchen. No one was there. She wondered if she could be too early for the household. But the fire had been stirred. She removed her outer wrappings, and left them at the hearth. Then she walked through the hall to Longfellow's study.

This, too, was empty, and as yet had no fire. She

supposed he could have decided to take his coffee in the sunny front parlor. As she walked on to the front hall, she heard low voices, and her nose informed her that coffee was nearby.

"Good morning," she said boldly at the parlor door, intending to make her presence known before she overheard what seemed to be a close conversation. She saw two men holding china cups, leaning forward in their chairs so that their heads nearly touched. They turned at the sound of her voice. One rose quickly—the other took his time.

"Edmund?" she asked in amazement. "How is it that you're here?"

"Good morning, Mrs. Willett! You didn't know I'd been summoned?"

The captain came and took her hand and kissed it gently. She went further, inviting him briefly into her arms.

"He sent for you?" she then asked, while her neighbor watched with an expression she could not quite understand.

"Richard? Yes. I presumed you knew that. Have you two had a falling out?" Their silence caused Edmund to nod slowly. "Possibly an oversight."

"It was intentional, Carlotta, I'm sorry to say," Longfellow offered.

"There's no need to tell me anything you wish to keep secret," she said. But her look assured him she was not entirely easy.

"I have *never* wished—" he began. Recalling his own injured feelings, he reconsidered. "Perhaps I did. But only after . . . well, the truth is I sent Edmund a message on Tuesday. It had to do with something odd I found by the ice—a piece of silver."

He watched a flush of crimson mounting Charlotte's cheeks, as if he'd touched on something to embarrass her. What that might have been, he could not imagine. Perhaps, he thought, she would tell him later.

"I wasn't sure," he continued. "And I thought you might already know about it, at any rate."

"Know about *what*?" she demanded. "I've begun to feel I know very little lately—and, that there's a good deal you've not told *me*. I have been forming my own ideas. But how," she added as a new thought rushed into her head, "could you have known on Tuesday of either of the—of either death?"

"I didn't." Her neighbor paused, considering her precise choice of words. Then he plunged on. "I presume you can keep a secret, Carlotta. Will you keep the one I'm about to tell you?"

"Of course, if you ask me to."

"All right, then. First, let's all sit down. Would you like some coffee? Here—take mine. By the way, did you see anyone in the kitchen when you came in?"

"No. Where are the others?" she asked, entering the covert spirit of the discussion she'd interrupted.

"Diana is still in bed," said Edmund Montagu. "Reed, as well." He brought a third chair, and sat beside her.

"Cicero," said Longfellow, "is out in the glass house, stoking the stove. Lem should still be shoveling out front." He looked through the window, and was satisfied to see the young man at his task. While the wind took some of each raised shovelful of snow, the rest was tossed to one side of a lengthening passage.

"I've had several aggravating moments recently," Longfellow admitted as he came to sit with the others. "But the thing that united my growing suspicions was this." From his waistcoat, he produced a shilling. He gave it to Charlotte.

She took the coin and examined it briefly. Then, looking straight into her neighbor's eyes, she held them.

"Is it counterfeit?"

"A lightning conclusion, Carlotta. Unless you know something else that led you in that direction. Something you have yet to tell me?"

Instead of answering, she turned to the captain with a question of her own.

"Edmund, is *this* why you've come? And not for Diana's sake? Are you, too, interested in this silver?"

"Yes and no," he answered truthfully. "I will admit I was glad to have another reason to visit. My wife, you see, bolted from our home, leaving only the briefest message for me to find. From what little it said, and its vehemence, I had to assume she had no wish for me to follow."

"Oh—I'm sorry."

"After we had watched one another suffer for several weeks, I truly believed that a separation might help both of us to mend. It was necessary to let some things settle, I supposed, before we could hope to begin again, on better footing."

"I should have told you earlier how—how affected Richard and I both were, to hear of your loss," Charlotte told him earnestly.

"You both must know . . ." The captain looked now to Longfellow. "We all fear losing what we love one day. It's a hard thing, but loss must be felt by all whose lives are not very lonely. Or very brief, as my son's was. I hope Diana learns to accept this."

"Perhaps she already has, to some extent," said Longfellow. "But you'll not mention to my sister that I called Edmund for quite another reason, Carlotta?"

"I suspect you only found a roundabout way to be helpful. You could have waited a while, after all, before calling for assistance. I wonder what will happen now that you have," she finished, a new concern in her voice.

"What will happen, do you mean, to our good villagers? That remains to be seen. But if you, too, have felt as if you were kept in the dark, then just how did you learn of this criminal scheme?"

Charlotte started at the beginning, telling them—though she was thoroughly sick of doing so—of her recent visit to Boar Island. She saw the two men grasp the arms of their chairs while she briefly mentioned falling through the ice. They remained speechless as she went on to describe her visit with Mrs. Knowles, and her observations of Magdalene's circumstances.

The discovery of the silver spoon beneath the landing seemed the culmination of her story. But she assured them a little breathlessly that this was not all. She'd learned that it belonged to Rachel Dudley, who'd lost several others—though every one had now, mysteriously, come back to her. She'd also been told that women from Bracebridge to Concord had found silver or pewter objects missing within the last few months. Each, however, had been discouraged by her husband from accusing anyone of a crime.

"Small wonder!" Longfellow finally exclaimed. "For I don't doubt their husbands were responsible! Never was much 'lost' or taken, I presume—and what was gone would soon have come back to the household in newly struck shillings, each remarkably close to the real thing. This one I suppose, like many others, is mixed with pewter—tin, a little copper, more lead—debased enough in value to earn each of those who participate in the scheme some small profit."

"But how did *you* know?" she asked, examining the shilling she held between her fingers more closely. "It seems to me no different from any other."

Holding the coin so that it caught the strong sunlight, she saw the familiar profile of the late king, large pouches under the eye and chin, a laurel wreath resting atop long curls. She read around the curved edge, "GEORGIVS II DEI GRATIA."

"This may help," said Longfellow, offering her a pocket lens he'd taken from a table; she presumed he and the captain had already scrutinized the coin together. She re-examined the front of the object, then looked at its back. Coming out to the edges were the usual four emblems, surmounted by crowns, and a date—1758. Between these ran a series of letters: M-B-F-ET-H-REX-F-D-B-ET-L-D-S-R-I-A-T-ET-E.

"Do you suspect anything yet?" asked Longfellow.

"No. But I've wondered for years," she admitted, "exactly what these mean."

"The letters? Ask Edmund to reel it off for you. He's been at court far more than I."

"The letters," said Captain Montagu, "stand in place of Latin words. The translation is, 'King of Britain, France, and Ireland, defender of the Faith, Duke of Brunswick and Luneburg, Arch-Treasurer and Elector of the Holy Roman Empire.' Their four emblems make a cross, you see, with a sunburst at the center."

"A remarkably close match to the genuine article," said Longfellow. "And one showing an excellent hand. But to the carefully observant eye, the whole is not entirely successful. You'll note that this coin does seem to have been milled, for there are diagonal cuts all around the edges. In the course of wear and handling, such indentations naturally become tarnished, and fill with minute amounts of oil and other debris. The edges above them, like the faces, are more exposed to abrasion, and so they should be shinier than what lies below. However, you'll see that on this coin, which must have been intentionally soiled, the inner marks are still bright in many places. This indicates that they've been newly minted—yet the date is several years old, and for good reason. The year of 1758 was the last in which a large run of shillings was made."

"Then how—?"

"I believe this shilling was created in a mold with at least one set of faces. And I suppose the 'mill marks' were added by hand. Look closely and you'll see they're somewhat irregular. There, I think, is where the nub, which once attached the piece to a pouring chamber, has been filed off."

"But how did you come to look for these things?"

"As soon as I picked this up from the snow, early on the day of the ice harvest, I thought it strange no one nearby would claim it, though one of them must have dropped it from a pocket."

"Who was there?"

"Flint and Tinder, Jonah Bigelow, and young Ned."

"I see." Charlotte felt her heart beat faster. "But Edmund, this hasn't come to your attention, I hope, in Boston?"

"Once," the captain told her. "I've not yet learned enough to tell Hutchinson; as you know, he sees himself as quite an expert on the currency question. But several found their way into a bagful about to be melted down by one of the town silversmiths. Seeing that the weight was not right for the number of coins on his scale, he looked more carefully, and then let us know what he suspected. Some coins were heavier than they should have been, no doubt because your coiner's pewter had a great deal of lead in it. I understand much is re-melted in the colonies, and eventually becomes so. Not surprising, since there are no guilds here to assure the quality of metals."

"Many of us do exchange spoon molds," Charlotte admitted. "I, too, have been taught to re-cast damaged items . . ."

"I'm willing to wager," said Longfellow, off again on his own path, "that each man who is a part of this scheme has agreed to spend no more than one or two at a time. Given that, who knows how long it may have gone undetected?"

"What puzzles me," said the captain, "is why they've chosen *shillings* to copy. The profit must be next to nothing. Far more sensible to forge large notes, or to work with gold, as most moneymakers do."

"Yes, but gold is relatively rare here, especially in ordinary households. Silver is more common—yet we see less and less of it. And now that your Currency Act has forbidden the further issuance of paper money in the colonies—"

"Because of the criminal inflation you've caused! We hear complaints daily, though you're not the only ones to suffer. On the frontier even wampum has been cheapened, for now a New Jersey enterprise has found it can bore stringing holes with steel drills. *Silver*, Richard, is a far better system than shells, or paper. One day you may find yourselves pleased that we've insisted you stick to it."

"But how can we, when most that comes from England is hoarded, or goes back to pay for goods your merchants are so happy to send us? Yet you insist we find it somewhere, to pay our taxes!"

Charlotte sighed, for she had heard all of this before. It was part of a larger argument beloved by the village, one concerned with the new stamps, colonial representation in Parliament (or the lack of it, actually), the increasing power of King George, and the strained tempers of lesser men a great deal closer than he. She wondered how often Diana had been plagued by much the same thing in Boston, though perhaps from the opposite side.

"The scheme we've uncovered here, Edmund," his brother-in-law countered, "could be one of a hundred operating quietly. Don't forget that among desperate men, a little extra may count for much."

"Desperate?" the captain responded with a bitter laugh. "I don't doubt most involved in this scheme are chuckling up their sleeves like intolerable children! But Richard, have your own finances been greatly affected by this latest downturn?" he asked with new concern.

"I won't throw myself on your charity just yet. My sister should be left something, in the event. . . ."

"In what have you placed your faith?"

"I wondered, Edmund, when you would finally ask. I am well invested in the London funds, a Dutch cloth firm in the lowlands, some small weaving concerns in Scotland, and the Dutch West India Company. All far better, I think, than my father's trust in the Triangle Trade, which still leaves much misery behind."

"Then you, too, have the interests of London's merchants at heart."

"In mind, let us say. At heart, my sympathies are with those who would tweak Parliamentary probosces—as well as the noses of certain provincial officials. In this, I'm hardly alone."

"A good many in these colonies might pay for such a privilege, if it were offered."

"A new source of revenue, Edmund, in place of the stamps? But this spoon." Longfellow turned suddenly back to Charlotte. "You say you found it on the island. Was it dropped by Alex Godwin? If *he* was involved in this affair as well—and I've heard he meant to bring me some sort of information on the day of his death—do you imagine his plan was to expose this moneymaking ring?"

"That, I can't say."

"Lem said nothing more to you of what their argument was about?"

"I haven't had a chance to speak to him since Alex Godwin was found."

"But you suspect something there, I think."

"That would be hard to say."

"Yet you're sure he said nothing about the scheme earlier."

"No one did! In fact, I supposed *you* knew, but wouldn't tell *me*."

"While I suspected the same." They continued to examine one another silently, until Captain Montagu began anew.

"What I wish to know, Mrs. Willett, is this. Do you suspect anyone else of having ties to this business? You've known these people far longer than your neighbor, after all."

"I—" She stopped, unwilling to speculate further. Could she accuse John Dudley of anything with certainty? Or with safety? Lem and Ned might have discussed any number of other things while chatting beside a fire. And while it was true Jonah Bigelow knew something about metals, surely *that* was not enough to prove he'd been involved in any business as serious as counterfeiting?

"There's little I know for certain, Edmund," she replied. "But I do suspect these shillings came from Boar Island.

And I'm not entirely sure our constable should be in charge of looking into the matter."

"I wonder if he isn't the ringleader," said Longfellow. "He lives there on the north road, not far from the island. I think we should look into who may have been 'assisting' the law, too, in the last several months."

"John Dudley," said Moses Reed, whom they turned to see standing just inside the room, "is someone whose word I'd prefer not to count on, even under oath. I agree that you'd be doing the village a service by helping him to accomplish his job."

"Which reminds me," said Longfellow, "there is another interesting thing that Mr. Reed told us last night, which neither of you has yet had a chance to consider."

"Before you begin," the attorney broke in, "may I ask, Mrs. Willett, how Magdalene Knowles does this morning?"

Charlotte then recalled that Reed, too, had heard the terrible accusation made by Catherine Knowles, of which Richard and Edmund might yet be unaware.

"Did she come with you this morning?" he asked further.

"No—I left her sleeping."

"Alone?" asked Reed, his expression an uneasy one.

"Perhaps I should go back," she replied, beginning to doubt the wisdom of her earlier decision.

"Is there an objection to my going to her myself? We might speak quietly there, and then I'll bring the lady back to this house for the rest of the morning. After her rest she may enjoy some companionship."

"A fine idea," said Longfellow. "We'll soon have breakfast. Please tell her she would be most welcome."

"That I'll gladly do," said Reed, bowing as he moved backwards through the door.

"But now, Carlotta, for the rest," said Longfellow, his hazel eyes more intent than ever. "This time, I think you'll find what I have to tell you quite unexpected."

Whether that would be a good thing or not Charlotte tried to imagine, as Richard Longfellow began.

Chapter 23

"LAST NIGHT," SAID Longfellow, "while you were with Magdalene Knowles, and Edmund was finding his way to us through the snow, Reed told us something about a will. He is, or was, Catherine Knowles's attorney."

"Ah!" said Charlotte, while Captain Montagu maintained a watchful silence.

"Catherine made her first will, it seems, little more than a year ago. Recently, however, she sent him another."

"Then—who is her heir?"

"Reed won't yet tell us. But I've heard Alex Godwin claimed he would receive more than wages, one day, for his care of the two women."

"Yes, I've heard that myself. But then, you don't suppose whoever killed him could have been angry simply because he might have come into a fortune?"

"Men being the covetous creatures that they are, it's possible. But I'm curious to learn the name of the *previous* heir, if we assume Godwin was the latter."

"When will we know that?"

"Soon, is all Reed will say. It seems he has some dainty concern for legal proprieties."

"Then while we wait, you may be interested in something else that I've discovered."

"What is that, Carlotta?"

"Two things, really. Mr. Reed told you no more last night of Catherine's death? Of her last words?"

"No. What were they?"

"She claimed she had no accident, but that she was *pushed* into the fire. She also instructed me to investigate something. Her exact phrase was, 'Find out if the boy was—'"

"Pushed! Good God! A horrible thought! But . . . find out if the boy was *what*? And *what* boy?"

"I'm not sure. Later, Magdalene also told me she once had a lover. He wasn't allowed to stay with her on the island, but a seed was planted. And she bore a son."

"So that was why she watched, as you told us, from her perch?"

"I think so."

"And yet no son lived with them all these years?"

"No."

"A romantic story," said Edmund. "Did this boy die?"

"No, I think she believes she's seen him."

"Recently?" asked Longfellow.

"I can't say, but it's what I suppose."

"On an island she never leaves," he said quietly. "That supports my earlier idea. Godwin *must* be the one in the will."

"I wonder," Charlotte replied. "Why did she make two wills in such a little time?"

"The elderly often retain strong convictions, while they

sometimes lose the ability to judge rationally. Reed will probably have his own ideas. One thing, though, seems certain. He will want to visit the island soon, to look through the rest of his client's papers. We might go along, I think, to help Magdalene claim her possessions."

"Is it possible that she was the beneficiary in the last will?" asked Charlotte.

"Reed assured us she has no more than a small trust, which he'll continue to manage for her."

"That's what I thought. Catherine said she'd been passed over before."

"I'm not sure," said Montagu, "how this business of heirs will turn out, or if the old woman was pushed or not. But let us suppose whoever did murder Godwin decides to fly. Should that happen, Richard, we may never get our hands on him."

"Perhaps we should ask no more about Alex for the moment. Nor shall we tell the village just yet what Mrs. Knowles imagined. That doesn't stop us from pursuing the other matter. This moneymaking ring includes too many, I think, for it to remain hidden much longer. We may make some progress there with a few discreet inquiries and a little pressure. Before long, we'll learn who's at its head."

"And yet . . ." Charlotte began.

"Yes, Carlotta?"

"Think of the position of anyone who agrees to tell what's been done, whether he was a part of it or not. Wouldn't many call him less than honorable? Especially if an oath has been sworn?"

"Lem, for instance?"

Her expression told him he'd guessed the source of her anxiety. Longfellow nodded slowly, for he supposed that she was right. He had no wish to shame the boy, even in the eyes of less scrupulous neighbors. "But just who *are* we to ask, then?"

"I think I may have a way . . ."

Sounds at the back of the house caught their attention. The captain then made his way up the stairs to see his wife, for he'd heard movement above as well. Orpheus led Longfellow and Charlotte to the kitchen, where they found Moses Reed helping Magdalene out of the woolen wrappings wound around her feet. The woman gazed at her new surroundings with more interest than she'd shown the night before, when she'd come into a darker kitchen.

"You're very welcome here, Miss Knowles," Longfellow told her, smiling calmly. "I hope you'll feel as you do at home." This sounded highly inappropriate, and so he tried again. "Whatever you need, you have only to ask for. We're glad to have you with us for as long as you wish to stay."

Magdalene nodded. Moses Reed led her to a seat by the fire, where she began to warm herself.

"Have you spoken with Miss Knowles about the rest?" Longfellow asked the lawyer quietly, once he'd walked him a little distance from the hearth.

"She seemed not quite ready."

"Reed, do you know she gave birth to a son?"

"Yes, I know of the birth. It was accomplished without the benefit of a ceremony. Or even a midwife, I believe."

"Was it, by God?" Longfellow's eyes went to the lost woman by the hearth. "Do you know what became of the boy?"

"Quite soon, you will hear reasons for what Mrs.

Knowles insisted on doing, when he was only a few months old. In this, I must admit, I assisted her."

"When?" Longfellow demanded. "*When* may we know the rest?"

"Later today, I promise you. It can hardly matter if we wait a little longer. This afternoon I will explain it all. But I must prepare the way, and do the thing properly. For too long this unfortunate woman has been abused! Let us not be guilty of the same thing."

Longfellow said no more. Instead, he turned to practical matters.

"We'll scrape together a breakfast. A ham hangs in my cellar, and there are eggs. We have cheese, preserves, plenty of flour, and cornmeal. What do you say to a hasty pudding with cream and maple sugar, Mrs. Willett? Or do you suggest biscuits?"

Since the oven had not been used for some time, pot pudding was chosen. Cicero and Lem returned to the house, and there were plenty of hands to help in the heating of various dishes at the fire. Those not involved in the cooking arranged tea tables in the front parlor. When Diana descended, eight sat down to breakfast.

After all had been satisfied, they made their plans for the rest of the day. Longfellow invited Captain Montagu to accompany him on a visit to Nathan Browne, the blacksmith, whose forge stood behind the Bracebridge Inn. He also announced his intention of visiting the Blue Boar tavern alone, some time later.

Softened by Lem's pleading, the selectman decided to allow a visit to the Sloan household, as long as it was made in the company of Mrs. Willett. This condition she accepted, since it would give her a chance to see how Hannah progressed. Both promised to return well before dinner. However, Charlotte made it clear that first she would go and speak with Nathan, as well.

Diana and Magdalene would stay indoors, as neither had any need to go out. Together, they would be able to help Cicero with the dinner.

Cicero agreed, realizing their assistance would be minimal once they'd found something to talk about, and that they would then be little bother, after all.

Chapter 24

SINCE NEW PATHS through the snow had by now been made in much of the village, Longfellow and Captain Montagu had no difficulty escorting Mrs. Willett to the circular drive before the Bracebridge Inn, and on to the smithy beyond the carriage house.

Smoke signified that Nathan Browne was hard at work. Little wonder, thought Charlotte, for this was his busiest season. She often visited the place, but avoided his shop when most farmers brought in their tools and plows to be mended and sharpened for spring. Frequently they stayed far longer than they needed to, conversing and enjoying the warmth.

Today Nathan had only one customer, who wished to pay for the sharpening of a pair of shovels and a pick he'd brought in a few days before. He left them behind, however, for he'd come with neither horse nor wagon. In something of a rush, he lifted his hat and hurried out, as soon as the new party came through the door.

"A very good day," the blacksmith said, adding coins

to those in a pocket that already bulged and jingled. "The snow seems to have made men feel generous."

"Why do you suppose that is, Nathan?" asked Longfellow.

The muscular smith pulled a heavy hood over the fire to slow it. He approached his visitors with a questioning look of his own.

"I don't know," he answered. "But I wonder if you have an idea, sir?"

"How much have you taken in recently?"

"Of that I'm not sure—but far more than usual. I'm often paid after harvest, for as you know, farmers are always behind. And yet, since yesterday morning, several have come to pay their debts, and a few have even advanced a little cash for future services! Silver has been pouring into my pockets." He gave the coins another jingle and laughed out loud.

"Most of it in shillings?"

"Why yes, as a matter of fact."

"I wouldn't be surprised if you weren't the only one having luck today."

"Oh? Why is that?"

"I doubt," Charlotte said, "that Nathan *would* know, Richard. After all, he's the first person you'd be expected to ask. Isn't he too obvious?"

"Asked about what?" The smith rolled down his sleeves, for the atmosphere had cooled.

"We've only come to ask for your help, if you'll give it," Longfellow replied. "Something unlawful has been occupying the village, of which only a few are unaware. This makes it necessary for me to suspect even those I consider my friends, at least until I find some answers. Would you mind if I took a look at those shillings of yours?"

The smith reached into his pocket. He then set the

coins down on a nearby bench, and spread them with a quick movement of his strong fingers.

One by one, Longfellow picked out silver that far outweighed a few coppers, and took it to the window. Looking for information of another sort, Edmund Montagu walked around the shop, observing implements that hung along the walls.

"Mrs. Willett?" Nathan appealed. He pulled a keg forward and offered it as a seat. "This has nothing to do with the boy's death, I hope?" he asked suddenly.

"All eleven shillings are counterfeit," Longfellow announced, setting them on the sill.

"What?" Nathan cried. "What is that you say?"

"Several of our neighbors appear to be less scrupulous than we about the law," replied the selectman. The captain approached with his pocket lens and made his own examination.

"How do you know this?" Nathan asked warily. Edmund Montagu handed him the lens, so that the smith could take a better look himself.

"By the shine within the false mill marks," Longfellow said helpfully. "And, if you would care to bite down on one, you'll find it somewhat softer than you'd expect."

"I would have to agree," Nathan said eventually. "But you say you have no idea who to suspect?"

"That may not be entirely true—you're the first I've questioned. No suspicions of anything else unusual? None of your customers has dropped a hint?"

"Many men come in here, of course. But I work alone while they pass the time of day with one another. Since I came to this village no more than a few years ago, there are things they won't tell me—not yet. I've often been glad of it, for it frees me to think my own thoughts, and keep my own council."

"That is an advantage," Longfellow agreed, having long enjoyed the same benefit. "But you might tell us this: in your opinion, would such a moneymaking scheme be difficult to accomplish? What tools would be required, and what sort of talent?"

"As for the tools, plenty of farmers have small forges; they often make and mend things at home. And you're right about a need for talent. Ordinary coins, I believe, are pressed from sheets of silver. Here, someone seems to have poured them into a finely etched mold, most likely one of steel. I myself might have suggested one with room to make several coins at each pouring. I expect inferior metal—pewter, by the look of it—was added to the silver, once that was well melted. The marks along the edges, now, seem to be cut with some sort of small knife; but they're not quite alike from coin to coin, are they? So perhaps more than one man was involved in that tedious job."

"As we, too, suspect. Does anyone come to mind as a possible candidate for casting these things?"

"Well, now! To begin with, your friend Mr. Revere can tell you that even a master silversmith such as he may not be much of an etcher. That is something a man is born to—like being able to paint, or carry a tune. Even after working at it for years, a master may do no better at the task than a promising lad."

"You think, then, that a young man—?"

"Who knows? He would surely need to know how to handle a firebox and bellows. But with a little practice, silver isn't difficult to pour, for it melts with less heat than iron, which is hard to work. That's the reason most of us buy iron bars and rods of different sizes. Then, we need only heat them to the point where they can be hammered out."

"That's some help—"

"Beyond anything else," Nathan decided, "I think your man would need a delicate, steady hand to make his faces. And to etch several, he'd need to spend a great deal of time, probably for little reward. He would surely make more at honest labor, if he'd only apprentice himself. Unless, for some reason, he was unable to do so? He—or perhaps she?" he asked, looking to Charlotte.

That was a possibility, and one she'd overlooked.

"An interesting idea," said Longfellow. "Yet unlikely. The women of the village have been carefully kept from hearing of this endeavor—by their own husbands. Where do you think something like this could be carried out, Nathan?"

"Not in the village, I would agree. Or neighbors would see the frequent smoke, and then, wouldn't one of the women have gone to see? Nor along the main roads, I should think . . ."

"How about Boar Island?"

"Now there's an interesting thought. Somewhere Alex Godwin went quite often." The smith considered the idea. "Do you think he's been doing this?"

"No—though it could be someone he knew, and planned to expose. Mrs. Willett found a silver spoon near the island's landing a few days ago, something with no more business there than she. This spoon was stolen from John Dudley's wife, with several others like it."

"Trouble for someone! What does Dudley have to say?"

"I plan to ask that, the next time I see him. But you're sure you've heard no gossip? No suggestion of anything improper going on?"

"Sir, if you were to ask me to come and tell you of everything of that sort that's said in this place, I would

take up far too much of your valuable time. But about
these coins, no."

"Well, you have your business to attend to. But I
thank you for your thoughts, Nathan. And please—don't
make this common knowledge just yet."

"I promise you I'll keep my eyes open and my lips
shut," said the blacksmith.

"That would be appreciated. I think we'd better leave
you now, or you're likely to get no more visitors today."

"The shillings?" asked the smith uncomfortably, looking toward the window sill.

"Evidence, I suppose." Longfellow turned to the captain who'd thus far kept silent, though he'd listened
carefully to all that had been said.

"Hold onto them," Edmund said flatly, surprising them
all. "Some day, if you wish, you might sell them for the
silver. But don't spend them. Accept any others you're
given, and put the names of those who've had them into
your head."

"I won't guarantee I'll be able to keep them there,"
the smith replied.

"But such knowledge could be useful one day, if it
helps us to identify a murderer."

"That's hardly something one can overlook, like a
pocketful of queer coins, is it? . . ."

Nathan Browne watched them leave, then whistled
softly as he went back to uncover his waiting forge.

Chapter 25

WALKING ONLY A little further, they came to the kitchen door of the inn and entered noisily, clearing their boots of snow. Elizabeth turned from the wide hearth to exclaim at the intrusion. She then greeted the arrivals as neighbors and friends, while her daughter Rebecca made a curtsy.

"What may I do for you, sirs? A pie for your dinner? I have some fresh made, of beef and kidney—"

"Thank you, Elizabeth," said Longfellow, "but it's the landlord we've come to see today. I'm sorry to make a corridor of your kitchen—"

"Don't apologize, sir! It's good to see you all, though Captain, your return is a *special* pleasure. Is it not, Mrs. Willett?"

Charlotte reddened, but did not deny they both enjoyed the sight of this handsome officer in military coat and breeches, whose high black boots and gold buttons shone impressively in the firelight.

Once again, Longfellow pondered a curious fact.

Though the village had little respect for most members of the British military establishment (hardly surprising since they'd followed so many blockheads during the last war) it did seem to crave the approval of this one, a son of an English lord who had married, if not quite one of their own, at least something of a compatriot. As to his sister's ambiguous reputation in the village, Longfellow had little doubt.

"Possibly," he added, "you'll be able to feed the captain at the inn soon enough. My house has become a little crowded, of late."

"So I hear," said Elizabeth, giving the captain a new look, full of pity. "To have Mrs. Montagu come to us again, only to find all of this! First the lad, and now an old dame she tended herself, right up to the end! Shocking, that is. I do hope your brave wife is well this morning, Captain?"

"She is, madam. I will tell her you asked."

"Oh, she would not wish to know—! But I thank you, sir." The modest woman lowered her head to hide a blush, and kept it so until the others had gone on.

A visit to the taproom showed nothing unusual this quiet morning, except that the place did seem strangely brightened by the new snow, some piled up along the windowsills. Tim, the message boy, sat enjoying a day on which no one, as yet, had asked him to venture out. At a sign from Longfellow, he came to the table as the three sat down.

"Would you know where Mr. Pratt is this morning?"

Tim nodded, his eyes examining the party as he tried to decide what they had come for at this hour. Most in the room were travelers who had little interest in continuing until the roads improved, and instead nursed warming drinks after their large breakfasts.

"He's in his office, sir, working the figures for year's end. Good morning, Mrs. Willett. Glad to see you again, Captain."

"If he can be bothered, you might tell him we would like a word about another financial matter."

"A financial matter?" Tim repeated, still curious.

"Exactly."

"Yes, sir. Then I'll go and see." Wasting no more time, the boy left with his usual dispatch.

"Your welcome holds, it seems," Longfellow said to Edmund Montagu. "I wonder how long it will last."

"Oh, I'm sure they'll all despise me soon enough, as most in Boston do."

"Has it been difficult, Edmund?" asked Longfellow, a touch more sympathy in his manner.

"The patriots of Boston are always difficult, Richard. Yet I must say that I now begin to doubt the motives and methods of my own side, as well."

A young woman, newly arrived from Framingham in search, Longfellow suspected, of a husband, came to serve them.

As she approached her skirts swayed gently, and her expression was especially welcoming to the gentlemen. This Charlotte noted briefly, before her attention returned to Edmund's weary face.

"Punch," Longfellow said abruptly. The young woman retreated. "Recently I've been somewhat lax," he went on, "in following the news from town. Have things worsened so much?"

"That depends on what you mean. Since August, of course, nearly everyone who's taken a position has cried out against the stamps; Bernard is now governor in name only. I've heard he doubts he could command ten men in the town. I believe he's right."

"That would depend on what they were wanted for."

"Well, the militia can't be raised. The man they call 'Captain' McIntosh has been released from custody, yet everyone agrees it was he who led the mob that destroyed the lieutenant governor's home this summer—for which Hutchinson has yet to receive a penny! It seems some have decided that if McIntosh is tried, the Liberty Boys must tear down the custom house. At the moment, it contains some six thousand pounds of the King's sterling. *That*, I'm sure, would never be seen again."

"Perhaps not. But with Boston ordered closed to shipping for six weeks, it did seem only a matter of time before starvation might—"

"*Starvation!* It would have been many months before your gouty friends felt a pinch in anything but their waistcoats! Their wallets are another matter. Most cried famine when they saw docking fees for their sitting ships rise, though *all* they needed to do to clear them was agree to buy the blasted stamps! Don't forget, we in Britain have had to purchase the things ourselves, for a number of years."

"Yes, but the problem is, we *here* have not. For good reason—"

"And it is largely a means for financing the troops stationed on your western borders, where the French might still—"

"That is your affair now, since the King has ordered *we* may no longer settle west of the mountains."

"Legally, that is correct—but whom does it stop? Hordes continue to go there anyway, against all sense."

"Bracebridge is close enough to the frontier for my own taste, as well. But let us both be reasonable, Edmund. We hear Mr. Oliver, the Stamp Distributor, has resigned; the stamps are still out in Castle William, and in fact

Parliament has *yet* to send us copies of the Act officially—making this little more than a French farce!"

The serving maid arrived with a flounce and put down her tray, then set out glasses and a hot jug. Longfellow quickly gave her a coin, but no further reason to stay. Dropping the payment beneath her neck scarf, she smiled nonetheless.

"I can't argue with you there," said Montagu when she'd left them. "Frankly, I've come to believe both sides are equally ridiculous in the way they behave. Every official in Boston seems to fear upsetting his own boat—and so the governor sends the stamp question to his Council, which forwards it to the judges of the Superior Court, who decline to sit and defer to the House of Representatives. These gentlemen consult the townsmen, who speak with their lawyers, who wish the judges first to give advice before they risk their licenses. But the judges will not meet until they are scheduled to do so some time in March—and so it all starts over again! This has been thrown from one hand to another like a hot ingot, while the town hopes someone, *anyone*, will decide what is or is not legal, or at least what Parliament may accept. A loss of respect for all authority, I'm very sure, will be the consequence. I can tell you it's a thing I've begun to feel myself, with my own home put in jeopardy."

"Perhaps you take it too much to heart, Edmund," said Longfellow as he raised his glass. "After all, no one has yet been hanged—except in effigy. There is, after all, a comic side."

"Oh, yes. The strategy of the Attorney General of Massachusetts, your old friend Trowbridge, is particularly amusing."

"What has he done now?"

"For weeks he ducked the issue of how, or if, the courts

might legally do business, with stamps unavailable for their documents. Finally he had a friend pay a visit to Town House. There it was explained that due to rheumatism of the arm and shoulder—on the right side—the Attorney General had been forced to abandon all business, as he can no longer sign his own name!"

"And you don't think? . . ."

"Do you?"

"No," Longfellow said amiably. "I suppose I don't."

"But perhaps you're right. Friends inform me a growing number of Whigs at home speak out against this business of taxing the colonies, at least for general revenue."

"And since we all suppose the Whigs will regain power some day soon, it seems preferable to have friends among that party, rather than the thanks of an ungrateful king . . . whose health is questionable."

"The reality is, the port is again operating as usual. So your men have already won. The remainder of the courts will soon be opened, as well."

"Without the stamps."

"Without the stamps. I, for one, look for the repeal of the Act in the spring."

"Perhaps," said Charlotte, catching the men by surprise, "this might have some bearing on our own problem. Of the shillings, I mean."

"How so, Mrs. Willett?" asked Longfellow.

"If the governor and his men, and our own legislators and judges, have all avoided their duties, and overlooked the law . . . then can the men of Bracebridge be made to pay too dearly for doing much the same?"

"But here," Longfellow retorted with a new uneasiness, "surely, it is different. When a whole town participates in illegal activity such as this, and when they have acted against—against—"

"You?" asked Montagu. He smiled suddenly, pleased to see the shoe on another foot. "It does seem that you have been hoodwinked, Richard, by much of Bracebridge. Though perhaps Reverend Rowe is also in the dark. That may be of some comfort."

"Delightful company," Longfellow replied with a grimace.

"Oh, I think there are quite a few others," Charlotte reminded them. "Remember the ladies . . ."

"Well, yes," Longfellow admitted.

"The real question," said Montagu, "is this: what will happen if we throw a large portion of Bracebridge onto a legal system that barely functions? We can no more do this, than Bernard can afford to do what he really wishes to do as governor. He recently believed that the people of Boston were his worst enemy. Now, my sources assure me country men may be even more ready for violence, if the stamp issue is pressed further. Should things worsen, some say, they will refuse to accept Britain's sovereignty entirely!"

The rest had been considered with a sense of amusement on one side or the other; this was a sobering thought. Such a declaration might lead, after all, to a state of open warfare.

"The issues are heady ones," said Longfellow slowly. "And they're likely to cause passions to become overstrong. But when chaos becomes the acknowledged tool of politicians, and punishment becomes impossible, what do we call the thing we're left with, I wonder?"

Then, they saw Jonathan Pratt, who apparently had troubles of his own.

"Good morning, good morning . . . good morning," said the rotund man as he approached them. A hand went to his bulging waistcoat, as if he'd suffered a twinge of dyspepsia.

"Hello, Jonathan," Longfellow said airily. "How are you today?"

"Not well. The recent excitement has affected my digestion."

"To which excitement do you refer?"

"The idea that there may well be a murderer in our midst!"

"Of course. Yet rest assured we will get to the bottom of it. At the moment, there is a slight delay—but soon, soon we will begin to move forward. Perhaps by then we'll have sorted out another little matter."

"You and the captain . . . have found something else that concerns you?" the landlord asked hesitantly. "Something that goes on in Boston?"

"Partly in Boston, yes. But I believe the root of our trouble is here."

"Here?" asked Jonathan, his voice strangely hollow.

"Not on this very spot, no. But then again, it's difficult to say. Especially when one has been told very little."

"I see. Or shall I say, you see? Ha, ha. I myself scarcely know any of the details that might help you. But have you proof?" he asked, suddenly inspired.

"Of a sort." Longfellow took the shilling he'd found from his pocket, and held it before the landlord's shifting eye. "Would you care to examine it?"

"No need," Jonathan said slowly. "For I've found many others in my strongbox, while counting up my profits. They are all rather soft, it seems. When I attempted to use one to pry off the frozen cap of my inkwell some days ago, it bent. I might have told you, Richard—but would the knowledge have done more harm than good?"

"Then you weren't told their secret either. I feel just a little better, Jonathan."

"I'm glad. No one, as you say, has told me anything—

but now that I've examined my records, I realize a large number of our neighbors have given me shillings in payment for old bills, though silver has become difficult to find. It seems I now hold many pounds of counterfeit coins— enough to pray it's not confiscated one day! I feared to have it melted down, let alone to pass it on—though I'm sure I've already done so unwittingly. Is this . . . is this something you feel strongly about, Captain Montagu?"

"We shall have to see. Have you anything else to tell us, sir?"

"I will think very carefully, Captain, and let you know," Jonathan answered. "But how did you gentlemen discover it?"

"I'll tell you later," said Longfellow. "One evening, while we share a bottle or two of something rare and mellow, from your cellar."

"I will be delighted to provide just the thing."

"Good. Now, I've thought of another question or two, which I shall put to one of your clients. If you will excuse me?"

Slowly, Longfellow put his shilling back into a pocket, unwound his long legs, and rose. He made his way to a table by the fire, where Jack Pennywort had planted himself not long before. Already, it seemed, the small man was in his cups. He gave the approaching selectman a nearly toothless grin.

"I was hoping to see you here, sir, for I've read all of it now!" said Jack. "A lively place Otranto is, too. Full of wonders, and interesting Science."

"Science, Jack? How is that?" Longfellow asked with some surprise.

"Well, Mr. Flint and Mr. Tinder have told me that's what must lie under most of the things the book sets out, after all. And I agreed with them, as I don't suppose you'd have anything to do with the kind of foolishness this *seems* to be, sir, not unless there was something real and true beneath it. Maybe you will explain to us at the tavern, one day. Gunpowder, I suppose, is involved—and perhaps brimstone, as before?"

Jack paused to chortle, for he'd recalled an unusual event of three years ago, in which he'd been a central character. "That was very good of you, sir, and it was then I first wished I had more learning myself—for it can be a useful thing, I see now. I was double pleased when you lent me that book to read, and offered to pay me for the privilege! Only I think, if you would be so kind, sir, you need not trouble my wife with the rest of what's been promised. You might save yourself some steps, if you will, and give it directly to me."

Jack sat up, attempting to look steady and responsible, while his moist eyes continued to weave.

"Well . . ." Longfellow hesitated. He'd not been unmoved by the praise he'd heard. In fact, he felt a little ashamed of himself for what he'd asked of the small man before him. An education was, after all, a privilege, and not one to be taken lightly, or mocked in its absence. Still, had Pennywort seen fit, recently, to share what *he* knew, concerning certain local activities?

"How would you like it then, Jack? In shillings, I suppose. But what kind of shillings?"

"What kind, sir?"

"The regular ones? Or would you prefer some that are a little heavier and softer? Those that are, like yourself, of local manufacture?"

After a few moments, Jack jumped—for the information had taken its time reaching his brain. Only a cunning instinct for survival kept him from babbling what he knew.

"Have they got a mint now, in Boston?" he finally asked with a sweet, inquiring look.

"I don't think so. However, there may be a new one open out on Boar Island."

"That *would* be curious, wouldn't it, sir?" Jack answered with a crooked smile.

"It would indeed. You're not going to tell me, are you, Jack? Even for your last payment?"

This made the other man consider carefully. He licked his lips, as he imagined the additional spirits he might buy over the next several hours. Then a look of resolve crept over his face. He shook his head, and clamped his lips together.

"Hmm," Longfellow responded, pleased in spite of himself. "But tell me this, Jack. Why did no one tell me? Was it because I'm a selectman? Or do you mistrust me for another reason?"

"Well, you see . . ." Jack looked as if he were trying to remember the honest truth. Longfellow waited patiently, supposing this to be a rather rare occurrence. "You see," Jack decided at last, "it's because we *do* trust you, sir. You are a man we all respect—and we expect you to do what's right. It's what I feel in all of our dealings, for you've never been unfair with me, even if you do come to us from Boston. I feel the same about Mrs. Willett, who I know I wronged once—but she forgave me, didn't she? She's a good, honest lady. But that's another reason why we never told you. For we thought then *she* might find out, as well."

"About the shillings?"

"About whatever it is you may mean, Mr. Longfellow, sir."

"Yes . . ."

"And it wasn't your being a selectman, sir. For most of

them *do* know, and in fact joined right in! With whatever you may be imagining."

"Ah-ha! That is interesting. Well, let it never be said I took advantage of a man over a glass of—what is that you've got there, Jack?"

"Rum, sir! Today it is rum, for I remembered a seaman once told me it will ward off anything. And that is how I plan to continue, as long as I can afford it," he finished bravely.

"Rum, then, it will be, until this fails . . . or you do." Once more, Longfellow retrieved the tainted shilling, and set it down on the table. Giving the matter a second thought, he picked it up and replaced it with another of full value.

"What we remember, Jack," he said seriously, "is worth more than silver, or gold. Remembrances of friends, of kindnesses, of love—even of shameless flattery. All of these retain real value, I think, in the midst of chaos."

"Whatever you say, Mr. Longfellow, sir!" Jack cried as he raised an arm, summoning the young lady from Framingham, who came immediately.

Chapter 26

RICHARD LONGFELLOW STOOD for a moment on the snowy road, watching the others return to his home. Captain Montagu, he felt, would only be a hindrance in what he planned to do next. And he could see Charlotte had another idea of her own, though she only admitted she'd go and ask Hannah about her sciatica, while Lem saw his young lady.

Longfellow raised his scarf and began to walk into the brisk west wind, hoping to catch a ride. Before long he had his wish. Once over the bridge, he strode to the north on the road to Concord; this soon took him to the swinging sign of the Blue Boar.

The air inside was full of warmth and talk, but the latter ceased when Longfellow entered. He was not a regular here, and when he did come in, others might ask why. Yet he supposed word had circulated concerning the tenuous state of the village secret—now that he'd begun to look into other affairs connected with Boar Island. The tavern's patrons would ask themselves what he knew . . .

much as he had wondered about them in weeks gone by. Good! Better to fish in troubled waters. Doubt might soften their resolve, eventually helping the truth to burst out like—well, like the thing he'd observed on John Dudley's stump of a neck.

Anticipated success put a smile on the selectman's face, which he imagined gave most of those watching additional discomfort. When the time was ripe, he would pounce. Until then he would wait like one of his cats, and watch for further developments.

Phineas Wise came toward him between the tables, carrying a jug of ale.

"Good day to you, Mr. Longfellow. Have you come to see how we do in the other half of the village this morning? After our little snow?"

"Good day, Mr. Wise. Half of the village is on my mind, I admit. Due to the weather . . . and a few other things I've been looking into."

"Would you like something to warm you? I'm about to make flannel."

"At your stove?"

"Yes."

"Fine."

They made their way past the fire where Flint and Tinder seemed to be reading their newspapers, though this Longfellow doubted. As he passed, new smoke rose up from their pair of long clay pipes, yet their eyes would not meet his.

"Gentlemen," he said as he went by. In return, he received startled grunts, and a rattling of pages.

In a tiny space built onto the main room, Phineas had a cast-iron stove blazing. Onto its top he set a pan, taken from a board crammed with several others. Into the pan he poured the contents of the pitcher which was, in fact, a dark brown ale of strong fragrance.

"What do you know of this shilling business?" Longfellow asked. Wise paused to look up, his eyes steady as he considered.

"All that I need to know. Pass me four eggs from that basket behind you." Longfellow obliged. He watched the lean and rawboned fellow crack the eggs into a bowl, then beat in several spoons of sugar.

"You've taken them and said nothing?"

"As often as the next man. I'm not constable this year, as I was the last. So I felt no need to look further."

"They didn't tell you?"

"They know that I know, and I leave it at that. I don't think," Wise continued as he began to grate a furrowed nutmeg, "it's as well planned as you might suppose. Things of a hidden nature expand, if there's no one to stop them." He took up a smaller gray jug, and poured a cup of dark rum into his spicy mixture.

"Just how many *are* in on this, would you say?"

"Two dozen? Perhaps more. Few with much to lose, I'd say."

"And who, Phineas, is behind it? Do you know that?"

"I've overheard enough to guess. But I suggest you go out yourself, and hear what you can."

Seeing the ale on the stove steaming, the landlord poured a little into the bowl, stirring quickly with a large spoon to keep the eggs from curdling.

"I doubt I'd learn the time of day talking with your customers this morning, Phineas. As you already suspect."

Wise smiled at that, for it was true. He poured the rest of the ale into the bowl and blended it thoroughly.

"From what I can tell," said Longfellow, "the shillings are coming from Boar Island. And John Dudley, constable or not, has something to do with it. Where is he, by the way? Still upstairs, sleeping amidst his fumes?"

"Gone. Got up early—ate some cold pork and gravy from that pot there, while I was up a ladder pulling down snow drifted over the door. When I came back in, he was finishing a bottle two gentlemen abandoned last evening, telling me I could hardly charge him for what another had left behind!"

"And?"

"I could, and did. He gave me this for the night, and a small debt built up over the past week." Reaching onto the shelf above the stove, Wise took down a shilling and handed it over. Longfellow brought it close to his eye.

"Like those given to Jonathan, and Nathan Browne."

"I should think so." Wise poured the rest of the pan's mixture into the bowl, then poured the concoction back into the hot pan. A moment later it had returned to the bowl. This process was continued until the liquid became smooth and glossy.

"There," said the landlord, when he was satisfied. "A yard of flannel, as they say, to warm the stomach and the heart."

Longfellow picked up a glass from a shelf, wiped it with no fear of offending his reasonable host, and allowed it to be filled. The drink was as smooth as silk, and pleasant on the tongue.

"I just spoke with another of your regular clients," he told Phineas a moment later. "Up at the inn."

"Who was that?"

"Jack Pennywort."

"Just as well," said the landlord. "He'll hear less there to cause damage, should he repeat it."

"I take it, then, you hope this secret won't come out?"

"There's little hope of that. *How* it comes out concerns me. When it does, will they all begin to nip at one another like dogs, trying to stay on top? Will this business with Godwin and Old Cat Knowles enter into it, and bring us even worse? I only know I wouldn't want to be the man who informs on all the rest."

"That's what someone else recently told me."

"Well, she's right. My business is a rough one. Some farmers come in here feeling barely Christian. They may leave in worse shape. I've even heard it said the young man's death may have been the best thing for us all."

"A cold thought."

"It's been a cold year for many, as you know. Even before the snows."

Longfellow recalled his earlier sympathy for his neighbors' struggles, increasing with each new season.

"What do you know of Boar Island, Phineas?"

"I know it's a rock set in a marsh. Now it appears to be something worse. A good place to stay away from, I should think."

"It might be, at that," said Longfellow. Despite another sip of flannel and the warmth from the stove, he felt a chill as he contemplated a visit of his own.

AFTER HE'D HELPED Charlotte to a fireside chair in Hannah Sloan's kitchen, Lem Wainwright set down a basket that contained fresh milk and cream, and a packet of cheesecloth filled with dried hop flowers. Hannah looked to her daughter Martha. She alone among her sisters and brothers had stayed indoors this morning, no doubt hoping for a visit.

"Take this bag, Mattie," said her mother. "Pour boiling

water over it, and let it brew—then squeeze it out for me. I can hardly move today, for the pain!"

Martha found a bowl and began to do as she'd been told, then took what she'd made to a table across the room. Lem followed, admiring her second-best petticoat, and curls the color of ground ginger tucked under a nearly transparent cap. Orpheus, too, went to sniff at the hops, and sneezed at their unpleasant odor. The couple sat and gave a conspiratorial look back toward the fire.

"They're not holding you, then?" Mattie asked, fingering a ribbon at her ear.

"Well, not exactly," said Lem. For the first time in days, he felt at peace. It was not to last. "Though I am staying with Mr. Longfellow. And I'm still not supposed to go out on my own."

"Good," said Mattie. "We'll all know where you are, for a change. I've been hearing stories . . ."

"What kind of stories?"

"On Sunday, after the sermon, a girl I know who lives north of the village told me she'd seen you up there last week."

"That's not so strange, is it? My parents live north of here, you know. And my brothers and sisters."

"Whom you rarely visit, as you've told me yourself."

"Sometimes I do. Occasionally Mrs. Willett gives me something to take to them."

"When, exactly, was the last time that happened?"

"A while ago," said Lem, praying it would be enough. He stuck a finger into the bowl that held the poultice—and withdrew it suddenly, hissing his discomfort.

"It's not as hot as all that," said Mattie. "I should think you'd be used to hot water, by now." She lowered her own hand into the water to move the cheesecloth around, but withdrew it immediately. "There," she said, biting her lower lip in a way the boy found most attractive. "We'll let that sit. But she also said," the young woman continued, sliding easily back to her first subject, "that you'd passed her without a word, and even turned away—as if you didn't want anyone to know you were there. Why, I wonder, was that?"

"Who was it?"

"I'll not tell you. I can keep secrets of my own."

"Oh," he returned unhappily. "I'll tell you this, if you would like to know. It's not much good keeping a secret, Mattie. It's far better to have none in the first place."

"That, I'm sure, is true," she sighed. "Especially between people who are married."

"Married?"

"Yes, as an example."

"I'd not keep anything from you, Mattie. If we were ever—"

"To marry?"

"Well, as an example."

His smile, she thought, had become almost witless. Perhaps she had baited him too long. When his hand felt for hers behind the bowl, she let him take it.

Meanwhile, by the fire, the two women glanced over. They said nothing of what they saw, but returned to their own quiet conversation.

"I was sorry to hear about the Godwin boy, of course," said Hannah. "Still, I doubt he's much of a loss to his parents, if they sent him away from Worcester."

"Did they? Why do you suppose that was?" asked Charlotte.

"Samuel says he got himself into some sort of trouble. When they managed to get him out of it, he came here to start over. *That* didn't work out well. Some are born bad, it seems to me."

"There's something else I came to talk about," said Charlotte, not wanting to make a judgment on the information she'd just received. "It's something you'll find irritating."

The larger woman tilted her red face, putting her best ear forward. "Just what I need to distract me. What now?"

"It seems there's been a scheme of sorts going on in the village, perhaps for some time. It's one many of the men have organized, and neglected to mention to the rest of us."

"There's little news in that!" Hannah leaned back and gave a groan; her hand then went to her lower back to give it a rub. "Not here, nor anywhere else in the world. When have they *not* conspired to have things their own way, at our expense? Though I'm fond of a few of them, I can't say I've trusted any man for years . . ."

"But this is something rather unusual." Charlotte supposed, too, that what she was about to divulge would end this particular problem within their little society—if events took their normal course.

"It's not about the spoons, is it?" asked Hannah suddenly. "Have you found out what's behind all of that?"

"Yes. I have."

Hannah's heavy bosom began to heave. Eagerly, she waited for more.

"It seems several of our neighbors have been filching silver from their wives. And pewter, too . . ."

"Yes . . . go on."

". . . melting the objects down, then bringing them back."

"Back? How?"

"As counterfeit coins."

"Ahhh!" cried Hannah. She rocked back, causing her nerves to issue a new pang. She winced but otherwise ignored it, for she'd begun to imagine something far more painful.

"Shillings, actually," said Charlotte.

"Shillings!" Hannah's new exclamation caused Lem and Mattie to pause and look over, though their own conversation had become ardent.

"Mattie! Go upstairs and get the purse that's under my pillow."

Amazed by her mother's request, the young woman quickly left her corner.

"My Samuel," Hannah assured not only the kitchen, but the world at large, "will pay for this—and not with shillings, either!"

Charlotte glanced at Lem, and saw that he seemed resigned to what was happening. When Mattie returned, Hannah opened a leather purse and spilled several shillings into her lap.

"Like this?" she asked. Charlotte took one up. She looked at its edges carefully.

"I'm afraid so," she said as she returned it.

"And this?" asked Hannah, thrusting out another.

"That, too."

"Samuel 'confessed' to me that he'd won these playing cards at the Blue Boar. My father's silver snuff box! Ohhhh!" While Hannah's brows knitted themselves together, her eyes seemed to sink further into her weathered face.

"Samuel is not the only one," Charlotte assured her.

Lem had turned the color of a boiled crustacean. The young woman beside him also seemed affected by the news.

"Who?" Mattie asked.

Lem shrugged, then saw that this was not the right response.

"Who else knew?" she demanded. "You?"

This time he nodded, watching her face darken. He was reminded of a woman he'd read about in Tacitus, while he studied in Boston—one Boadicea, who'd led British warriors against the might of Rome. That had not turned out well, either. And this fight, he supposed, would unite all of the women of Bracebridge against the entire male population. It wouldn't take a sibyl to see who would lose. At least he would have plenty of company, while he lived out his life hungry and dirty.

"John Dudley, among others," said Charlotte to Hannah. Her friend realized at once the implication of this, and finally understood how such a man had been elected to uphold the law. "A travesty—nothing more!" she cried.

"Perhaps something more," Charlotte replied softly. "It's likely the coins were made on Boar Island. So they may have been connected with the death of Alex Godwin . . . and perhaps that of old Mrs. Knowles."

"You don't mean to say *she* was murdered? There on the island?"

"It could easily have been an accident, so I really shouldn't have said—and Hannah, please say nothing of what I've told you to Samuel, or to any other man in the village. Not yet. I think we might surprise them after we learn a little more—for one thing, I would like to know who else has lost something of silver or pewter. For another, we should find out who has lately been to the island, and knew about this scheme. Shall we form a conspiracy of our own, for a time? Lem, I think, may be counted on to keep our plan to himself—at least for a few days more."

"But *not* Mr. Longfellow? He wasn't—?"

"No. He knows now, and so does Captain Montagu.

They're conducting their own investigations. I only thought we might assist them."

"So we will! Every woman here will want to get her own back, even if she has to hold her tongue at home. For a few days, you say?"

"That should be enough."

"All right, then. You may as well leave this to me! I'll go and enlist Emily Bowers; Rachel Dudley will be more than glad to alert those north of the village."

"Ask them to try to account for the whereabouts of all the village men, as far as they can, on the afternoon of the ice harvest. And, on the day of the storm, between ten and two."

"That's far more serious business," Hannah objected.

"It is. But that part of what's happened here *must* be considered, in case they're connected. I'm still not sure, as I told you, about the second death, though it's what Mrs. Knowles believed. It's likely she was wrong. Yet Alex Godwin *was* murdered."

"Of course," said Hannah. Neither spoke for several moments.

"Lem Wainwright," Mattie then said quietly, as she began to back him further into the corner, where he'd found it natural to stand.

"I—" he began to protest. The words he wanted wouldn't come.

"Lem Wainwright, *what* have you done?" asked Mattie, voicing for every woman in the village a question nearly as old as mankind.

Chapter 27

SHORTLY BEFORE NOON, Charlotte and Lem were met by Cicero outside Richard Longfellow's door, where they shook snow crystals from their clothing, and clumps of heavier stuff from their boots. Taking up cups of tea, they went to sit by a welcome fire. There, Orpheus chewed at the pads of his feet, before enjoying what was left of a beef knee brought to him from the pantry.

"A profitable morning?" Cicero asked, his face wreathed with pleasure at seeing a woman who appeared to have nothing *seriously* wrong with her.

"We'll see," Charlotte answered mysteriously. "I don't know yet, myself, but I think so. What have you to report?"

"Mrs. Montagu and Miss Knowles have been together most of the time, lately in the study. Diana took Magdalene on a tour of the house before they settled on amusing one another at the pianoforte."

"Really? I hadn't realized—and where is Mr. Reed?"

"Retired to his room. He mentioned correspondence."

"We've been busy, ourselves." Was Cicero aware of

what had been discussed earlier that morning? It turned out that Edmund Montagu had already spoken of the shillings with his wife, while the old man was dusting behind a door. He'd heard, too, of Jonathan Pratt's pain at his discovery of the counterfeit coins. It was news to him, however, that Hannah bore up reasonably well under her sciatica; Cicero shook his head, and described the state of his own rheumatism.

Lem next took a turn, telling of their first stop after leaving the house. They'd paid a visit to Christian Rowe, and Mrs. Willett had asked the minister to arrange for the removal of Mrs. Knowles's body later that day. He'd said he would see what he could do—but what would be done with it? It didn't seem right to place a respectable dame from a wealthy family in a cellar, especially with a young man who'd been murdered. Rowe finally decided that until the ground could be prepared, Mrs. Knowles would be placed much as the Montagus' child had been, her coffin left to wait for spring, in a quiet corner by the respectable stones of village ancestors.

The minister went on to say he'd called for a general meeting of the village on Saturday, in two days' time. By then he supposed all who'd attended the ice harvest, and any others who had something to tell, would be able to make their way to the meeting house. Lem and Charlotte had promised to attend.

Now Longfellow came home, leaving a sleigh whose muffled bells jingled as it continued up the hill. He reported that nearly half the roads for which Bracebridge was responsible were passable, after fresh teams had come out to relieve the first oxen and their drivers. There had been a blaze in the home of one of the elders who lived by the common; it was quickly smothered by neighbors who'd flung carpets full of snow onto a padded settle.

He would say little about his visit to the Blue Boar. Yet he did propose to Charlotte that they talk alone, some time before dinner. He excused himself, and went up to speak with Moses Reed.

Knowing he might not be long, Charlotte felt a rising sense of pleasurable excitement. Would he tell her what he'd learned? Or had he something else to say to her? Would he ask of her own quest for information? At least in discussing the shillings, Richard had again taken her into his confidence. Aglow at the thought, she went to the study to find Diana and Magdalene looking over a stack of magazines.

Mrs. Montagu pondered what she might wish to buy for her new home in Boston. But Magdalene seemed stunned by a world she'd nearly forgotten. Not for the first time, Charlotte wondered what the effect of a rebirth might do to such a simple woman, and whether she would be likely, at last, to find happiness.

"Miss Knowles," she asked, "would you like a fresh cup of tea? Perhaps in your room, while you rest before dinner?" Magdalene rose with apparent stiffness, but seemed relieved to go.

Indicating to Diana that she would return, Charlotte accompanied the older woman to the kitchen, and then up the stairs. After that she returned to the study, to find out what else might have been learned that morning.

"I've been prying, of course," Diana told her with no sign of regret. "I should think Edmund would be proud of me; but for now, I've decided not to tell him anything about it. Though there isn't much, really."

Charlotte replied by telling her of the conversation she'd had with Hannah. Diana approved, but added that she could see little wrong with the making of coins on Boar Island. After all, if Parliament in London could do it, what was wrong with a similar plan being undertaken in Massachusetts? The secrecy of the thing in the village, though, the part of keeping the scheme from wives especially, did seem to her quite wrong indeed.

"Has Lem learned his lesson?" she finally inquired.

"I haven't asked him about that—or a few other things," said Charlotte. "I took pity on him after Mattie's scolding. But we all supposed he deserved it."

"I should think so!" said Diana, as she flipped an auburn curl from her face. "It's a good thing he seems to have found someone else to take care of him one day. You can't be expected to do it forever! Did you know Magdalene can do most things to run a house, by the way?"

"I thought she must have done what was needed on the island, beyond the heaviest work."

"She can sew and cook. Cicero was surprised at the extent of her help this morning. They prepared a stew, and put a pudding into a bag to boil, while I supervised. And then I played Richard's pianoforte for her, thinking she would be astonished—but it was I who was surprised! She plays well. No doubt that's because she's had time to practice on the island, where there is a harpsichord—and she's not had the trouble of living in society, as one does in Boston."

"Probably," Charlotte said kindly, well aware of the limitations of Diana's own musical skills.

"We also built this fire together, after all of you left us with no help but Cicero this morning! On the other hand, she shows little knowledge of fashion. It seems she's never even seen an umbrella—"

"Diana, do you still think Magdalene may be dangerous, in some way?"

"Dangerous? Oh, no, I think not. Whatever gave you that idea?"

"I wonder. You suppose, then, she's no more than a little backward, in social things?"

"She doesn't talk much, that is sure. But then, perhaps she hasn't been allowed to," Diana decided shrewdly. "What little she said of Mrs. Knowles makes the woman sound like a tyrant, with no interest in anyone but herself!"

Before she could go on, her brother entered, clearly in high spirits.

"I've spoken with Reed. He tells me he'll explain all that he's withheld from us as soon as we've had our dinner. He's gone in to have his talk with Magdalene, supposing she's calm enough to understand what has happened. Dinner, by the way, is nearly ready."

"Then I'll go in and help Cicero," said Charlotte, sorry to have found that Longfellow had nothing more to offer her.

Soon she stood before a polished table in the small papered room not far from the clattering kitchen. Outside the west windows, ice crystals still flew by, but the sky over the village seemed blue and peaceful. She wondered, as she set out a cloth, then silver, china, and linen napkins, whether the death of Catherine Knowles had been an accident after all. She suddenly wished to think so. For a moment, she concluded that it was, to see if something within her would object strongly.

There would be plenty of time after dinner, she told herself, to reconsider the other, more dreadful alternative.

Chapter 28

THE MEAL WAS a hurried one, as everyone seemed impatient to hear more of the disposition of Mrs. Knowles's fortune. All, at least, but Magdalene, who ate quietly, her eyes cast down.

What, Charlotte asked herself, had Reed said to her during the previous hour? Whatever it had been, it had caused a return of her previous melancholy. Diana, too, noticed. She sent Charlotte significant glances over the stew and corn bread.

When Cicero brought in the boiled pudding, it was admired, then hurriedly dispatched. The study's clock struck two. Magdalene, at the advice of her attorney, went back to her room, to be spared hearing what he would tell the others, some of it of a delicate nature. At Longfellow's request, Cicero took Lem off to help him stoke the glasshouse stove. The rest retired to the front parlor still brightened by the sun, though its light had lost the exuberance of the morning.

"The wills, then," Moses Reed began. He stood before a

window stroking his beard; Longfellow, Charlotte, Edmund, and Diana sat in chairs arranged before him.

"As I have already said, it appears that Catherine Knowles wrote two wills in the space of the past year, each of them brief. Magdalene assures me she witnessed the first, though not the second, of which she knew nothing. The first document was witnessed as well by Alaric Jones, who delivered it to me in Boston shortly before his own death. The only witness to the final will was Alexander Godwin. It was he who came to me with the document several weeks ago. Godwin, in fact, was the sole and final heir, at the time of Catherine's unfortunate death."

"As we've already deduced," Longfellow informed the lawyer.

"Yes, I thought as much. Now for the rest. I assume, since Magdalene informed Mrs. Willett of the fact, and I have since discussed it with several of you, that it's no longer a secret she bore a son some seventeen years ago. After a short time, the boy was taken from his mother. Upon this, Catherine Knowles insisted."

"I would like to know exactly *why* that was the case," Diana interjected. Her face, Charlotte thought unhappily, had the intensity of an avenging angel, bound on righting injustice in the world.

"I'm sorry to tell you of this, Mrs. Montagu," Reed said with a grimace of concern. "I'm aware that you, too, recently lost a child. Nor do I wish to open Magdalene's wound, though it came to her long ago. However, she assured me this morning that it has greatly lessened, since—" He stopped, as if to reconsider.

"But perhaps I should not go ahead of my story," he continued. "First: Magdalene is unmarried, though her lover did hope to return one day and claim her. For whatever reason, that never occurred."

"But how did the *child* come to leave the island?" Diana asked once more.

"I must admit I took the boy away, as Mrs. Knowles instructed me to do. You ask why, Mrs. Montagu. I will try to explain. Catherine Knowles held strong views on hereditary rights and duties. As I recall, she felt she owed her husband's family something better than—well, than a bastard, and one who quite possibly would not have developed a full mental capacity, or a full moral sense. She felt it would be better for the boy, as well, if he had no chance to inherit wealth and power, if in fact his blood carried his mother's affliction, and his uncle's. She believed it would have been a sort of pollution. In this, she refused to take part."

"She believed, then, in *primogeniture*," said Longfellow, looking to see Edmund Montagu's reaction. The captain's face was an unchanging mask.

"But again I jump ahead," said the lawyer. "Mrs. Knowles insisted it would be far better if the Philadelphia family did not *know* what had happened—that Magdalene had been secretly with child when John Fisher died, and had been delivered of that child some time after the return of Peter Knowles to Philadelphia. Catherine then asked me to repay her father's earlier kindness to me. I was glad to be able to do so. And, because of the trust she placed in me, I was able to establish myself in Boston, where I have since acted as her attorney and advisor."

"But Reed, *what did you do with the boy?*" asked Longfellow.

"I took the child to a place where I was sure he would be well looked after. Again, at the request of Mrs. Knowles, I did not tell her with whom the boy would live. Nor was Magdalene ever to know. I've often wondered if I made the right choice, in following this plan . . ."

"His name, man—his name!" Longfellow insisted, sensing that the lawyer still did not wish to give it. "Was it Alexander Godwin?"

"Godwin? No. The boy's name, the new name he was given, is Edward Bigelow."

"Ned?" cried Longfellow. "It can't be!"

"I think Mrs. Willett suspected as much," said Reed, as Charlotte felt his eyes examine her own.

"You gave him to old Jonah?" Longfellow asked, his voice still full of disbelief.

"To Jonah and his wife, who had long been my neighbors. I knew they'd lost their own children to illness, some time before. They were very glad to take Ned, as they called him, and to raise the boy as a child said to be related to Mrs. Bigelow. Then, when Abigail died, only Jonah knew the secret."

"And Ned?" asked Charlotte. "Do you suppose he knows?"

"I think—I hope—that he does not. Nor that he was for a brief time Catherine's heir. The first of two."

"Was he!" Longfellow exclaimed, enlightened on that point, at last. "I'm not certain I'm glad to hear it—but tell me this, Reed. If Catherine Knowles didn't wish Ned to inherit from the Philadelphia family, why did she leave him her own estate?"

"I believe that with her end in sight, she wished to make amends for his earlier rejection, which she came to see as unfair. She asked for his name, and I gave it to her— though she had no wish to see the boy. And at last, she wrote out a will. Perhaps, too, she had Magdalene in mind. She never told her what would happen after her death, but it seems she never quite trusted the Philadelphia family to see to Magdalene's happiness."

"Did they know, in Philadelphia, that Ned would be

revealed as Magdalene's son? Or that Catherine changed her mind a final time?" asked Longfellow.

"She never told me. In either case, the head of that family was still her secondary heir, should something happen to the first. She had no one else. Now that Godwin is gone, I suppose they will be glad to learn they'll lose nothing to the widow of Peter Knowles, after all."

"The old woman did Ned a great disservice, it seems to me," Longfellow said soberly. "That boy is anything but simple. He's learned much on his own, and has an admirable spirit. Though lately—"

"But she had good reason to question his abilities, Richard, given the circumstances." This came from Edmund Montagu, and he continued forcefully. "I've seen some who were not up to the task destroyed by the assumption of wealth—worse, they've often caused innocents to fall with them. When a first-born lacks physical strength, or mental ability, how can he do justice to his family, who depend on him? . . ."

Montagu let the thought drift away. Had he gone too far? Would his wife see his true meaning—the one that had been seared into his memory, into his heart? Their own son had been too weak to survive. Had he lived, could he have faced life squarely? Would he have been able to handle the family wealth, or the title if it had come to him, one day? And should his father have hated himself for having such a thought, when young Charlie, small and sick, lay dying?

"At any rate," said Reed, "the final document did not favor Ned Bigelow."

"Why," asked Longfellow, "do you suppose that was?"

"I don't know. Perhaps Mrs. Knowles learned of something that made her feel Magdalene's son was unworthy, after all."

"A charge of counterfeiting?"

The lawyer's reaction told Longfellow that Reed, too, had realized what had been going on in the village. Damn him!

"That is possible," the attorney replied quietly. "As I agreed to defend Lem Wainwright, I will now offer my services to Magdalene Knowles to protect her son, if anyone sees fit to charge him. With anything at all."

It was no more than Longfellow had expected from a member of the legal profession. "A charge will wait," he returned, "until other things are sorted out. In all probability, it won't take long."

"I'm not sure I understand," Reed said uncertainly.

"But you will, sir. Soon. Very soon."

Giving the attorney a meaningful smile, Longfellow rose and turned to Charlotte. "Mrs. Willett, I believe Lem will need to attend to your cows. I think it might be advisable for you to go along."

Realizing that he wished her to ask Lem what *he* knew of the coins, and the island, and anything else he may have kept hidden—knowing, too, that it was time— Charlotte rose and went out before the others.

Chapter 29

THE SWEET SMELL of fodder surrounded them while milk began to hiss into empty pails, inside the dark barn. With their lanterns nearby, Charlotte and Lem settled once more into an old habit. Happily familiar, it gave them a chance to think with their hands busy.

Today, both knew something unusual would be expected.

Charlotte began by saying they'd been told Ned Bigelow was once in line for an inheritance, though that would now go back to Philadelphia—and, that Magdalene was the boy's mother. When she'd finished, Lem whooped from the next stall.

"*There's* something I never expected to hear!"

"Do you think Ned knew?"

"If he did know about his mother, he never said. As long as I've known him, he's been worried about money. So as for this inheritance, I'd say probably not. Though I'm sure he *wished* for one."

"Oh?"

"He and Jonah never had much, and he talked about going off one day, traveling by sea, exploring places he's read about. He often asks Mr. Pratt for old newspapers, or the *London Gentleman's Magazine*, which sometimes gets left behind by the guests. Stories about pirates and the like, he sometimes reads aloud."

As the milk continued to shoot, Lem fell silent, possibly considering his own future, which was far from sure.

"You know Ned goes to Boar Island?" Charlotte asked.

"I would have told you—but I swore an oath to tell no one. Especially not any woman!"

"That's what I'd imagined. But why do you suppose Ned confided in you?"

"Because we've been friends since we went to dame school together. My mother never liked him—she said he sets a bad example. But no more than my brothers, it seems to me! And when I came to live with you, our paths often crossed in the village, so we started to talk about things other people don't seem to understand. Things he'd read about, and ideas I'd learned from Mr. Longfellow. And other things, lately," Lem added, his voice less certain.

"The counterfeit shillings?"

"Sometimes I wished he'd never told me! But we were friends, so it would have been hard for him not to. It wasn't his idea. The whole thing was urged on him by a few others—who, exactly, he never would say. But he did worry about money, so he went ahead."

"When did you see him last?"

Lem got up and moved to another animal, kicking his stool through the hay before he replied.

"He came to Mr. Longfellow's last evening," he finally answered. "After he heard the constable wanted me kept there. He waited until he saw me by a window, and threw some snow. I went out when I could. I'm sure he didn't come for fear of what I'd say—he knew the truth would soon come out. He only wanted to see how I was."

"Did Ned ask you to help him make the coins?"

"No. Well, he did let me help him score the edge of some of them, once or twice, while we talked with Jonah. He's a fine old man," Lem added warmly.

"With a colorful history."

"The foundry, you mean? Yes, he does have interesting tales. Is that what made you suspect Ned was involved in making the shillings?"

"Partly. When I visited Jonah, I saw Ned had a burn on his hand. He said it was from the discharge of his fowler—but I noticed he had no gun when he came in. Later, I wondered if he might have received the burn while working on the shillings."

"That's more likely. He never was one for hunting, especially in the cold. He can't stand the wait."

At least, thought Charlotte, the coins had been one explanation that came to mind to explain Ned's injury; and it did lead her to suspect he'd been on the island that morning. As yet, neither of the two young men had been told of the final accusation of Catherine Knowles.

Find out if the boy was— Was what? On the island that day? The boy Catherine had disinherited, who may have killed her new heir, only the day before? The one who then could have come up behind an old woman at her hearth, and pushed her into it?

"But how did the scheme get started?" Charlotte asked after a long silence. "Who knew what to do, exactly?"

"Jonah was able to tell Ned how to set up a forge in

the house I told you about, after someone else went over and made repairs."

"Did he make the molds?"

"That part was easy. Ned has a good eye and a clever hand; he's often sketching pictures he finds in books and magazines. Though for learning how to work with the metal—the engineering of it—I think he had the help of someone in Concord who makes etchings for the newspapers. A friend of Sam Adams. You remember I met him at the Green Dragon Tavern, this summer."

"That, too, is interesting. But did you see Ned on the island yesterday?"

"No. Before I got there, smoke was coming up from where I knew the forge to be—and Magdalene told me she'd just come from there. But by the time we left, the smoke had stopped. I thought he'd already left for home."

"Magdalene saw Ned at work there?"

"He told me he first met her there in the spring. She gave him a fright, peering in at a window; but he soon found she wanted to watch. He finally coaxed her to talk a little—but did *she* know?"

"That Ned is her son? I think so. For fear of losing him a second time, she still won't say."

Her son's dancing eyes, Magdalene had told her, came from his father—whom she would not see again. And Ned did have a warm, joyous presence; Charlotte had seen that often enough herself.

This time they moved together to new stalls, after emptying their pails into a vat on wooden runners.

"Did John Dudley come often," Charlotte tried next, "to bring Ned the silver he needed? And the pewter?"

"It was usually Dudley. He left things in a hollow under

a tree, in case anyone else should come by. He even brought his wife's spoons, and then lost one somewhere. Ned said Mrs. Dudley got it back from you. Did you find it that day you fell into the river?"

"Please don't remind me! Did Ned say how Dudley got the other spoons back?"

"He brought them from the island when Dudley told him he'd better, or his wife would have someone's ears! On the day of the ice harvest, he ran home and returned with them in his coat. And he slipped them into the bag I'd left by the bonfire, thinking Dudley would take them out when he was sure no one else noticed. But Dudley pulled the bag under his feet, and took it home at the end of the day."

"Then whoever removed the hatchet took it *before* Ned came back—or he would have seen it when he put the spoons in? . . ."

"I'd say he would have had to."

Charlotte stood once more, patting the brown rump before her as she waited for Lem to finish draining the last udder. "Did Alex Godwin know Ned visited the island, and why?" she asked finally.

"Oh, he knew. That's what he threatened to tell Mr. Longfellow—to get both of us into trouble. I don't suppose, though, that he ever really would have dared to."

She hadn't yet told him she'd also learned that Alex had stood to gain Ned's fortune, after Catherine changed her mind. If he'd known that, would he have spoken so freely? She told him now.

Lem's reaction was a long, quiet look, and a slow nod. He understood and readily forgave her—just as she had forgiven him for his own recent omissions.

"But you will try to help him, if he needs it?" the young man asked, watching her earnestly.

"Of course." She only hoped such a thing would be in her power. She prayed that what she suspected might be wrong.

"I will," she said once more. "If I can."

Chapter 30

W HAT DID HE say?" asked Longfellow.

Minutes before, Charlotte had returned and walked alone down the corridor to Longfellow's study. She'd found him gone.

Cicero informed her, once she'd found him in the cellar selecting a bottle of port, that Longfellow was out inspecting his glasshouse. This stood against the barn, to which a path through the deep snow had been made; still, she felt like grumbling as she took off her house shoes and put her boots back on, then slipped a cloak over her shoulders.

The inside of the glasshouse was hardly warm, but at least the wind could not get in. A Baltic stove with several branching conduits rising from its firebox served to keep one corner well above freezing, if it was regularly tended. This, Longfellow was seeing to now. The smell of green that surrounded them in the darkness was especially enjoyable at this time of year. The fronds of the tree fern and a few other specimens seemed to droop somewhat, but they'd survived here for several winters, and she knew it would take a hard frost to damage any of them permanently.

"He said," she finally replied, "enough to make it clear that Moses Reed was right about one thing. Lem should have nothing more to fear, even from someone who may have wished to harm him, or to spoil his name."

"Ned Bigelow, however . . ."

Her spirits sinking, Charlotte waited. Longfellow shut the iron door with a clang, and went on.

"There does seem to be something there. Could he have known about the inheritance—and, that he'd lost his chance? Magdalene may have told him of the first will. Jonah could also have decided he'd reached an age when he should know his own history. Then again, if Alex Godwin unsealed and read what he'd witnessed, and was about to deliver? . . . He might even have found a way, I suppose, to go through all of Catherine's papers. In that case, he may have taunted Ned with being excluded once again."

"Alex did know about the counterfeiting scheme. He even threatened to come and tell you." She then told him the rest of what Lem had revealed.

"I see," said Longfellow with a frown. "So Ned is implicated in that, as well." He escorted her to a stone seat behind the iron apparatus; there, warmth and a soft glow came from air vents in the iron box. She felt the encouraging pressure of his arm at her waist, until he politely moved it away.

"But we also have John Dudley to consider," he said at last. "He went to the island, you say. And with the hatchet there at his feet—"

"But if he took the hatchet and used it, would he have taken the bag home, to draw our suspicions? Beyond that, when Mrs. Knowles fell into the fire, Richard, the constable was with you."

"He seemed shaken at seeing the hatchet, when we were all in Rowe's parlor . . ."

"But that may have been no more than a fear of blood, which is fairly common," she returned.

"Hmmm," said Longfellow, disliking it himself.

"If I'm completely honest," she admitted, "I would say I'm greatly interested to know what Ned was doing at the time of each death. Magdalene saw him on the island yesterday morning; I saw him return to his grandfather's house later, his hand burned. He said he'd had an accident while out hunting. But if someone pushed Catherine Knowles into her fire, that someone may have found he had to keep her there for some while—waiting for her wool skirts to burn," she finished in a small, unhappy voice.

Longfellow grew concerned for the kind woman beside him, long his friend. She was struggling admirably to be impartial. From a knowledge of her heart he knew, too, that she would be slow to forgive herself, if her suspicions led to Ned Bigelow's downfall. He would miss the lad, he thought suddenly. It would be a shame to find him guilty—and especially hard on old Jonah. Lem would be deprived of a companion with a fine brain, and that was something rare enough in Bracebridge.

"But Carlotta," he continued, putting his arm around her shoulder to warm her. She was shivering, he noted with new alarm. He drew her closer. "Though it looks as if Ned may have had opportunity, even reason, that doesn't mean he must be the *only* one. Let's give this thing time, before we say more. As to the shillings—"

"I did hear what Edmund said in the taproom," she replied. "But what might Mr. Hutchinson do, if he hears of them? I'm afraid life has taught us that things have a way of changing."

"For the good, very often," he replied, moving back a strand of hair that had fallen across her worried face. "Take Edmund, for instance. Though once a staunch supporter of the rights of first sons, I believe he's reconsidered that faulty British tradition, and it may mean he'll give his future children, and Diana's, a more equal chance in life. In yet another case, someone else we know quite well seems to have turned a different corner . . ."

Was it time, at last, to admit his own fault? For weeks he'd suspected his unreasoning jealousy of his summer visitor, Gian Carlo Lahte, had been more than a little unfair. In the matter of courtship, he himself had been unable to act as he might have liked—*would* have liked. And so he'd nearly abandoned his neighbor, just when she *should* have been able to rely on his friendship, while she examined rekindled passions of her own.

What an ass he'd been!

Yet in some ways it was understandable. He knew Aaron Willett remained oddly alive in his wife's mind. He had liked Aaron—had even begun to love him as a brother, toward the end. With Aaron and Charlotte for neighbors, and her sister Eleanor his fiancée, he'd known for the first time the joys of a family. Certainly, life with his father and stepmother had lacked this kind of warmth and comfort. And then, his family had been sundered, leaving him alone with Charlotte, to mourn.

Now Diana had grown and married—and it seemed there were four again. Such an arrangement was almost too easy; it even felt as if it could have come at the expense of the other. He recalled how one day Charlotte and Aaron had laughed together, ambling through the fields. Walking behind with Eleanor, he'd found the sight of their pleasure added a conviction to his own. He'd assumed he and Eleanor, too, would share a spiritual and physical unity, which would last forever.

It had all been a house of cards. But it seemed he must try again. For months, years, he'd asked himself if he were willing to chance such happiness a second time. Yet now, he knew that losing even a portion of the closeness he felt for the woman beside him was unthinkable. He *must* do whatever he could to keep her affection, and slowly add to it. And he had better begin soon, he decided.

Charlotte imagined her neighbor was about to add something, perhaps of a more personal nature. He bent a little, and she suddenly felt his lips on her own. They lingered, and she began to suppose he offered her a new sort of endearment, a different kind of beginning. In a few moments, she drew a long breath, and thought she saw him smile in the faint light.

"But in any case," he told her, "I don't believe you should continue to worry about Ned Bigelow, or Lem . . . or anyone else who may have vexed you lately. Now, will you stay with me tonight? Good. Let's go in and try a bottle of old port, one of my best. I've asked Cicero to bring a pair up from the cellar. May I walk you home, madam?"

"Please, sir," she replied, rising and pulling her cloak more tightly about her. Then, with his arm at her waist to guide her, they walked out into the ancient magic of a starlit night, making their way toward a glow of candles across the yard.

Chapter 31

THE ORMOLU CLOCK on Longfellow's mantel struck eight. Yet not one of the four friends sitting around the study fire made any sign to say that it was time for bed. Each couple seemed lost in private speculation, as they recalled the events of the day.

Diana Montagu fingered an attractive volume on the subject of Roman history, one her brother had set down some time before.

"There is much, I suppose, to be learned from the past," she said, wondering if anyone would comment. "And yet most of the time it only confuses one, and can have little to do with the present, after all."

"Ancient history perhaps," her brother replied. "Though I find it restful to be reminded that our own troubles are scarcely new."

"What do you think, Edmund?" his wife asked, hoping to draw the captain from his own musing.

"I think," he answered her, "that history makes us what we are. But I was pondering something of recent history, shown to me last week at Town House. You might be familiar with the story, Richard, as a Bostonian. Do you recall Owen Syllavan?"

"Indeed I do," said Longfellow, re-crossing his long legs. "A most dedicated moneymaker."

"I was given a copy of a remarkable document published in Boston ten years ago, taken from his own words. Though self-taught, it seems he succeeded in making above fifty thousand pounds in counterfeit money, spread about for him by a network of unscrupulous men."

Charlotte raised her eyes, for she'd been thinking of Lem's involvement with Ned Bigelow, in what appeared to be a plot fostered by John Dudley. Had he always been as drunk as he seemed, these many years?

"Didn't Syllavan begin with Boston bills of credit?" Longfellow asked.

"With one Spanish dollar, actually—molded for amusement, he claimed, while he worked as a silversmith. He was earlier a seal cutter, and before that an armorer in the King's service, where he learned to engrave. During his later career he was imprisoned regularly, but still managed to create new bills while in jail—each by hand! For some reason, they would not bring him a rolling press."

"There is often, I fear, a certain laxity in such places," Longfellow replied to this irony.

"So it would seem! For he would also escape regularly. Even when he had been pilloried, branded on both cheeks, and had his ears cropped, he continued—though legally he could have been hanged years before. I doubt he would have had such an illustrious career in England."

"Money is a sensitive subject with our juries," Longfellow said helpfully. "Perhaps because most who sit have rarely seen much of it."

"What has happened to him?" Diana inquired. "By now he must be a rich man."

"He was hanged in New York, having copied bills of that province, and of New Hampshire and Connecticut, too. He seems not to have profited from his work. Instead, it kept him running from place to place, hiding wherever he might, hoping none of his friends would reveal him out of fear, or for reward. That is what finally happened, of course."

"A life of crime is fraught with difficulty," Longfellow said lightly.

"Something you might impress on a pair of young men not far from here."

"That, I will do. I shall also tell them that if they contemplate such a life, they should have sufficient standing, or at least enough backing, to change the name of what they do. Like Clive, first 'protecting' India for the Great Mogul, then returning this past summer to effectively steal its vast wealth for Britain."

"Clive, in many ways, is a man of greatness. His better qualities will probably ruin him in the end—for he's hardly as greedy as most," Edmund finished with a sigh. At any rate, it was not to his taste to look for boys to catch up in the nets of Justice, such as it was here, especially for what seemed to them little more than games. On the other hand, what might happen when young men followed leaders like Sam Adams, and the enormously wealthy Mr. Hancock? At least in Bracebridge, the "leaders" were no more than a few farmers.

"It is strange," he remarked, shifting back to the topic of history his wife had advanced, "to find two ends of such formidable English families interwoven in this province."

"Which families?" asked Diana, always interested in society.

"Dudley and Knowles. Robert Dudley, as I hope you know, Diana, was made Earl of Leicester by Elizabeth. And Knollys, which is where Knowles comes from, was that lady's chamberlain and treasurer, and the keeper of Mary, Queen of the Scots. I'm personally acquainted with another, Sir Charles, who is an admiral. Once the governor of Louisburg, he now supervises Jamaica. I suppose he'll become accessible to his new relation—though Ned Bigelow, or Knowles, is to receive little else. The Navy, at least, pays scant attention to which side of the blanket one has been born on."

"Often having something to do with it in the first place?" Longfellow asked.

"Lately," said Charlotte, startling them all as she came to life, "Ned has become interested in sea travel, and the southern islands."

"Has he, Carlotta?" Longfellow inquired.

They all waited for more, but she seemed to retreat back into her own thoughts.

In fact, she wondered if that could mean Ned had known about his blood relations for some time. And she wished Richard and Edmund would not talk so blithely of Mr. Syllavan, for it seemed to her that a similar noose might now be tightening around the neck of a certain young fiddler, fascinated by warm and distant climes.

"A Knollys of *our* century," Edmund continued, "was the notorious Earl of Banbury, who killed his brother-in-law in a duel."

"Shocking behavior," said Longfellow, making the captain wince at an unpleasant memory of his own. "It does begin to sound as if the Knowles clan in Philadelphia may have something odd in their veins, after all."

That, thought Charlotte, was another theory Catherine Knowles had advanced when she'd taken tea with the old woman, dressed in her dated finery. When the dark mirror had seemed to dance . . . and she'd first seen the sorrow of Magdalene's life.

"Speaking of history and black sheep," Longfellow added, "I've just finished Horace Walpole's peculiar story."

"*Otranto*? I would have guessed that far too romantic for your taste," said the captain with a smile.

"And you would have been correct."

"Oh, yes," said Diana. "The book with the castle. What is that all about, Edmund? Richard tells me any day now one of our Boston friends may ask us about it."

"Walpole claims in his introduction that his reason for writing it was an artistic one," Edmund replied. "But that may be as fanciful as the rest. Its true purpose is no doubt hidden."

"Well, what do you suppose it is?" asked Longfellow, wishing he had something to pass on to Jack Pennywort one day.

"It's not far, I think, from what Mr. Reed brought us, with his talk of wills and responsibilities." He stopped and looked to his wife, fearing the subject might distress her, not quite sure of his own feelings.

"Go on, Edmund, please," he heard her ask. Could it be that Diana was even more beautiful tonight, with this new display of bravery?

"For you, I will try—though much of it is foreign to the way things are thought of in Massachusetts. Walpole, you must realize, is no longer a young man—he's also a martyr to the gout, which may have something else to do with it—but in his time, he's seen great change in Britain. Kings, lately, have become more powerful than they once were, at the expense of those who share their power of governance. In the current king we have an example of the sins of the fathers, newly magnified. Perhaps Walpole wished to call attention to the fact that the Hanoverians, who were invited to England, have nearly worn out their welcome."

"That could be part of it, I suppose," Longfellow considered.

"Yet there's something else that concerns Walpole. I believe the rest of us should be aware of it, as well. In England, indeed in much of Europe, lesser men have for some time been gaining influence and power—"

"Lesser men," Longfellow interrupted. "Those of us without hereditary stature, Edmund?"

"Those with less investment in family, Richard, yes. Those with less interest in chivalrous behavior, too. Merchants, city traders, men with fleets of ships, investors in new canals and other works that benefit the public—and change it. This trend threatens men like Walpole even more than irritable kings, who might be replaced. *Otranto*, I think, shows us the unhappy effects of an old, corrupt system. And yet it should also remind us that even our children's children will be marked by today's injustices, which will continue to haunt them."

"And will there be no escape?" asked Longfellow with a gentle smile at this foolishness. "Who, exactly, does Walpole wish to expose?"

"For a start, those now turning whole villages away from

the land, forcing enclosures so they may enrich themselves
without responsibility—building gigantic farms, and exclu-
sive pleasure parks where they may hunt and otherwise
amuse themselves, all at the expense of poor cottagers, and
the older landed aristocracy. Increasingly, they do this with
the help of Parliament—"

"I've no doubt," Longfellow said soothingly, hoping to
stem the tide. He'd seen before that his new brother enjoyed romantic philosophy. However, while it made the
captain more heated, it somehow left him cool. Some
curious natural law, no doubt. "Beware, Edmund," he
added, "or you may one day awake to find yourself a revo-
lutionary."

"I still maintain the novel is about social injustice,
Richard. Do you not agree this is something we should all
attempt to define, and address?"

"I do. The question is, what are we to make of Walpole's
bizarre attempts, if that is what he's up to? What of
his apparent passion for gigantism, and spectral inva-
sions?"

"Those are rather difficult," Edmund admitted. "Yet I
think he implies that power, grown too large, can be top-
pled only by something greater—something grounded in
family and honor."

"Family, honor, medieval chivalry—rather than Nature,
Science, and the Rights of Man. An interesting plan, if
one's aim is to march backwards. I seem to recall that
Voltaire, several years ago, wrote a work in which our
planet was said to have been visited by beings from Saturn.
Life for our philosopher-novelists seems a riot of fantastic
events! In fact, now that I think of it, I may write a novel
myself. Something in Walpole's new style—for it seems to
be selling well. I believe I know just where to begin. Let us

look more deeply into the fire; most of our candles seem to have guttered out, anyway. And I think my sister has fallen asleep—"

"I have not!" Diana said indignantly.

"Then nudge Mrs. Willett, will you? A story, in the style of Mr. Walpole—just the thing to prepare some of us for a visit to Boar Island tomorrow. As an Anglican, Edmund, you will have no faith in ghosts, but do your best to follow. Now . . ."

Longfellow leaned back and put his feet closer to the dying fire, while he examined the plaster overhead.

"A very long time ago, when gentlemen still controlled the world and ladies knew their place, a nobleman set sail from one of Europe's barbaric regions—a little west of Calais. He wished to see the end of the earth, but found instead a great island populated by people hardly unusual, yet oddly smaller than he. Lesser men, it seemed to him as he tottered about on high heels, his head covered by an immense court wig far grander than anything with which these Lilli-puritans, as they called themselves, were familiar."

When even his poorly schooled sister had groaned at this, Longfellow went on.

"Eventually this great man built a damp castle, in which he installed his family. One ominous day, during which it rained nearly a foot, in a fit of terrible cruelty, he promised his only daughter to a fellow from Philadelphia."

"Against her wishes?" his sister asked.

"Yes, Diana. Then, however, as romance will rise like cream in a bucket—a reference for you, Mrs. Willett— the daughter foolishly disobeyed her father and formed an entirely unsuitable attachment herself. Because the neighborhood lacked any really good families, she decided to trust her fate to a brown bear of the forest—"

"Richard!" his sister cried reprovingly.

"It is only fiction, Diana . . . or perhaps a natural history. Yet as it turned out, this was a visiting coal merchant from Newcastle, and quite a wealthy one, too—which was not quite as bad."

"Though very nearly," Montagu interjected.

"As the case may be. And yet—and yet! A dark and mournful force had come to haunt the castle, nightly walking the corridors, sighing and moaning and leaving wax drippings for which small boys were frequently blamed. Life is indeed full of injustice, Captain Montagu, as you say. But one young fellow, I believe, grew up to find that he was entitled to everything the castle contained— yet only if he married at once, and swore upon his honor never to forget his wedding date, to the end of time. That idea will touch the sensitive reader, I think, and provide you with a reminder, Edmund. Now tell me, is this a new species of romance?"

"It is a new species of something, Richard. And a fine soporific. I am going to bed. Diana?"

"A very good idea—before my brother thinks of something worse, which I know he's quite capable of doing. Thank you, Edmund." She took his offered arm and rose to her feet, glancing as she did so to Charlotte, who still seemed lost in a dream of her own.

Longfellow bent and touched his neighbor's hand, causing her to look up into his eyes.

"Oh," she said, her gaze lingering.

"Ah!" Diana suddenly exclaimed, in a manner so forceful that Edmund stepped back to examine her.

"Are you all right, dear?" he asked with some concern.

"I'm well enough," his wife told him, smiling somewhat smugly, he thought. "Don't worry, Edmund," she then said as they walked toward the door. "It was only a pin, popped out of place. Let us go to bed. I believe Richard and Charlotte will do well enough now, on their own."

Chapter 32

ON FRIDAY MORNING, Charlotte awoke to discover two things that seemed curious. First, she was in Richard Longfellow's bed, a large piece of furniture with no curtains, but plenty of feathers. It was admittedly comfortable, yet she herself was not—until she recalled he'd sent her to bed after a final glass of port, saying that he intended to camp out next to Cicero in the kitchen.

She heard a stirring below, where they must have begun breakfast. Perhaps that was why Orpheus was not with her as she'd expected. Rising, she closed the door the clever dog had found some way of opening, washed quickly in water from a pitcher, and looked carefully at her face in a mirror, to see if she was in any way changed. Then she dressed, and went to join the others.

Next to the east room where she'd slept, she passed one claimed by Diana on all her visits, where she and Edmund were probably still asleep. Next to that was the room given to Moses Reed. Cicero's at the west end had been offered first to Lem, who'd now moved out to accommodate Magdalene Knowles. It was a full house, to be sure.

As she stooped to re-buckle a shoe, Charlotte reminded herself that Longfellow had acted as a gentleman. And yet, she did feel a little disappointed. That was nonsense. They were old friends. And if they were to become something more, it would not happen overnight. At least, it had not happened *last* night.

In the kitchen, Orpheus bounded to her side, his tail flashing.

"Up at last?" Longfellow asked. He continued to toast pieces of bread in a wire basket while Cicero made fresh coffee, nodding his own greeting.

"At least before the sun."

"Barely, for it's after seven. Lem has gone to do the milking, and I've already been on a mission to the inn. I had to beg Elizabeth for breakfast provisions for our little army."

"I'm surprised you woke so early."

"A straw bed on the floor makes sleep something of a challenge."

"I'm sorry to have kept you from your own bed, which was delightful."

"Was it?" he asked with a smile. Cicero made a noise of sorts, and delivered a cup of coffee. Charlotte accepted it gratefully.

Bringing the basket back from the embers, Longfellow set it down, opened it, and gingerly offered her a piece of dark bread with gleaming raisins.

"There's clotted cream," he pointed out, "and preserves. We should fortify ourselves for our jaunt. The weather promises to remain clear, and the road north is open. We need only walk a mile or two from where we'll leave the sleigh. Jonathan has one ready to lend us."

"Who else will go?"

"Reed and Magdalene, and Lem. Edmund feels it would be best for him to avoid any connection with the place. Magdalene can pick up what she needs, and your presence will comfort her, I'm sure. Not that I thought I could leave you behind! Reed and I will search for whatever documents Mrs. Knowles may have kept, to see if there is anything else to shed light on recent events. Lem can hold the horses on the road, to atone for his sins. We'll also be able to take a look at the place the shillings were cast."

"It will do no good," she told him, sipping more of Cicero's brew.

"But I'll have done my duty. And our curiosity will be satisfied."

"Where did Lem find himself last evening, by the way?"

"He shared a bed with Reed. I doubt he rested as well as you. Though I hope he slept more quietly."

"What?"

"We might go into that some other time. But tonight, you'll again have Lem for company, unless? . . ." He watched carefully for her reaction.

"It will be good to have things back to normal." To that, Longfellow said nothing.

At the end of another half hour Lem had returned, and Moses Reed came down to join them. Edmund descended soon after to help himself to a plate heaped with griddle cakes, kept warm by hot bricks in the bread oven. At last, Magdalene and Diana arrived together, having finished more elaborate preparations than the others had attempted. It seemed to Charlotte, who felt her own want of attention, that Diana had made Magdalene more than presentable.

"Let's be off," said Longfellow, after everyone had shared in the coffee, cakes, butter, and syrup. "My thermometer tells me the air is warmer today. And melting won't help the roads."

The party for the island crossed the road, and in a few minutes saw a pair of large horses, one of which Reed had ridden out from Boston, hitched to a wide sleigh. This was furnished with robes and even charcoal foot warmers the ladies might set under their skirts. Longfellow and Lem climbed up onto the front, while Charlotte and Magdalene sat behind, the attorney between them. With a shake of the reins and a warning jingle of bells, they were off.

THE TRIP ACROSS the bridge attracted a number of eyes, for there were quite a few villagers already about their business this Friday morning. But once they'd turned north on the Concord road, there was little traffic on the newly compacted snow, shining like smooth satin.

For a few miles they admired the frosted countryside. Nothing, it seemed, broke up expanses of snow deep enough to bury all stubble from the harvest. Overhead, hawks could be seen wheeling, searching for a meal, while the blue mountains in the distance stood out with new brilliance.

But all too soon, enjoyment changed to anticipation, and concern. There to the right was the island, dark, rocky, robed with coned trees whose branches had already lost much of their new coating. Between island and road lay well over a mile of brush, reeds, and river ice, which would have to be negotiated carefully. Knowing this, Longfellow had brought along a length of rope, to be used in case of emergency.

They passed the house of John and Rachel Dudley, where they saw Winthrop busy with the eternal chore of chopping firewood. At least Rachel and the children would stay warm, thought Charlotte, whether the constable returned home or not. Still no word of his whereabouts had reached the inn, according to Longfellow's information that morning.

They stopped when they reached the point of land nearest to the island. Lem remained where he was, better able to watch their progress from a high seat.

Climbing down, Longfellow helped the ladies who each, he was again glad to see, wore stout footwear. Their capes looked sufficient for the day; he and Reed, he supposed, would need to open their great coats before long, due to the exertion of walking.

This proved true as the sun rose higher, shimmering on the ice around them, forcing them to squint through the crisp air. They reached a few small rocks within the hour, and sat for a few moments to rest. Then they moved on, and with surprising suddenness seemed to be upon the main mass.

Observing a sharp shadow, Longfellow led them around to the south, until they could see sunlight penetrating a thin cleft.

Charlotte realized this must be the place Lem had told her about, which he must have described to Richard Longfellow. She watched as her neighbor strode into unknown territory, with a strong curiosity that took him well ahead of the rest.

Longfellow looked about to see bare vines, and a mixture of trees that seemed to hang above him. Through the cleft was the small meadow he sought. On one side, snow had fallen heavily; on the other a projecting cliff offered protection, so that brown fronds of wood ferns still poked through the new layer of white. Over all, climbing bittersweet with orange berries had drawn several sorts of birds, all chattering busily, ignoring the new arrivals.

They came to a stone building. It was square, with a sloping roof; some of it was newly repaired and mortared haphazardly. A new door, too, had been attached to the old rusted hinges. It was partially open.

Of whatever had once been inside, little remained. Someone had come before them, probably on the day of the old woman's death, for there were no tracks in the snow beyond distinctive hoof marks.

Longfellow imagined a few men had hurried over after hearing of Alex Godwin's death, to clear away all trace of their illegal activity. They found a hearth, but no bellows; a bench built into a wall, but no chair, nor implements to tell how someone might have created the shillings. However, a few candle stubs were still melted onto shelves of flat rock projecting from the wallstones. These were recent; mice had only begun to gnaw them.

"If you ladies are chilled, we might find some fallen wood and make a small fire. No? Fine. It will be a warm walk up to the house. And since there's little here to see, we might as well go."

Leaving the meadow as they'd come, they again took to the ice, and walked further to the east. They eventually reached the wooden landing. Today, only its upright columns were visible, for the rest was covered by several inches of glittering snow. Finding the path to the house, they started to climb.

At the top, though the air was still, they heard little beyond their own labored breathing. Then an insistent crow cawed as it flew far below, over the sunny marsh.

"I see nothing ghostly," Longfellow said aloud, causing Charlotte to wonder what, then, had brought the idea into his mind. "An old manor, sorely in need of attention. We'll give it our own for an hour or so. Shall we go in?"

He opened one of the great doors and stood back to allow Magdalene to enter first, though she hardly seemed anxious to do so. Facing her home of many years, she appeared less than pleased with it.

"You don't have to go in," Charlotte assured her. "If you like, I'll bring out whatever you ask for. But you might want to choose, yourself, what you'd like to take back to the village. To Mr. Longfellow's house. Or to mine."

Magdalene looked to her lawyer, who nodded his approval. Then she disappeared through the pointed portal.

Surprised at the amount of courage she, too, had to summon, Charlotte went next. Nothing had changed. Yet today the house seemed even less inviting than it had been before. She realized it had become a dead thing, a relic with no meaning. No person remained to give it a glow of warmth, a pulse of daily activity. Yet perhaps she did feel *something* here, after all.

"By all that's holy!" Longfellow exclaimed. He'd looked first across strips of dark carpet on the broad stone floor, up the walls to where weapons shone dully. The tapestries beyond had made such an impression that he stood staring, his mouth open. Finally thinking to close it, he turned to regard the others. "I imagined," he said, "that there were furnishings here, of a primitive sort. But this!"

"Are they very old?"

"*Undoubtedly.* Such skills no longer exist. The classical scenes are a delight—but I wonder how he got them here? Wrapped around a mast, possibly. I suspect our lieutenant governor would give his eyeteeth for such decorations! The weapons add a curious touch. It's as if Fisher hoped to keep the medieval past alive, far from where it once belonged. All in all, it's an amazing collection."

"There is more," said Moses Reed shortly.

"Then let's go and see it," said Longfellow. He took a few steps one way, then turned another and began to stride toward the room Charlotte knew would lead to the hearth where she'd taken tea.

Once in the dark antechamber, he went to the windows and grasped a curtain. Turning to Magdalene, he asked for permission to let in the light. She nodded and he pulled, only to find the material falling in a heap at his feet, setting dust flying all around. However, he'd lightened the room so that the paintings on the walls seemed to come to life, and the chairs made of antlers and tusks stood out against the darker wood paneling of the walls.

"German, certainly," said Longfellow, dismissing them for the moment. Turning on his heel, he went on through the far doorway to enter the larger room beyond. Here, he and the lawyer both took hold of sets of curtains, and let them fly. These held, sliding on iron rings over their rods, so that the air remained reasonably clear. The next thing to draw their attention was the portrait of Catherine Knowles, whose blue eyes fell upon the room with an icy sentience that caused Charlotte to shudder.

"I see now why Horace Walpole imagined a portrait might leave its frame, to walk among us," was Longfellow's first comment. "I only wish it could speak, so we might learn exactly what happened to old Mrs. Knowles."

Charlotte was about to reply. She saw movement just above the hearth. She felt her stomach lurch. The mirror had renewed its gamboling. In its dark reaches, between spots of blackened silver and the overlay of rosy glass, she again seemed to see colors swirling.

"Look!" she cried.

"A lovely old thing, to be sure," Longfellow answered. "Venetian glass, I would say. Older than the one in my study, but similar. Do you admire it particularly, Carlotta? I might find one for you one day, during my travels."

"You—you see nothing unusual?"

"How do you mean?" he asked, his nose wrinkling.

"Nothing moving?"

"Well, Reed, behind us." Longfellow turned to make sure. "Yes, looking at a small chest on the table there. Meant to hold letters, do you think, Moses?" he asked, going to investigate further.

"Possibly," the lawyer replied. He found that the jeweled lid needed a key, which none of them had. "Magdalene, do you know where we might find something to open this?"

"She wears the keys at her waist," she answered. Charlotte then recalled putting such a set away, in her desk at home.

Removing a small folding knife from his pocket, the attorney inserted it into the brass lock. He rocked it back and forth, then applied a prying motion, forcing the mechanism to give way. Inside were folded letters; the seal to each had been lifted gently, to keep the wax impression of a signet ring intact.

"It seems," said Reed a few moments later, "that they're all letters of love, addressed to Catherine by a man named Donald."

"A good Gaelic name," Longfellow said, allowing the matter to drop. "Let's move on. I see nothing to help us understand what has occurred here."

Charlotte pulled her eyes from the mirror, and saw that the rug before the hearth was singed and stained with ashes.

"It's a terribly sad place," she said suddenly, looking up. Longfellow stooped to examined her face. "Are you all right, Carlotta? You look as if you've seen a ghost."

Though she had not, she heard once more the sound of faint music—a harpsichord jingling, voices joined in song. Looking to the others, she saw their concern for her, but nothing more.

"I'm quite well," she assured Longfellow, taking her skirt in her hand, making her way quickly to the sunlight by an uncovered window.

"Then let's keep moving," he suggested. "Magdalene, do you know where Mrs. Knowles kept her papers? Those that dealt with legal matters, and finances?"

"In her bed chamber," the woman replied without hesitation. "She has them there."

"Will you lead the way?"

Magdalene turned and looked about the room, as if for the last time. Straightening her back, she walked with new resolve along the way they'd come. In the vast entry she began to climb steps against a gray wall, past windows with colored glass, toward a second floor. The others followed, enjoying a closer view of the niches full of weapons and spiders, and the tapestries above.

At the top, they came upon a long gallery. Clear glass in small, high panes let in enough of the noon sun for them to admire portraits of several gentlemen and their ladies, in two long rows that faced one another. Most seemed very well done.

Charlotte felt especially drawn to one whose etched plate identified its subject as Ermengarde Fischart, wife of Johan. This, then, was Catherine's mother. It strongly resembled the young woman in the larger painting below them. Yet this woman had been more slender, and seemed resigned to an unhappy fate—no use to her a gown enriched with a fortune in pearls, embroidered in thread of gold.

"Here is old Johan himself," said Longfellow, coming to stand a few steps away.

Next to Ermengarde, they saw a man whose face showed great force of will, and a contempt for the world he took no trouble to hide. Something of him, too, had been given to the young woman below, though here was a more sensuous set to the forward lips, and a gleam of appetite in the eyes. He appeared to be dressed for the hunt. Thick leather straps ran over a heavy doublet, and on his head perched a hat made with small curled feathers, which Charlotte suddenly recognized.

"It's the hat Alex wore, isn't it?" she asked. "On his last day."

"In the cellar now, rotting with the rest of him," Longfellow returned cruelly, moving away. His voice, she thought, had sounded like that of someone else—someone frightening. "Carlotta," he ordered. "Come here."

She did as he asked, and felt as if fingers of ice had penetrated her skirts, chilling her legs and thighs. With a shocked gasp she stepped back, and found herself as she'd been before.

"You felt it, then."

"Oh, yes!" she assured him. "How do you explain it?"

"A draft seems improbable, and could hardly account for the strength of the cold," he said in his usual voice. "Actually, I have no idea what has made it."

"None at all?"

"Well, it is a stone house. Perhaps a magnetic force, from embedded ore, has set itself up in a column, with its center here in the building's core. I may come back one day, with tools for measuring the drop in temperature. Or I may not," he finished with more assurance.

"It does seem oppressive, doesn't it?"

"Worse, even, than below."

"You felt something there, too?" she asked in surprise. "Didn't you?"

"You didn't say—"

"And just what, I wonder, did you find so special in an old mirror?"

Finally she told him.

"I see. Or rather, I didn't—but there was an oppressive smell, I supposed, that grew more horrible as one neared the hearth. Possibly from the burning . . . but was that something you noticed?"

"No," she admitted.

"Perhaps we should finish our business. I wouldn't want to keep Lem waiting too long," he added, giving them yet another reason to move on. "Miss Knowles?" he called out. "Will you show us the bed chambers?"

No one asked for more time to examine the considerable number of portraits. Instead they moved off in a close group, each glancing to the left and right as they moved on to a corridor that was smaller, and darker.

Chapter 33

Magdalene's chamber was of a more pleasant nature than Charlotte had imagined. Beside an ample bed sat a chair with bright cushions; others lay along a wide sill that formed a seat by a window. Here, it seemed, the curtains were often shaken, and they appeared to be less dilapidated than those below.

By a small hearth, enough wood was stacked to ensure a comfortable fire, the next time one might be wanted. There were no candles, but it would matter little, for there were no books in evidence. Yet the needlework on the cushions was lovely, shining in the window's light. Had some of the metallic threads of silver been carefully plucked from old garments? Several colors, too, had been used to create patterns depicting ferns and spring flowers, which Magdalene might well have seen in the island meadows during her daily walks. These, thought Charlotte, were especially pleasing, and something of a relief in a house that held little else of softness. While their maker had a troubled mind, her eye, at least, was subtle and imaginative.

Without a word, Magdalene took a few simple robes from a clothespress that stood against a wall. She picked up a silver hairbrush, and two pairs of silk slippers, their worn soles replaced with felt. A chest of drawers held undergarments, and then she opened a box whose lid had been inlaid with nacre, to form a white rose. From this she carefully removed an infant's shift. It, too, had been beautifully embroidered. Magdalene held it up, allowing it to be admired. Her own eyes seemed to caress the garment—or perhaps she recalled the child who'd worn it. She then put it back into its special box, which she added to the small pile on the bed.

Meanwhile, sounds came from a larger room at the end of the hall, where Longfellow and Moses Reed had found work of their own.

"I have seen rats," said Longfellow, "make tidier nests."

"She could have noticed little," Reed reminded him as he lifted a reeking shawl, thrown over the remains of a meal left on remarkably fine china. All about them were bits and pieces of a life declining—not neatly, as a mantel clock that slowed, but stumbling into darkness.

"She had a nose, after all," Longfellow retorted, wondering at his harshness. *What had gotten into him?* He hadn't felt any great distaste for the old woman, to whom he'd never even spoken! But something now seemed to disgust him in the very air—

"Here!" cried the lawyer, pulling a miniature chest from beneath the bed. "This looks as if it might hold correspondence." Disdaining the soiled quilt on top of a sagging mattress, Reed lifted the chest to a dressing table, shoving back odds and ends already there. He then began to open its many small compartments.

Meanwhile, Longfellow went to look out into the hall, wondering if he'd really heard distant footsteps, as he'd supposed.

When the attorney had gone through every drawer, he drew together a pile of papers which included copies of both wills. Other than that, they were mainly lists and receipts from chandlers and suppliers of food, wine, and cloth, sent from Salem and Kittery, Philadelphia—even London. A few were of great age; none had been marked paid.

"That would seem to be that," said Reed.

"Then I propose we do a little more exploring below. Not for long, as Magdalene, at least, may wish to go."

"You don't think Mrs. Willett—?"

"Her curiosity is something of a local legend," Longfellow informed the lawyer. "She would stay, I think, to view the place from top to bottom, if we gave her the chance. Although today, I wonder—"

"Another day," said Reed, "when there is time. For now, another twenty minutes or so?

"I, for one, will be waiting at the front door."

With that, Longfellow went out of the room and down the gallery, leaving the lawyer to go wherever his own feet might take him.

MOSES REED WENT first to inform the ladies that they would all be leaving shortly. Charlotte then felt a heightened desire to explore. She left Magdalene with her attorney and walked back along the corridor, looking into each room.

There was little to see. Furnishings more useful than beautiful had been provided for visitors, although one or two chambers did have something more. In these, decorative hangings were flanked by tall stands that might take several candles. Carpets, too, had been provided; the others made do with bare wood floors.

When she had seen enough of the west wing, Charlotte hurried back through the picture gallery, avoiding the mysterious spot of cold. In another minute she stood below and frowned, unsure of where to go next. The second floor of the east wing could be reached only by another set of stone steps. Somehow it seemed wiser to remain where she was, or to descend. She chose the second option when she noticed another doorway, and a smaller flight of steps leading down. She'd wondered earlier about the kitchen, and decided to see it for herself.

The lower level was lit by high windows that faced the south. It contained a cavernous room with a gigantic hearth, complete with a spit large enough for roasting an entire boar, as well as several side ovens for baking. Rusting utensils hung about the walls, but seemed usual enough. She saw a set of pipes coming down from the ceiling; they probably supplied water from a rooftop cistern, so that at least some water need not have been carried up from the marsh. This reminded her that the house was no more than a half century old, though its appearance, especially above, suggested great age. It was almost as if she were behind the scenes of a theater, she thought, something she'd heard Longfellow describe on occasion, from his travels.

Further exploration showed her a huge pantry, nearly empty. At its end stood one more door. Upon opening this she felt a draft, and saw that she stood at the top of yet another set of stone steps. Below, there were no windows. Could it be a dungeon, used for torture by a man obsessed with his tiny island? Had he been like the duke in Horace Walpole's story, caring little for the lives of others, while he sought his own pleasures? She shuddered to think of it. And yet she felt herself wanting to learn more . . . if only to be sure.

Someone had conveniently left both a candle and a tinder box on a table near the door. She lit the candle, supposing its presence indicated the lower room was still used for something; in the kitchen itself she'd seen no such amenities. That thought was strange enough to cause her to put a foot onto a stone step, and prepare to follow the rest down into the darkness.

She stopped when she heard a sigh from below. Changing to a moan, it caused the hairs on her arms to rise. Could there be someone there in pain—even in chains? If so, should she go and see? Or should she retreat to safety, while she still had the chance? As she tried to decide, she felt a light hand settle onto her shoulder.

She knew without turning that she would see no one there. And she'd recognized the familiar scent of horehound, a favorite remedy of Aaron's when he'd been alive. For several months, she'd missed her husband's lingering presence. Now, it seemed, he had returned.

Again, the moan came from below.

The hand rested quietly. Aaron's memory was still a comfort. When had she truly realized he was no longer a part of her life—or any other she knew? She'd loved her husband deeply, yet this was less than a shadow. And she wondered now what it cost him, to come back to her. Wrenching a last hope from her heart, she confronted whatever it was that remained.

"Would you keep me from finding more?" she asked gently. "Would you stay, when you need not?"

Finally, it was done. She felt his presence diminish, as if it slipped silently away. In a few moments, he was gone altogether.

Her heart was in her throat, and it suddenly occurred to her that Aaron might have come with a warning. The candle she held continued to flicker; the moaning went on. With a breath, she took back her life, and walked down into the void.

As she descended she felt the loss, too, of what little warmth the windows gave the kitchen above. A new coldness enveloped her, though it was less than the frigid spot in the gallery above. A wind seemed to blow—with no windows to give it entry.

When the stone steps ended she smelled earth beneath her feet, and then the bitter scent of snow. But she had come upon nothing dire, nothing uncanny. Instead her candle showed her a room full of old furniture. Next to a jumble of chairs in need of repair stood a stack of several rods, once used for fishing expeditions—wine casks missing staves or bands served as supports for a pair of long ladders—tackle for horses lay strewn in a corner, though where animals had been kept on the island, she could not guess.

She found herself drawn to an ornately carved headboard, taller than she was. It seemed to have been the back of a box bed. And where it leaned against a wall, a new moan seemed to have begun. Long and deep, this soon suggested a body in the throes of intense passion.

But there was no one there! She stared at ornate carvings of stag and doe, garlands of leaves and acorns, all cut into joined planks of heavy oak. Her candle flickered violently, and she felt a fresh draft. Something, it appeared, was behind all of this—possibly behind the headboard itself?

She bent down to set the candle on the floor. Then she stood to lean against the tall object before her. The whole bed would have been heavy enough, she supposed, to collapse the floor of a simple cottage. It might even have been the last resting place of old John Fisher. By squirming, she was able to see a little behind the wood, where a passage of some sort began. That, at least, explained the moaning of the wind. At its end, she glimpsed a faint light.

As she had no hope of lifting the headboard, she decided to try to slide it enough so that she might slip behind. Shifting her position, she lowered her head and applied a shoulder to the wood. In another moment she felt it give, and then it began to move across the hard-packed floor. Elated by her success, and curious to see where the passage might lead, she renewed her effort.

Then it seemed as though she'd been plunged into a painful night, under a sky full of swirling stars. The ground came to meet her with a crash, and she lay for a moment in a sort of twilight. Did she again hear music? Or was it only a roar of blood in her ears? Laughter seemed to sound as she continued to sink into a deep well. On its sides were faces, illuminated, laughing, passing by as the stars above receded. And there was a sound like the whirling of skirts, lulling her to sleep.

Beside her still form, the candle danced. Something brown scurried past her skirts, frightened from its burrow. But Charlotte was unaware of anything that might have harmed her further.

Some time later, she begin to revive. Someone called

out to her from far away. The familiar voice drew nearer. Before long it came clearly.

"Mrs. Willett? Mrs. Willett!"

"Here!" she called back, but her voice sounded no more than a whisper. She stretched her neck to view the stairs. Soon a pair of legs strode toward her.

"*Oh God—Charlotte?*" His exclamation was rather strange, she thought, and it seemed that a part of his voice, too, was trapped in his throat. Could something have happened?

Richard Longfellow swooped to enfold her in his strong arms, protecting her at first, then settling his cheek against her own. She heard him murmur thanks as he cradled her, felt his warm breath, and saw a most unusual fear in his lovely hazel eyes. She recalled her earlier hesitancy on the steps, when she'd felt another hand on her shoulder. This touch felt far more urgent, and wonderfully real.

While an arm continued to support her, a hand began to run searchingly about her face and into her gathered hair, where its fingers prodded gently. She felt a sharp pain and cringed, giving a startled cry as she fully recovered her senses.

"I'm sorry, Carlotta," he responded, his attention drawn to a growing bump that had caused her discomfort. "It seems there's no break in the skin, and no blood. By the sound of the crash, I imagined you'd found a way to bring the entire house down around you. What happened? And how did you nearly manage to crack your skull?"

"I'm not sure," she said, feeling the bump herself, amazed by its size. "I was only trying to move the headboard—"

She looked to see that it had fallen to the floor; now it lay in several pieces. Pale tongues that had held the joints together were exposed.

"The thing must have been dried and warped, waiting to spring apart when you touched it," Longfellow decided.

And yet she'd barely moved it, she recalled, while trying to see into the hidden passage—

Soon Longfellow, too, arched his neck to stare at what she'd uncovered. A haze of light still beckoned from beyond, while an eddy brought air from the outside.

"You saw no one else here?" he asked suddenly.

"My head was down," she admitted. "But I . . . I don't think so."

"I'm glad it was no worse. You gave me the devil of a fright. Do you suppose you can stand, Carlotta? I'll support you. Or I'll carry you, if you like."

Her attempt to rise gave her a new thrill of pain, but it passed quickly. She tried putting one foot in front of the other, testing her weight. It seemed nothing else had been damaged.

"I'll recover soon. But where do you suppose this leads?"

"It looks to be no more than a few yards long. Shall we see?"

Longfellow picked up her candle and shielded it carefully, for they had no other. Holding her arm, he began to walk slowly into the mouth of the tunnel. In a few feet, it narrowed. It seemed they would have to walk one behind the other.

"Can you manage alone?" he asked.

"Yes. No one's been here before us; the floor is sandy, but there are no footprints."

"It would seem so. This slight rippling must have been caused by the wind."

They walked on, along the walls of a cleft filled from above by roots that clutched at fallen stone, while they fed on sifting soil. At the tunnel's end they met a high boulder. Rounding this, they found themselves on an airy platform, now in cold shadow. Both looked down. Far below were snow and dark branches the wind had freed.

Looking above, they discovered a slope that could be climbed with no great difficulty. There were even clumps of vegetation one might use for hand holds. But a more striking sight was a little to the right. There, Magdalene Knowles stood at the edge of a precipice. Charlotte knew this to be at the end of a small yard, just beyond the room with the tall portrait, and the mirror.

"See, here," said Longfellow, drawing her attention to a spot a few feet above them. A branch had been torn from a stunted pine rooted among the rocks. Resin, still fresh, had oozed from the white wound. "It's been torn away, and could have helped someone to climb down, to enter the tunnel the other day," Longfellow said with a frown. "It might also have been used as a broom, I suppose, to cover his steps as he left."

Charlotte peered back at Magdalene—and saw that Moses Reed had come for her. He held out a hand and took a step back, inviting her toward the house.

"Hey there, Reed!" Longfellow called out. The lawyer gave a start. Advancing to look over the cliff's edge, he saw the movement of a waving arm.

"Are you nearly ready?" the lawyer called down. "I believe we really should go."

"We'll meet on the front path."

"So," Longfellow mused as they walked back through

the great kitchen, "someone *may* have come into the house unnoticed, while Lem worked on the opposite side."

Charlotte nodded, keeping a new worry to herself. At the moment, she had little wish to pursue anything further—at least until they were all away from the island, and safe at home.

Chapter 34

IN THE MORNING, Charlotte lay again in her own bed, watching a dagger of ice slowly drip its brief life away.

Touching the receding egg at the back of her head, she reconsidered her visit to Boar Island. She'd seen places where Ned and Magdalene spent many hours. She hoped some of them had been happy. What the future held for each might be less so.

Climbing down from the cheerless house on top of its perilous crag, she'd imagined Magdalene leaving earlier—then circling back, entering through the underground passage, and doing what she wished to Catherine Knowles. Ned, too, might have done such a thing, if he'd discovered the passage . . . or if Magdalene had told him of it. Each possibly had a motive. Yet what had happened need not have been planned, after all. What if one of them had only gone to persuade Catherine to change her mind? But if that was so . . . why not go in through the front door?

Outside the window, a cardinal seemed to strike a

pose on a nearby branch, pulling her thoughts back to something else she'd seen. For yesterday, she'd finally met one of the island's fabled inhabitants.

They'd nearly reached the bottom of the trail when they heard a snort. Then they saw him, lit by the low sun, standing upon a flat rock. The boar was a yard high at the shoulders, and appeared neither cruel nor demonic, as she'd guessed it would. He did have impressive tusks, but they seemed given for protection. Most creatures, after all, had enemies. Though his body was substantial, he had small legs and hoofs. Particularly surprising were large ears, soft and supple, standing in peaks. His tiny eyes stared, as if they did him little good, but his nose twitched busily while he considered their unknown scent.

It suddenly seemed a shame this was an animal most often encountered as a head on a platter, or a body turning over a slow fire. Charlotte decided that in future she would imagine these creatures doing no more than living their own simple lives, away from harm.

She had been shocked to see Moses Reed reach into his great coat to one below, and pull out a pistol. This he cocked, and it seemed he aimed to shoot. But the slight click of the mechanism had been enough to alert the animal above them. He turned abruptly, showed them a tufted tail, and leaped from the ledge to the brush below. They heard him crash about a while longer, as he scrambled away.

Slowly Reed lowered the weapon, to find Longfellow regarding him. Magdalene had backed away, her eyes grave. She must have known what firearms could do, Charlotte imagined, from the time she'd lived with hunters. But according to Hannah, the attorney beside her was no stranger to the ways of the forest—and, presumably, of wild boars.

"No need, I think," said Longfellow. "He's no threat to us now."

Reed assented, uncocked the pistol, and put it back into his clothing. "Better safe . . ." he remarked.

"Do you often use that thing?" Longfellow asked.

"No. But I might, sir. Some would rob a man who travels regularly, as a lawyer must. In fact a circuit judge suggested to me the idea of carrying one, as he does."

"Yes, of course," Longfellow replied. But Charlotte wondered if his look implied a greater concern. Had Reed feared for his safety when he came to Bracebridge? Or onto the island? Did he perhaps think someone else might join them there, uninvited?

After their return to the village, the rest of the afternoon had given Charlotte a chance to stay home alone, while Lem visited Hannah and Martha, telling them the news. With Orpheus at her side, she'd gone into the blue study and built a fire.

What, she'd wondered, had their visit proved, after all? That there were still some things that could hardly be considered natural, even by Science? She had not told Longfellow of her initial sensation that something was in the house with them, something other than the comforting spirit she'd encountered. But what did it matter? She'd seen the tunnel, and its newly brushed floor. Had someone used it on the day of Catherine's death? And if so, had that same person killed Alex Godwin?

There was yet another possibility to consider. Yesterday, she'd felt that Aaron had given her a friendly warning at the top of the cellar stairs. But had she been given another, far less friendly, below? Again she touched her head, glad that her pinned hair had cushioned what could have been intended as a deadly blow. Had Moses Reed been right, after all? Was there cause to worry, still?

Charlotte continued to watch the icicle beyond the window, realizing that today many other questions, at least, might be answered. For it was Saturday, and Christian Rowe had invited the village to the meeting house, to discuss what was known of the events that took place on the day of the ice harvest.

Since she herself had earlier made certain suggestions to Hannah, and because wives had ways of finding things out, she expected that some progress had already been made. All in all, she decided as she rose to wash and dress, it promised to be a most interesting day.

THE MINISTER'S MEETING had been set to begin at eleven. But by ten-thirty, the space between the long, white-washed walls of the meeting house, lit by several plain and tall windows, had begun to fill. Certain of the boxes in the front waited for tenants who paid extra for them each year. Behind these, villagers with smaller savings, or a lesser sense of responsibility, sat in knots on pews, and on chairs added to the side aisles. Men and women together were strangely quiet, while groups of a single sex talked quickly, if softly, raising their eyes to see who else might join them. In a rear loft, youths and maidens mingled with more animation, occasionally admonishing younger children for complaining.

Thus far, thought Charlotte, it was what she'd expected. With Lem at her side, she'd come in before those of Longfellow's household. She was glad they'd arrived early, for as she'd guessed, the village saw no reason to wait for the appointed hour to discuss what had happened to Godwin, where the base shillings had come from, and who might be to blame for either, or both.

As she and Lem sat down one voice rose above all others, catching the attention of the room.

"Where is John Dudley?" Sarah Proctor asked loudly, causing a good many who nodded and grumbled to look about.

"He's not here," called one of her neighbors. "He's not been seen in the village since yesterday morning! His family's not here, either. Maybe they felt it best to stay away—"

"Dudley's whereabouts are known to some of us," a farmer retorted. Today, like several others, he wore his grandfather's long white wig for warmth, and perhaps in honor of the special occasion. "Even if he didn't see fit to inform the women!" he finished from under his fall of curls.

"Where is he, then?" Mrs. Proctor demanded.

"Well, Sarah, it happens he went off to Worcester! *Somebody* had to tell Godwin's family what happened to him. And he is, after all, the constable. Said he'd be staying at the Three Ravens, if you care to go after him—looking for the young man's murderer!"

"He'll be back, as soon as Thankful Marlowe decides he's drunk more than the selectmen will likely pay for," predicted a wise man.

"Here comes Mr. Rowe," Lem told Charlotte, for he'd been turned about in his seat, waiting for Hannah's family to arrive. Christian Rowe indeed hurried to the front of the room, to the stand where he usually delivered his sermons.

"*We must have order*," he insisted loudly. "Let us wait until the hour. There's no need for hurry, with the boy dead some days—"

"Fine," said a large woman from under a pink quilted

bonnet, "but what about these shillings? And what about our housewares?"

"I've heard Ned Bigelow was the one," called another, over an infant's wail.

"But he never decided to do it on his own," insisted the first. "No, he had to be led by someone!"

"It will be the same men who've left maids lying down in the meadow sweet, I suspect, after they've had what they were after," said Mrs. Proctor dourly.

"Or those who keep secrets from wives, and their poor mothers—" Jemima Hurd added.

"And who make everything we own liable to seizure, under the King's law!" cried Esther Pennywort. This last observation was a truly frightening one, and it started fiercer rumbling.

"Ladies, ladies!" the minister called bravely, holding up his hands. "There has been, I agree, a terrible breach of trust—one committed against myself as much as any other! Yet a charge of murder is even more worthy of our careful—"

"But what if Godwin was killed because of these shillings?" Sarah Proctor interrupted. "What if he was about to tell what he knew? He did threaten Lem Wainwright with something, and said he would tell Mr. Longfellow what some were up to—though why he supposed any of the selectmen would care is a mystery."

Charlotte saw Lem squirm in his place, and look to the minister to defend him.

"If," said Rowe, "there is blame—and I am sure there is!—then, we must ask ourselves who had the most to lose by the discovery of this moneymaking scheme. Can that be young Wainwright, when so many older men are obviously involved?" He gave an oily smile in Charlotte's direction, before returning to the fray. "And, we must ask ourselves this: what might happen if Crown officials, rather than our own, begin to ask the questions here? As we all know, Boston cares little enough for *us* . . ."

"You should be asking, as we've asked ourselves, who else *could* have killed Alex Godwin that afternoon," said Sarah Proctor. A hush fell.

"Constable Dudley," Dick Craft replied, representing the thoughts of the Blue Boar, "claims it may well have been some stranger off the road, coming by to look for trouble."

"John Dudley!" cried a woman who lived on the north road, and felt she knew her neighbor. "The sot could barely see his feet that afternoon. And he never picked the boy up and took him into those trees. He probably pissed in his own boot that day, to avoid lifting so much as a finger—"

Charlotte blushed and looked away, glad that Rachel Dudley and her children had not come, after all.

"But if some of you men," said Rowe uneasily, "can give us ideas as to who was in a position to do such a thing—?"

"There is no need, sir," said Emily Bowers, rising from a collection of her own nodding supporters. "The women of the village have already counted heads, and we can't see that any of our own men would have been able to get away with such a thing, even if they had good enough reason. It may be, for once, that John Dudley is right."

"Except for the boy," Sarah Proctor intoned. "Ned Bigelow has neither wife nor mother to look after him, or to wonder where he's got to. Jonah surely can't follow him far! And he may have wished to stop Alex from talking about what we now know of the shillings—he may even know more about other goings-on, up there on that island . . ."

This new suggestion, reminding them of the sad fate of Catherine Knowles, quieted the crowd.

"Well, where is he, then?" asked Rowe. "And where is Jonah? It is still a little early—but some of you men, go and fetch them; we'll ask for their explanation."

"There's no need for us to pull Ned into this," Phineas Wise objected. "We all know the lad, and he's got as good a heart as any man here."

"Better that than let someone else examine him, Phineas," came an answer from near the back doors.

"How do you mean?"

"I mean," said Samuel Sloan, though Hannah tried to pull him toward their usual seats, "that it would be a shame, as Reverend Rowe says, if the sheriff in Cambridge got the idea to come here and listen to what's being said about murder, and then began to ask about the other thing. Still, he'll find no proof of that, I think."

"No proof?" objected Reverend Rowe. "No proof! *We all know*—"

"You may think you know, Reverend. But where is this mold? And is there a forge on the island? I wouldn't be surprised if there was nothing there at all."

"There isn't," said Richard Longfellow as he walked briskly up the center aisle. "I was there yesterday and saw no sign of recent activity, though I was told where to look. But there still remain the coins, gentlemen. And the body."

Again somber tones grew among them, until a further cry arose.

"I say bring back old Bigelow and his grandson. Let's get this over with, *now!*"

With the meeting house nearly full, it seemed most of the town agreed. A handful of men then rose and went out together, satisfied that they would miss little, while the rest waited in suspense for their return.

Chapter 35

Longfellow gave Lem and Charlotte a look, but went on to sit alone in his box at the front of the meeting house, apparently lost in thought.

Charlotte heard a rustling, and saw that someone else had come to sit beside her. For years Moses Reed had been a stranger to village meetings. Now, he asked if he might join her.

Yet today she hardly recognized the lawyer—for he had shaved off his full beard! His face, quite bare, seemed terribly pale. She even wondered if he might not feel the weight of some new concern; his bearing, too, appeared altered. She was relieved when he leaned before her and told Lem calmly that he mustn't worry about what happened next, for it would give proof of his innocence.

"What is it, Mr. Reed?" she asked. He gave a small groan for an answer. "I'm very sorry," he told her at last, "that what I have feared most, what I fervently hoped would *not* be true, has proven itself to be so. They won't find Ned Bigelow. It was he who took Godwin's life—he has now admitted it to me."

"Ned? To you? Why?"

"Because I finally brought myself to tell him a secret of my own . . . one I'm hardly proud to have kept, all these years."

Her eyes played over the lawyer's face, trying to read something of his tortured thoughts. Then his pained smile confirmed a suspicion that had come to her. Without the beard, there was something about the lips and chin, something about the bones of his cheeks, that reminded her of another . . .

"I've already told Richard Longfellow," he said. "I discussed it with Magdalene—and then, I went and told my son the truth."

The resemblance, when one knew what to look for, was very clear. The eyes alone were different. They did not dance.

"I promised him I would help, when he swore it was done in the heat of the moment, and that he deeply regretted his action. Still, there is no going back."

"No," she said, swiftly calculating the consequences of what she'd heard. "Magdalene will suffer for this as well. But then, you and she—?"

"Were lovers, yes, many years ago. I was called to the island not as a guest, but as a young man who knew the local woods, and could lead hunters to the boars' lairs, or drive the creatures toward their waiting weapons. Not a pleasant job, but one with a certain amount of excitement to it. That is how I met Magdalene, for even then she walked alone about the island. Her love of nature, her sweet wildness—these things drew us together. And in the end . . ."

"When you learned she carried your child—?"

"I have never done a harder thing, Mrs. Willett, I swear to you. Yet I had to admit I'd wronged not only Magdalene but my benefactors. John Fisher had been good to me, had taken me from a poor situation in life, and paid me well. When he died, his daughter wished to be sure she had someone who would look after her interests. It was she who sent me to Boston, away from Magdalene and the boy, to begin my study of the law. For that, at least, I have always been grateful. Had Magdalene and I married against John Fisher's wishes, or even later, against Catherine's, Magdalene would surely have been given nothing. Her family in Philadelphia, too, would have shunned her, I was convinced. And for long years, I could have given her little more."

"Ned knew of this?"

"Exactly when he learned he was her son, I'm not sure. And I don't wish to know! No more than I want to believe Catherine Knowles was pushed, as she claimed."

Had Reed learned the truth about that, too? Charlotte could not bring herself to ask him more. One day, perhaps. But not this one.

He suggested again that they keep to themselves what Mrs. Knowles had insisted on her deathbed. Would it really make a difference? If it came to a trial, he assured her, an unclear mind would provide some defense, especially after years of torment.

Charlotte decided she would need to think further, before she could decide for herself whether to keep silent about Catherine's death. Ned, however, was no longer among them. In his case, at least, vengeance might be left to the Lord.

"And Jonah Bigelow?" she asked finally.

"Not even he knew for sure that I was the father. I sent him small yearly sums in Catherine's name, to help him raise the boy. That's another reason I came back to Bracebridge—to see if I might do more for them both, with Ned approaching manhood. Though I was ashamed to let him know why. As it turned out, I gave the boy a note good for more than enough to travel far to the south, where he said he'd long hoped to go. And I promised I would send more, if he would only write to me."

"What will happen to Magdalene?"

"She has no wish to go back to Philadelphia, and has asked me to continue to manage her small trust. And yet, Mrs. Willett, I *would do a great deal more*," he said, his voice breaking. "I would gladly marry her, if she would accept me. My feelings on seeing her again were rekindled; in my eyes, she has hardly changed. But it seems she no longer feels she's worthy of love. It is Catherine's damnable influence, I'm sure! One day, perhaps, I may be able to convince Magdalene of the truth . . ."

A clamor rose outside. The men who had left returned, four of them carrying Jonah Bigelow in the chair Charlotte had seen at the old man's fireside. Its occupant was much changed. Jonah seemed terrified—for himself, perhaps, and doubtless for his grandson.

"Ned's not there," reported one of the farmers, "nor any of his things, that we can tell. Jonah says he doesn't know where the boy's got to, but that he couldn't have done murder. Yet it looks as though Ned feared we'd find out, and ran away."

"What happened, Jonah?" asked Richard Longfellow, who had risen immediately. He stood watching as more misery etched itself into a face raised to accept further punishment.

"I don't know, and that's the truth, sir!" Jonah cried. He bent as one deep cough followed another. It took some time for them to cease.

"Ned carried me out earlier, to sit with the cobbler," Jonah began again. "As I do on a Saturday morning. Amos takes his cart out later, and sees me home. But this time when I returned, Ned wasn't waiting—nor were some of the things that should have been in the cupboard, I admit . . ."

Watching this poor soul about to break into tears, Charlotte felt her heart touched by his tragedy, truly that of an entire family. "What is it, Mr. Reed?" she then asked, for she had seen the attorney's face darken.

"I can give no sympathy to a man with so much to answer for! He might have seen Ned properly apprenticed, and learning a trade, instead of involved in this business on the island! How I wish it were Jonah, instead, who—" His voice sank dramatically. "And yet I know it must be my own fault, too—my own burden. For I came back too late, far too late—"

His head now in his hands, Moses Reed wept.

Longfellow came to them at that point, and sat down. "He told you?"

"Yes," Charlotte said simply. He reached out and clasped her hands.

"I know, Carlotta. A terrible waste. At least we've formed a plan to make the rest something less of a problem. Edmund and I have—"

Before Longfellow could go on, a hush fell over the house. There in the doorway stood Captain Montagu, his wife on his arm. Though not dressed in their Boston best, both wore austere expressions that might have accompanied such finery, while they accepted the stares of those who watched as their due. Not a man or woman dared to speak; all waited while the couple looked over the house, seeming to see no one. The silence appeared to satisfy them, proving their authority if it did not exactly give welcome.

They walked slowly to the front where Christian Rowe waited, his hands folded as if in prayer. Upon reaching him, Edmund and Diana turned to face the village. Now they examined certain faces before them, willing guilty eyes to look away. Some admitted later that while the Montagus could be warm enough when they chose, they were no doubt made of sterner stuff than most in the small world of Bracebridge.

"I heard, sir," the captain said to the minister hovering at his side, "that you would hold a meeting today, to look into the death of Alexander Godwin."

"That is what we are about, sir, yes," said Rowe.

"But that is not all you're discussing today, is it, Mr. Rowe?"

"You may hear accusations, Captain, concerning a certain scheme. They are unproven," Christian Rowe answered carefully.

"Men too often accuse one another, it seems, without proper proof. That is how our courts of law are always full, yet accomplish little. When, indeed, they are allowed to open at all."

The captain paused for whispers that came in response to this hopeful sign. Did he agree with them, after all, that the Crown had been unfair?

"You are aware, I believe, that my wife and I have come to Bracebridge to visit her brother?" he continued.

"Yes, sir," said Rowe.

"And that I have *not* come on the King's business?"

"Why, yes, sir. That is what I would say, if asked."

"However, were I to decide to *make* what I begin to see here the King's business—"

Montagu gave another look about the room. He could almost hear new fears rising over the illegal business still unmentioned. It was enough, he decided. "Were I to see the result of criminal activity about me, I would be sorry, sir. For then, it would be my duty *to make someone suffer for it*. I hope—I sincerely hope—that this will not be necessary."

The captain reached into a pocket of his waistcoat and pulled out a silver shilling. If the room had been quiet before, it now seemed full of dead men. No one dared to breath as he flipped the coin into the air, sending it to Richard Longfellow. The move was anticipated, the shilling handily caught.

"Do as I do," said Edmund Montagu, "and you'll have nothing to fear. At least for now." With that he looked to his wife. Diana smiled back serenely.

It seemed to Charlotte that Diana played a role she had been born to, standing at the arm of a powerful husband, who was also blessed with good sense and understanding. If he could be masterful, so might she; together they could regard a painful past, an uncertain future. This joining, and not the lonely role of Nemesis, would be Diana's strength. Charlotte only hoped that in future her friend would trust a sympathetic husband, and would not run from him again.

The captain led his lady out amidst the hushed crowd, and Charlotte wondered what sort of finale he and her neighbor had decided on. She saw Longfellow stand and hold the shilling high for all to see.

"For the good of my conscience, and quite possibly my soul," he told the assembly, "I am going to take this symbol of corruption from our place of worship. For the sake of your own, I would suggest that every man here do the same. What has lately occurred in Bracebridge has brought discord among us; worse, it has led to a loss of life, and the ruin of happiness."

No one seemed to disagree.

"Ned Bigelow is gone," he continued. "Whatever else he may have done, he took good care of his grandfather, who now has no one to help him face his final years. This shilling will be the first contribution to a charitable fund for Jonah's benefit. I know a silversmith in Boston who will melt down what I bring him, without question, and make it pure again. I will be glad if others follow my example. Or you may leave your shillings, later, outside my door; I will set out a basket. And I would advise the women here to check carefully at home, to see if they have lately come upon coins a little too heavy, a little too soft, with bright indentations around their edges. *These must circulate no longer!*"

"But if we give them all to you, some of us may starve!" cried a wary voice from the crowd.

"Starve? I think not. No one has ventured a great deal, after all. And there will be a surprising amount in the village poor fund soon, for any who are truly in need. A good exchange, I think, for keeping your ears, gentlemen, as well as your goods, and your reputations—dubious though some of the latter are. You have elected me, *and I will* keep the peace here!"

Longfellow began to walk through the throng, hearing the others rise to follow him down the aisle, through the entry, and out the door. He went to one side of the snowy path they'd earlier trampled. There he dropped the shilling, which made a final shining statement as it caught the sun.

The selectman walked a few feet further and turned to face the road, keeping his back to the rest.

A thaw continued to warm the air, but he knew it

would be months before the roads would be entirely clear. The village would see other freezes and dangerous ice; further storms would force them to depend on one another, as they scrambled to dig their way out. That was the way of winter—it was the way of life.

Sometimes, little things could happen to make one glad to be a part of it all. Something like that was happening behind him now, he suspected, for he heard the pleasing sound of silver on silver, more or less, as the pile of coins mounted. Many of his neighbors turned and passed before him, starting down the road with furtive nods, bolder bows, even tips of their hats, set back atop their ridiculous, rustic wigs.

What they had done had been audacious, brazen, shameless—and it proved they had no love for overweening authority. In the end, what he'd uncovered made Longfellow a little proud of living among these unruly and resourceful villagers, after all.

Chapter 36

THE BRIEF WINTER day was done. In Richard Longfellow's study, the ormolu clock beneath the Venetian mirror struck the hour of five.

Charlotte glanced quickly to the glass. This was something he had observed her to do for several days, when she supposed no one saw. Had she grown vain? Or did she consult the thing to see if someone crept up unexpectedly?

At least, most of what had threatened the village lately was now put to rest or to flight, thought Longfellow. Once again a villain—this time an unfortunate one, whose loss would be regretted—had left them. He'd rarely thought of Ned Bigelow before. Perhaps, he told himself, he should take time to become better acquainted with the other village lads, who seemed to grow like stalks of corn. At least he might try.

At the moment, though, he planned to enjoy the end to this latest flurry of unwanted activity. It would be a pleasure to become reacquainted with the old fellow who spent cold nights in the kitchen, tending his creaking joints before the fire, replenishing his mind with reading. At the moment, Cicero was in the taproom across the way learning the news from Boston, where each of them had friends. At his return, Longfellow would hear whatever news he'd discovered, hidden in his favorite nook behind the great hearth.

For a while, at least, they would be glad to lose their visitors and return to an occasional game of chess or backgammon, and the revolving arguments manufactured on a regular basis to learn all sides of questions both considered worthy of study.

"Diana and Edmund will leave soon," said Charlotte, thinking of the future as well.

"Yes—and be pleased to start over in their own humble establishment."

"Are they above?"

"They went to the inn with Cicero. To be served, as you know, is, to Diana, one of the sweeter pleasures."

"I've been left as well. Lem went out to see Mattie."

"I predict you'll often lose his company as the weather improves. And then, one day . . ."

"Orpheus and I may easily enjoy ourselves, as long as we can walk, and visit someone who will throw us a bone from time to time."

"Then we're all pleased by our prospects," he said, smiling.

"And yet . . ."

"Qualms, Carlotta?"

"Richard, do you think Magdalene will go back to Boston with Moses Reed?"

"He told me he would discuss the question with her today; that is what I imagine they're doing upstairs. She can hardly return to the island by herself. And since it will go, now, to the Knowles family, it might soon be sold. I wonder if they will auction or keep the furnishings?"

"She could live here with Jonah. Each of them will need someone. And as they both care for Ned . . ."

"You forget Catherine's death hasn't entirely been explained. He might not have her, if he suspects . . ."

"You and Reed did discuss the manner of Catherine's death?"

"And decided to say no more. We can't *prove* what she claimed was anything but a dying woman's imagination."

"Magdalene will suffer greatly, when she's told her son has been forced to leave her."

"She may also warm to Reed—even marry and bear him another son, I suppose."

"Do you think so?" Charlotte doubted it. During the night of storm, soon after she'd found Moses Reed once more, Magdalene had said she would not see her lost love again. It was almost as if she could barely recall the man who'd stood before her, though for years she'd pined for him. But was that really true?

"Richard," she said suddenly, "suppose Magdalene realized, long ago—"

Before she was able to voice her new thought, they heard a tapping at the window. A youthful face reflected their candlelight—they were doubly surprised to see that it belonged to Ned Bigelow.

Longfellow leaped to his feet and went out into the hall, then through the small dining room to a door leading to the piazza. He returned in a few moments with the young man they'd supposed was far away.

"I couldn't leave my grandfather alone, sir, after all,"

Ned began. "His illness, you see, has worsened, and he depends on me. I don't care what I have to pay for the shillings. I planned to find a ship at Providence, but once I got half way to Framingham, I decided I'd better turn around and come home. I'll stay—though Mr. Reed told me I shouldn't."

"The shillings?" Longfellow asked, amazed. "What about the murder of Alex Godwin?"

"What about it?"

"But—do you now say?—"

"Wait," said Charlotte.

"Yes, Carlotta?"

"I think we all may have overlooked something important. Do you remember, Richard, that Moses Reed told us he would fight for Ned in court?"

"He did say that, when he thought the boy was innocent."

"But what changed his mind?"

"Well . . . Ned?"

"He said you'd confessed," Charlotte told him gently.

"That's not true!" Ned exclaimed.

"Could he have feared his defense might have been insufficient to save the boy?" Longfellow asked his neighbor in bewilderment.

"I would imagine Moses Reed is a man who fears very little—even the anger of those he's wronged. And I begin to suspect he's a talented actor, now that I recall the scene. But Magdalene *knew*. Richard, why do you think Alex Godwin returned to Bracebridge last year?"

"To find employment."

"Here, and not in Worcester, which is a far busier place? Catherine said Alex came to her with references. And yet, Hannah later told me Alex had been in some sort of trouble, before he was *sent* away. If that is true, who might have helped him out of it?"

"For serious trouble, I presume he would have consulted a lawyer—"

"And who is the *one* man Catherine Knowles appears to have trusted?"

"You suspect Reed sent Godwin there a year ago? But why?"

"What if—oh, how could he? But what if Reed himself wrote Catherine's final will?"

"If that's so, how was it we found a copy on the island?"

"Alex might have taken it there . . . or couldn't Reed have brought it with him, when he came to Bracebridge? He might have 'discovered' it in Catherine's bedroom—"

"While I was out looking for something spectral in the blasted hall! That could be. But wait a moment, Carlotta—do you suppose Reed is a murderer, as well?"

She stared back at him, hardly able to believe it herself.

"If he did plan for Alex to inherit Catherine's estate," Longfellow reasoned, "why would he then kill him, *before* she died?"

"A necessary change of plans?"

"Remember, too, that her fortune had been reduced to nearly nothing. And I saw the final will. Reed stood to gain control of no more than thirty pounds a year, for Magdalene—the rest, what little there was, will now go back to Philadelphia. Including, of course, the recent widow's portion."

"But what if he saw this added inheritance not as a blessing, but a curse? Better to allow the Knowles family the return of that portion, if it would keep their eyes from

Reed's other business, which may not have been exactly honest."

"Possibly . . ."

"He did tell us both earlier that Catherine's fortune was nearly gone. But do we know *where* it went? You saw the way she lived, apparently on next to nothing."

"And if he'd invested wisely twenty years ago, he would have seen her wealth grow enough to easily ride out this latest depression," Longfellow concluded.

"He told us Mrs. Knowles decided a year ago to give Magdalene's son his due—which might have encouraged Reed to make other arrangements. Would Ned, after all, have forgiven a father who had ignored him for years?"

"A father?" Ned whispered.

"He might have taken the hatchet from the bag at Ned's feet—" said Charlotte.

"—having no idea that it was Lem's, and not Ned's," Longfellow finished.

"Reed did come over to talk to Grandfather," the young man added. "Asking how he was, and then, when I would take him home."

"When he might rid himself of Alex," said Longfellow. "He could hardly have known Lem and Alex had argued earlier. It must have been an unpleasant surprise to see his plans go wrong."

"It could have been worse," said Charlotte, "to find Catherine Knowles dying in my kitchen, yet still able to speak—"

"That *was* somewhat disheartening," said a cool voice from the doorway. Moses Reed leaned there as they'd seen him do before, a placid expression on his smooth face. Then he brought an arm from behind his back, and aimed a cocked pistol toward the group before him.

"The story you've spun together is rather remarkable—yet only a little less than the truth. My congratulations especially to you, Mrs. Willett, although I do dislike an inquisitive woman! But what you know will make little difference. I helped young Godwin out of an embarrassing situation in Worcester, as you have guessed. I arranged to have a charge of theft ignored, and promised him a small share of an inheritance for bringing me information. And you were correct about the widow's portion. I knew it was a race between Catherine and old Peter Knowles—to see who would die first. If only I had acted sooner! One day I learned she was to have the Knowles money, after all. No doubt they would have sent someone to help her invest it, hoping it would eventually return to them. And once they'd seen she'd lost her own fortune—"

"How did you manage that?" asked Longfellow.

"Do not interrupt sir, or I may find you in contempt! You will know it all soon, very soon. You see, Godwin guessed more than I'd told him, and he became greedy. When I met him on the evening that preceded your ice party, he also told me he planned to tell *you* about those damned shillings! What better reason for his murder, by one of many in Bracebridge? That evening, too, the little pig threatened *me*, demanding one half of Catherine's fortune—which is, in fact, intact. What could I do but stop him?"

"And Catherine?" Longfellow asked warily, watching the pistol. "Did you then see to her, too?"

"Having started, it only made sense to finish the matter. I rode up the next morning and paid a visit, using the tunnel Magdalene showed me years ago. You see, unlike yesterday, when Mrs. Willett had her mysterious accident, I was once quite careless about 'covering my tracks.' Never expecting close scrutiny of my affairs, I'd simply kept a list of poor investments I might claim to have made; I was quite prepared to say they had drained away a little here, a little there. And while Catherine insisted on living like a hermit—Godwin assured me she very nearly covered her old bones in rags—I concocted invoices, as if she still enjoyed a life of splendor. Who, after all, would ever know? Eventually most of what I controlled for her did come to seem like mine. Considering the piddling amount I was paid to manage her estate, Catherine Knowles was a fool to imagine I'd *not* steal her blind. She may even have expected it—but she could never bear to come down from her eyrie to find out for sure. It seems she was satisfied with her immediate prey."

"Why did you never go back for Magdalene?" asked Charlotte, curiosity overcoming her fear.

"Because 'Mad Maud' had spoiled everything for me. Once she was quite beautiful, and I was willing to marry her for any settlement John Fisher, or even Peter Knowles, would have given us. But just before Fisher died, she began to grow big with child. She said it was mine, but did I know for sure? Other men were there, after all, and she was hardly wise or careful. In the end, after her brat had ruined my plans I was packed off to Boston to earn my own living, which I pretended to be happy enough to do. And Catherine had a reason to keep the silly girl captive, as she'd been kept herself."

"So you simply forgot her," said Longfellow, his voice carrying his contempt.

"But here's the real surprise! Now, when the little fool could make amends—when the family in Philadelphia might finally reward me for taking care of her, so that *they* need not—now, she *refuses* to marry me! Let her rot, then. I have my fortune tucked away where none will find it. All I need do is take the boy with me and pretend he has killed the two of you for revealing his crimes."

"Then you admit you tried to make us believe *that your own son* is a murderer?" asked Longfellow, to be very sure—and to gain time by keeping the lawyer talking.

"Certainly. I supposed he had more of his mother in him, and that he would run away, taking the blame. But he proved too intelligent—probably because I, too, contributed to his being."

"And now?" asked Charlotte.

"Now, we will proceed from judgment, to sentencing."

"How do you propose," asked Longfellow, "to accomplish our silence with one pistol?"

The attorney walked to an alcove where several curios were displayed. Among them was a rosewood box.

"Oh—" Charlotte breathed, as Moses Reed reached to open the lid.

"They're not loaded," Longfellow informed him. "I keep powder and balls hidden, after another guest took—certain liberties."

"But I've brought powder and balls for my own weapon. Earlier in my visit, I made sure that yours, too, were serviceable. In case I might come to need them." He cocked first one dueling pistol, then the other.

Longfellow's eyes went to the door. The lawyer laughed, and stepped to block it. Two cocked pistols were now in Reed's hands. A third lay on the tea table at his side.

"I don't care who you are," Ned cried defiantly. "I won't help you!"

"If you come with me willingly, boy," his father answered, "I will let you live."

"For how long?" the young man returned.

Charlotte gasped, and Moses Reed gave her a reassuring

smile. He could not see that Magdalene Knowles, wearing felt-soled slippers, had come into the doorway behind him, on her way to the kitchen with a tea tray.

"Have no fear, Mrs. Willett. It should be less painful than the other end of my pistol, which you felt yesterday. And your head will no longer trouble you. As for your heart, it may as well be taken by me as by another."

"And Magdalene?" Longfellow challenged. "What of her?"

"I have no further interest in what becomes of Magdalene Knowles. With no one left to care for her, she'll die soon enough. And that will be that."

"I doubt it," said Longfellow.

Reed turned at a slight sound, but he was too late. Magdalene had thrown the tray with surprising force; the man who had once claimed to love her raised his arms instinctively.

She launched herself toward him like a wild thing, causing Reed to stagger and fall, and cry out as he twisted a knee. Her full skirts flew over his face as she attempted to claim one of the weapons he'd dropped—the lawyer hung on to the pistol in his right hand. By some miracle, neither one had yet gone off.

Ned joined his writhing parents on the floor, clutching an arm that still threatened them with sudden death. For a few seconds he held on, until Moses Reed struck him a fierce blow with a clenched fist. The boy fell away, but by then Longfellow had leaped across the entangled bodies. Using a heel for encouragement, he made the attorney drop his weapon. He moved swiftly to reclaim a second, on the table. Turning to survey the scene, he saw Charlotte standing with a raised poker, her eyes flashing, much of her soft hair fallen down about her face.

Finally accepting what had happened, Reed sank back

with a groan. At last Magdalene straightened her skirts, then reached beneath them. In another moment, her hand emerged with the third pistol.

She studied it for a moment, seeming to consider, while the others froze. She turned so that the barrel faced the man beside her. Without even a flicker of expression, she then made another sudden move—and flung the pistol aside, into the fire.

The sharp explosion that followed caused a final moment of panic, until it was discovered that no one in the room had been injured after all.

"Well, Reed," said Richard Longfellow, as Ned rose to his feet. "It would appear that once more, your plans have changed. But none here will harm you further, as long as you stay still. We will all be glad, I think, to leave that privilege to the courts. Ned," he instructed, "go across to the inn, and tell Captain Montagu he's needed. Don't explain why. The village will soon know the truth—but not, I think, tonight. Tomorrow, perhaps, when Mr. Reed is on his way back to Boston, with a suitable escort. Wait a moment—tell Cicero, too. He'll not forgive me if he misses the rest."

"Gladly sir." Ned stared down at the man on the floor, but turned away without a word. Instead he went to his mother, to kiss her cheek in a manner that seemed entirely natural.

"I thank you, again," he said, "for my life."

At long last, Magdalene Knowles had reason to smile.

Chapter 37

CHARLOTTE WILLETT AND Richard Longfellow sat
together in her blue study, on the afternoon of his return
from a trip to Cambridge. Winter's grip had loosened;
they now sat with their sides, rather than their feet, to
the fire.

"Reed will be hanged within the month," he reported.
"Few were surprised that none of his Suffolk County col-
leagues offered to come and defend him—nor did any
here in Middlesex. He stood to give his own defense, with
the usual results. It seems even lawyers can't abide someone who has so thoroughly tainted their fine profession.
In fact, I heard John Adams made it a point to go personally across the Charles to chastise Reed, while the fellow
sat in jail. There is nothing a man of rhetorical skill en-
joys more than a captive audience," he finished with a be-
mused smile.

"Lem," Charlotte offered, "went to visit Jonah, Ned,
and Magdalene last evening. They've all decided Bermuda's
healthy climate would be best for their future home

together. That had been Ned's plan for his grandfather all along. And a physician he summoned last week from Boston gives Jonah every hope for many more years, if he no longer has to face the winter cold."

"That's good to hear. I'll go and visit them tomorrow."

"I'm sorry you missed our own excitement . . ."

During the time Richard was in Cambridge, Charlotte and the rest of the village had been roused one night by the meeting house bell, which rang out madly. At first it seemed there must be some mistake, for no one smelled smoke. A few supposed a superstitious neighbor had been unsettled by a magnificent display of the aurora borealis. This time, it sent down draperies of red and green from the northern sky.

And then, someone had pointed lower, to the marshes, where there was a yellow glow. It was soon agreed this must be the house on the island, consuming itself. What was not decided was whether the fire had been started by an earthly hand, or by one of the malevolent spirits still residing there.

When Charlotte finished telling Longfellow of the conflagration, he suggested that it might after all have been caused by old John Fisher, gnashing his teeth at the mess his daughter had left behind. Charlotte then asked if rot of another sort, perhaps logs left to molder, might not have heated itself to the point of combustion. This caused her neighbor to praise her astute application of Scientific law. And yet, neither knew, for sure. . . .

What was known before long was that the house, and all of its curious furnishings, had been thoroughly destroyed. As its new owner would soon travel to Bermuda, it was assumed the island would be home to no one for a generation, at least. Until then, the boars could rest easy.

"But now," said Longfellow, after he'd taken a last

forkful of admirable cherry pie, "I wonder what you'll find to do with yourself, Carlotta."

"I've wondered that myself. With Lem able to care for the dairy, I might try something new, I suppose."

"Bees, perhaps?"

"Well . . ."

"You might consider taking up the violin; we'll need a new fiddler. But you might do better to build something useful on your brother's land, to surprise him when he visits. You'll allow me, I hope, to help you start. I've a willing pair of hands."

"I know," she answered, smiling. "But by planting time, what assurance do I have that you won't have them full with new plans of your own?"

"Who knows?" said Longfellow. He stretched his feet further across the fire, until they nearly touched those of his neighbor. Through the south windows, the maples already showed swollen red buds that came before the green. He imagined the new season full blown, and found himself pondering how long he'd need . . . to find a reason to join Charlotte in something that would take them on together, so that he might always have her at his side.

About the Author

MARGARET MILES, now the author of four Bracebridge mysteries, is working on another. She and her husband live in Washington, D.C.

To learn more about Bracebridge and some of the subjects in the books, please visit her website at:

www.margaretmiles.com